Praise for *Courting an Amish Bishop*

Mindy Steele brings us another satisf̶ ̶ ̶ ̶ ̶ ̶ ̶ ̶ ̶that's rich in Amish culture and wisdom. We get a unique ̶ ̶ ̶ ̶ ̶ ̶ ̶ ̶ ̶ ̶ ̶ ̶ ̶ ̶ ̶ain people with the herbs and secrets of ̶ ̶ ̶ ̶ ̶ ̶ ̶ ̶ ̶ ̶ ̶ ̶ ̶eet romance will leave you wanting mor̶ ̶ ̶ ̶ ̶ ̶ ̶ ̶ ̶ ̶ ̶ ̶ ̶ ̶ ̶ ̶ hor

Fans of Amish fiction will enjoy *Courting an Amish Bishop*. Throughout Ms. Steele's character-driven, fast-paced story, I rooted for Bishop Simon Graber and Dok Stella Schmucker. Five stars for the book, and another five stars for the denouement!

~ Lisa Jones Baker, author of
The Quilt Room Secret and *Rebecca's Bouquet*

A warm, believable romance, *Courting an Amish Bishop* is a heart-tugging story sprinkled with laugh-out-loud humor and rich with fascinating details. You'll fall in love with Simon and Stella and the entire cast of delightful characters! Bravo, Mindy Steele!

~ Laurel Blount, author of the John's Mills series

A theme of healing is throughout Steele's compelling story. *Courting an Amish Bishop* is a beautiful story of compassion, love, friendship, and an overwhelming faith in God, the greatest healer of all.

~ Diane Craver, author of Amish Adoption Series

Embark on a heartwarming journey of second chances with Mindy Steele's enchanting love story. She beautifully captures the belief that each person deserves a second chance—a tale where the opportunity to leave the past behind and embrace a brighter future unfolds against the captivating backdrop of an Amish setting.

~ Tracy Fredrychowski, FHLCW Reader's Choice Award
for *Rebecca's Amish Heart Restored*

THE HEART *of* THE AMISH

Courting an Amish Bishop

MINDY STEELE

BARBOUR
PUBLISHING

Courting an Amish Bishop ©2024 by Mindy Steele

Print ISBN 978-1-63609-815-9
Adobe Digital Edition (.epub) 978-1-63609-816-6

All scripture quotations, unless otherwise noted, are taken from the King James Version of the Bible.

Scripture quotations marked NKJV are taken from the New King James Version®. Copyright © 1982 by Thomas Nelson, Inc. Used by permission. All rights reserved.

This book is a work of fiction. Names, characters, places, and incidents are either products of the author's imagination or used fictitiously. Any similarity to actual people, organizations, and/or events is purely coincidental.

Cover Design: Kirk DouPonce, DogEared Design

Published by Barbour Publishing, Inc., 1810 Barbour Drive, Uhrichsville, Ohio 44683, www.barbourbooks.com

Our mission is to inspire the world with the life-changing message of the Bible.

ecpa Member of the
Evangelical Christian
Publishers Association

Printed in the United States of America.

DEDICATED TO

The men and women who carry on the divine legacy
of being a balm to many through the ability to
minister to the sick, body and soul.

ACKNOWLEDGMENTS

To Miriam P. for helping get all the words right.
To Dok Dunnard and Dok Schwartz for giving me a look inside.
To Vicky and Dali for pushing me through the long days.
To Ms. Ellie for being my favorite muse.

NOTE TO READERS

While I live near the Amish and have a great many Amish friends, this novel and its characters are completely fictional. No resemblance between the characters in this book and any real members of the Amish community is intended. My desire is to bring realism to these pages through research and familiarity. However, each community is different. Any inaccuracies of the Amish lifestyle are completely my own.

That said, it has been the belief that the Amish refuse modern medicine, but that is simply not true. There are no traditions or beliefs that prevent them from seeking out modern health care. They are tied to their way of life—a life of simplicity, community, and great respect for the natural world. Modern medicine is simply a last resort rather than a first response. The Amish in general have less need for health care, as they do physical work daily and eat healthier than most. When a need arises, they treat most ailments with basic home care, prayer, and natural remedies. The use of vitamins, plants, and herbs is being embraced more and more by everyday people. Growing up Appalachian, I was already exposed to many basic treatments, and I know that God is the great healer. He has given us all we could ever need around us.

For generations, herbal knowledge has been passed down from one healer to another. They practice reflexology, chiropractics, and herbal healing. I can attest to all three as I ventured into researching for this book and now have an even greater respect for nature thanks to this opportunity.

The Amish do not attend local colleges for this knowledge, but they do meet and correspond with each other for support and further knowledge—sometimes gathering as far off as New York, where they meet other like-minded Amish healers. These healers have a vast knowledge that's not limited to just one thing. An Amish midwife is often sought out for more than when it's time to bring a child into the world, and a chiropractor (or muscle stretcher as they are called since no degree is obtained) can often tell you the best remedies for burns, the flu, and even how to detox your liver. I am a healthier, happier writer today, thanks to the wonderful healers and their wisdom.

Many blessings and health to you,
Mindy

GLOSSARY

ach vell: oh well

aenti: aunt

blut: blood

boppli/bopplin: baby, babies

bruder: brother

bu/buwe: boy, boys

daed: dad

danke: thank you

danke schon, geb mich sum meh: thank you, give me some more

dawdi: grandfather

dawdi haus: a small dwelling attached or unattached to the main family home, specifically for newlyweds or grandparents

die krank: the sick

dochter: daughter

doktor: doctor

du arma kleina ding: you poor little thing

Englisch: a non-Amish person

fatter: father

ferhoodled: confused

fisch: fish

fraa: wife

freinden: friend

freindschaft: friendship

gegisch: silly

Gott: God

grosskinner: grandchildren

grossmammi: grandmother

guten tag: good day

gut mariye: good morning

haus: house

hund: hound or dog

Ich vays naet: I don't know

Jah: yes

kaffi: coffee
kapp: prayer covering
katz: cats
kault: cold
kichlin: cookies
kinner: children
kuche: cake
kumm: come
maed/maedel: girl, young woman
mamm/mammi: mom, grandmother
mann/menner: man, men
meinda: remember
mudder: mother
muszer: a black suit or coat worn by men on Sunday or special occasions
nacht: night
naet: not
narrisch: crazy
nee: no
nochber: neighbor
onkel: uncle
rumspringa: the time for young people to run around before baptism
schtupp: family room or sitting room
schwester: sister
singeon: a singing or youth gathering
seltsam: strange
sohn: son
vell: well
verra: very
Wass iss letz: What is it? What's wrong?
wilkum: welcome
wunderbaar: wonderful
youngies: teenagers, youth

CHAPTER ONE

Simon Graber lumbered across the kitchen floor with the air of a man in complete control of his world. As bishop of Cherry Grove, Kentucky, it was best to always remain confident.

Kaffi in hand, he sat at the table and stared blankly at the steaming bowl of oatmeal. Perhaps his cooking skills did need tuning as his *sohn* insisted. In the next room, sixteen-year-old Michael still slept. Simon didn't mind indulging him on occasion. After all, Michael worked as hard as most men already, helping with the horses and working on his *onkel* Ervin's construction crew.

Pushing the overdone bowl aside, Simon opened his Bible and began feeding his soul instead. Reading the Lord's words was better taken in morning hours with kaffi anyway. It was one habit that was new, for his late wife, Lizzy, had always insisted kaffi only forced one's head to think, and all thinking should be done without stimulants.

"If a man desires the position of a bishop, he desires a good work." Simon inhaled a long breath as he read the words of 1 Timothy. He hadn't desired being a minister at the young age of thirty-two—or, better yet, a bishop just five short years later during a six-hour spring communion service. Lizzy had fretted terribly about how their life would change, but Simon ministered to others humbly, welcoming a life of service.

He recalled the day Bishop Menno Hershberger decided to suddenly move to Indiana. Simon had known a new bishop would be chosen from the deacons and ministers already serving, but he never expected drawing the lot twice so soon. Furthermore, he never expected God would place him as head of the church just months before losing his family.

Closing his eyes, he could see young William and baby Claire. Both had the look of their *mamm*, with Simon's deep blue eyes.

If only he had insisted Lizzy stay home and not travel with the group to attend a quilting frolic.

If only he'd insisted William and Claire stay with his sister.

If only they had all been wearing their seat belts.

If only the driver hadn't fallen into a fit of coughs, losing control of the van.

Opening his eyes, Simon wiped away the unbidden tear. He had long put away the questions and what-ifs. God had given him a family for a time, and for that Simon was grateful. He reined in his focus to the words before him. It was best not to dwell. God had allotted him a few scant memories, and he would hold tight to them.

The brown mission-style wall clock chimed, reminding Simon of the hour. He raised his head and glanced across the table. Twelve years gone, and he still had the habit of expecting to see Lizzy seated across from him, listening. She had been a great support in helping him sort his thoughts.

Right now Simon's thoughts were as scattered as a needle on the compass Michael always carried in his pocket. It had not escaped him that Mahone Miller still reeked of tobacco, though claiming he had smashed the horrid habit months ago. His chewing of matchsticks didn't mask the smell one bit.

Simon was also worried that yet another family had fallen ill. A summer's cold that seemed to linger longer than it should. If it was the flu, as some whispered, it was a mighty rough one, keeping so many laid up for days as it had. If there was only more he could do aside from prayer.

Jah, Lizzy's advice would be welcomed right now, just as it would have been when visiting the Glicks last evening. Lizzy would have instructed him on how important it was to decline any offer of lemonade

Betty Marie made.

Lizzy would have certainly known how to deter young Matthias Martin from his current plans. Fish farming wasn't farming. Simon shook his head as he stared at the empty chair. Without his *fraa*, Simon was drinking sour lemonade and watching a young man pour all his hard-earned money into. . .catfish.

Kaffi cold, Simon shifted his gaze into the far corner of the room. The worn couch needed to be replaced. A better chair would do as well. Then he caught sight of the old chest. It had been the first piece of furniture they owned. Simon remembered how thrilled Lizzy had been unpacking all the things she had collected over the years. Now it lay filled with the remnants of the past. Lizzy's wedding day apron. William's tiny straw hat. Simon had longed for the day he could take him to the bulk store for a second one. He swallowed back another run of emotions as he pictured the small dress and soft *kapp* Claire had worn. She hadn't taken her first steps yet and always smelled of applesauce with cinnamon, her favorite food.

You still have Michael, his inner voice reminded him. If his sister Verna hadn't insisted on keeping him that day to play with his cousins. . . Simon didn't want to think of that.

Michael was sixteen and attending gatherings, and would soon be courting. He was carving out his own future while Simon remained stuck in his past. No wonder he was feeling so melancholy these days. Far too many lonely days had collected like the cobwebs in the high barn rafters. Grief tiptoed into his mornings and tucked him in each night.

A knock at the door drew Simon back to the present. He set down his kaffi, closed his Bible, and got up from the table. Michael should be up getting ready, and most likely Ervin was at the door to pick him up to start on the new Shetler *haus*.

"*Gut mariye,* Bishop Graber," Judy Burkholder greeted. She held what looked to be a pie under a healthy wrapping of aluminum foil. The deacon's fraa wasn't one for stopping by unannounced, but seeing as she was not alone, Simon knew instantly that his quiet morning was about to be shaken up.

"Gut mariye, Bishop. We know you need to get on with your day, and hoped to catch ya before you got caught up in it," Mary Alice Yoder said, lifting a dish also covered in foil.

"Gut mariye to you both." Simon nodded curtly.

"We all like to be helpful, considering you have yet to remarry and Michael a child yet without a mamm." Mary Alice cocked her head. Michael was sixteen, not six. Simon pinched the place just above his nose to ward off a sneeze. It wasn't the flu, possibly allergies.

Currently Simon was starting to wonder if he wasn't possibly allergic to Mary Alice Yoder, but he quickly banished the terrible thought. A bishop had to keep a thankful heart even if it was a threat to his sinuses.

"Mamm sees that we don't go hungry for long," he reminded her. *Blessed Mamm.* Despite being the ripe age of eighty-four, she often insisted on making three meals a week for Michael and him.

"Jah, but to put such a burden on one Lena's age." Mary Alice clicked her tongue three times. "It's no kindness at all. You can always rely on my Pricilla to see you tended to." She lifted the dish just high enough to hide the grin on her face.

"She would have come herself, but she is helping at the school today. She's always one many can depend on."

"Mary Alice. . ." Simon tried to slow her fast-moving tongue as she pushed her way into his kitchen and set the meat loaf on his table. Simon knew it was meat loaf because it was always meat loaf, just as she knew he had no interest in her widowed daughter.

"It's terrible that Elaine and Dorie both came down with a *kault.* Thankfully, Pricilla stepped up. A teacher's heart, for certain sure."

"Mary Alice," Simon tried again, ignoring her continued praise for her daughter. Pricilla was a wonderful giver, but Simon had no interest in marrying her.

"All I'm saying, Bishop, is that my Pricilla is just a year younger than you, and with all this sickness going about, healthier than most, I reckon. A man needs a helpmate, and her *kinner* need a *daed.* I'd say that's a match, certain sure." She gave his sparse kitchen a long study and made a disappointed sound, her eyes resting on a sink filled with dishes he was in no hurry to see over.

Mary Alice came every Thursday like clockwork with meat loaf she somehow had conceived as his favorite dish in hopes to sway Simon's noninterest in Pricilla. Today, it seemed she brought reinforcements to help her plight.

"Mary Alice. . ." Simon didn't appreciate being prodded.

"*Ach*, you know kinner have need of both parents. I heard you tell Rob Glick just those words, and he married Betty the year you became bishop." Mary Alice lifted a sharp brow in confidence as she pushed his own words back onto him.

Simon looked to Judy for support but found none waiting there. He should have known the deacon's fraa agreed. For it was *Gott*'s will for man to marry, was it not?

"How is Lena?" Judy asked, changing the subject. Simon wished his mother were here right now, but at this hour she was probably eating toast and jam and knitting another kapp for *bopplin* as she most often did. Her sight was going, but her fingers still insisted every head be covered to ward off chills of the next season.

"She is *gut*."

"Lena is always one for good health." Mary Alice began inspecting his cabinets for staple goods. Simon had just done his shopping a couple of days ago, retrieving everything a widower and one *bu* required. Thankfully she didn't address how many containers of beans and jars of peanut butter currently lined the middle shelf.

"Man cannot live on bread alone," Mary Alice quipped and shut the pantry door. "A fraa would offer you much. You should start courting before you forget how it's done."

No one in the community tested Simon's patience this much.

"Mary Alice, it is not our place to instruct our bishop," Judy intervened. "And not everyone is comfortable courting at his age."

Simon lifted a brow. He wasn't old, and the space between his temples was starting to throb.

"We should go and let him get on with his day. We still have one more visit to make." Judy turned to Simon. "The Hooleys have this cold now, and I made chicken soup and zucchini bread for them."

Simon deepened his frown. *Another family sick. How many have fallen ill?* he wondered.

"What will *kumm* of you and Michael if Lena's health fails? I worry over you, Simon Graber. Lena cannot be raising a child at her age." Mary Alice had what many referred to as "selective hearing."

"*Danke,* Mary Alice, but worry *naet*, lest your faith weaken. Gott always provides," he reminded her before turning to Judy. "And danke to you, Judy. The Hooleys will be grateful for your gift. You are a gut *nochber*. And certain sure I have no plans on courting." It was the same response he offered Judy's husband and his eldest *bruder*, Ervin, Minister Fender, and his mother anytime the subject was broached. He should probably come up with a better reply in the future.

Simon had no time to worry with all the rituals that led up to marriage. His life was too complicated to consider such foolishness. He had to remain focused so as not to allow another young soul to jump the fence. And what of Mahone's habit? It would take some thinking to end his not-so-secret sinfulness. Simon had a responsibility to be an encourager to others, convincing others to marry, decide when discipline was required, ordain ministers, and baptize new church members. The spiritual health of Cherry Grove relied on him. Bishop Menno had left it all in his hands.

"Daed." Michael emerged from his room, and a parade of deep coughs spilled out of him, causing both women to move closer to the door.

"I don't feel so good." Michael stood wrapped in a quilt, despite the temperature already being in the upper seventies. His sandy hair stuck out in various directions. Simon turned to his visitors. If the illness had reached his haus, it was best they leave. Mary Alice must have read his thoughts.

"We should be going, Judy," Mary Alice said, leaving faster than

Simon had ever seen her exit a room before.

Simon went to his son, touched Michael's forehead, and felt the heat of a fever there.

"Let's get you back to bed, sohn. I don't think framing a haus today is gonna happen for you." Simon led Michael back to bed and went by memory to ready a cup of honey and lemon just as Lizzy used to do.

A fraa might better know how to handle many things, but the thought of marrying again, that was the least of Simon's worries. His sohn and his duty to his community. . . that was what he was married to now.

———————— ⚓ ————————

By the next morning, it was clear Michael needed something stronger than lemon and honey tea.

"He has the fever too," Mamm said, frowning. "Best be getting to your *schwester*'s store to fetch medicine."

"You can't tell *Aenti* Verna. You know how she fusses," Michael said in a congested voice.

Verna *was* a good fusser. She had taken on being as near as a mamm to Michael as she could after Lizzy's passing. Between Verna's coddling and Lena's prayers, it was a wonder Michael dared get sick at all. Simon tucked a blanket over his sohn as he shivered. Already the length of his bed, Michael's feet pressed flat on the footboards.

"But I will take her soup," Michael added before rolling over. Simon quickly ran through his morning chores, harnessed his horse, and aimed for Wickey's Bulk Foods Store just three miles away. One could get a fresh loaf of bread, a bottle of fever reducer, and all the comings and goings of Cherry Grove. It was a good place for a single father and bishop to get everything he needed.

"Hiya, bruder," Verna Wickey greeted as Simon stepped inside the dimly lit store. She was barely a year older and had been a healing balm to him after losing Lizzy, Claire, and William. Simon still struggled with the loss of his family and couldn't make heads or tails of the accident that claimed them so suddenly. Verna also called him bruder more than bishop, which Simon didn't mind, despite her doing so in jest.

"Is Willis already out in the shop this morning?" Simon asked. Verna's husband not only owned Wickey's Bulk Foods Store but ran his own cabinetry shop too. Talk of a shoe store was being whispered about the community, but Simon knew Willis had a good many months yet before he'd find time to move forward with the idea.

"*Nee,* he's helping Joel and Rachel put up new cabinets today." Verna beamed extra brightly at the mention of her married son. It wouldn't be long before Verna was a grandmother again.

Simon was happy for his nephew, but it never changed. Each time he married a pair of lovesick folks, a tinge of sadness fleeted through him, a reminder of his own wedding day and all he had lost.

"It is gut they have been healthy while so many are sick. Did you hear the Schwartz kinner have come down with this flu too?" Jah, Simon could always depend on Verna to know who needed called on.

"Nee." Simon removed his hat and ran his hand through his hair, strolling to a dim corner where medical supplies were, and Verna followed. Simon latched hold of a bottle of acetaminophen.

"Carlee Hooley has taken to the fever too," Verna informed him. Carl Hooley's daughter was no more than a child of eighteen, but hopefully Judy's soup and zucchini bread would help get them right again.

"Susie came by yesterday for a few things. I wish we had more medicine." Verna looked at the sparse shelf. Her vast store was filled to the rafters, yet held nothing that cured a simple summer flu. A few salves and ointments had a spot next to the Raber's Goat Milk soaps and lotions, but they would do nothing to help Michael right now.

"I had nothing to give her but my prayers. I remember Mamm making tea with yarrow and honey when we were kinner, but it's too late in the season."

Simon didn't remember that. He had never been much of a tea drinker, but perhaps Michael would do better with it. "Yarrow?"

"It's a weed." Verna waved off his question. "You just be careful when you and the elders call on folks. It's awful catching," she ordered in sisterly fashion.

"Gott's will, schwester," Simon reminded her. "I did hope you had something to help Michael. He's feverish. . .and coughing."

"Ach nee. Michael is *krank*?" Her voice suddenly grew concerned. Verna was a mother hen.

"He has a cough and no appetite."

"Have you tried soup? I've seen your oatmeal and burnt pancakes." Verna reached behind a line of pink-colored soap bars and fetched a dark purply bottle. "I have cough syrup but only one left." Before offering it to Simon, she glanced to the front of the store. "Perhaps Laura and Lydianne can see over things for today. I can make soup and come see over Michael."

"I can make soup," Simon replied, ignoring her lack of faith in his parenting skills. He had been both mamm and daed for a dozen years now.

"I will make the soup. We know how you are with a pot. Just don't be like Carl. If Michael gets worse, take him to the doctor."

"I will." Simon pulled out his wallet to pay for his things. He could never be as stubborn as Carl Hooley.

"Susie wanted to take Carlee to see the *doktor* in town, but you know Carl. I reckon you should remind him we must do what is best," Verna said, handing Simon back his change.

"He does not trust the *Englisch*, but if you are thinking I should speak to him, we both know his ears are closed to any thoughts I have." Carl Hooley was one of three parents who, during Simon's first year as Cherry Grove's new bishop, had lost a son to the outside world. The young men chose life away from their Amish upbringing, and Simon knew that Carl had hardened his heart toward him for it. A man could study Gott's words furiously to always have the answers to those seeking them, but sadly Simon couldn't find the right ones to convince Carl that his son's decision was his alone.

Worse, Carl's bitterness had grown to a point of refusing to sell his goods at any of the Englisch markets. When Englischers stopped to buy new spring plants, Carl shut down the greenhouse Susie so happily worked at to help bring in extra income. Now Carl wasn't selling any of his lawn furniture either. Slowly, their livelihood was shrinking, and soon they would have to depend on the church. Simon had no qualms with spreading out financial help equally, but it was a terrible thing when a man let his hurt eat at him to a point of suffering.

"Then go fetch the *dok.*" Verna's *dochter*, Lydianne, stepped from the back room. In her arms, little Sarah Rose tugged at her mother's kapp strings. "He cannot refuse help if it comes dressed Plain, I reckon." Lydianne was young yet but had always possessed an extra dose of wisdom beyond her years.

"They don't make house calls," Simon reminded her. "Or dress. . .Plain." Even if he sought out Doc Richmond himself, he knew he couldn't convince the Englisch dok to pay a visit, and the midwife who had been the closest thing to a doctor had retired and moved away.

"I know one who will," Verna announced abruptly. "Many have sought her out from time to time. I have been hoping to reach out to her myself."

"Why?" He narrowed his gaze. Was his sister ill? In the family way?

"For her herbs and medicine. She sells Nature's Sun products, and Willis' mamm insists they are to be trusted. No sense in folks driving all the way to Walnut Ridge for them if I have them in my shop." She grinned like a pup with an old sock.

Verna had a good head for business, but there wasn't much space for more, Simon noted, giving the store a quick glance. However, the idea of an Amish doktor not so far away piqued his interest. Simon would happily go fetch her himself if she could help Michael, and Carl Hooley would happily welcome an Amish dok over an Englisch one.

"Where do I find her?"

CHAPTER TWO

Stella Schmucker followed her faithful *hund*, Ellie, down the narrow path that paralleled Fox Creek. The land ran straight up and down, with barely a level break in between, but Stella didn't mind rough terrain, considering it was filled with the many wonders that enabled her to provide a livelihood for herself.

Early morning light was breaking over Sugar Mountain. The deep basket in her right hand already housed blackberry fruits and leaves, wild lettuce, and a few chicory roots she hoped to dry out now that her stock had been drained. The mild laxative helped remedy countless issues and always made kaffi taste a little stronger.

Taking her tenth of nature's bounty was the first rule in foraging. God had blessed Stella plenty, and she had never been greedy no matter how little she had. A person could always find what they needed within nature. Not so much with people.

Without a word, Ellie deviated uphill. Careful of her footing, Stella kept her eyes trained on the ground and took time to admire the various ginseng plants she'd been nurturing for the past seven years. Each stem branched into stalks with five toothed leaflets, and as August neared, red berries clustered the centers boldly. In springtime, the yellow-green flowers smelled like lily of the valley, but as the season waned, the plant turned an unclaimed yellow for which Stella had no name for.

Hiking her skirts upward, Stella stepped over a fallen poplar log and marveled at the unexpected five-prong plant waiting there. Ginseng had the ability to hide away with a quiet intelligence few could fathom. It would be another month before she could legally harvest the much-sought-after roots she was paid handsomely for, and this year the word was that eight hundred dollars a pound was the going price.

Jah, in times of less plenty, there was always seng to sell.

Unwed and thirty-eight, it all added to Stella's meek savings. She didn't mind finding new ways to provide for herself, but selling herbs and vitamins was barely enough to purchase material for a new dress. That alone was reason enough for helping the midwife when the need came. No matter how many roles she'd fill, she'd not fuss or fluster. Her life was full and served a purpose.

From Stella's earliest memories of mixing wild garlic and mud and letting the cakes bake under the sun, she knew she wanted to help others heal. The day she discovered jewelweed, a preventive and a cure for poison ivy, it had earned her a second helping at the supper table and freedom to roam after her evening chores. She even earned a few short weeks each year to spend with her grandparents in Kentucky without pesky bruders lurking. That's when her eyes had been opened to a new world and when she knew her life could be. . .different.

Mammi helped a good many folks with her gift of healing. Stella had thankfully found that she too possessed the gift. Amish and Englisch came with all sorts of ailments to her front door. From sore throats, digestive orders, headaches, insomnia, rashes, spider bites, and even thwarting off lice or fleas, Stella did her best to offer comfort. Of course, she couldn't charge them for advice or herbal teas that she put full stock in, but Stella never turned down a donation. That's why she started carrying Nature's Sun products. When you lived off the kindness of others, you had to think outside the box. It was not charity, she had told herself, but simply making a living. Her embarrassment of growing up with parents who lived off the charity of others had embedded deep the need for her independence. She would be a giver, never a taker.

July was bent on leaving its imprint before tearing out the calendar page and starting a fresh new one. Stella already felt the humidity rise, a sample of what the day had in store, but the steep grove she was aiming for, just above the ridgeline of her property, would provide a cooler respite.

She stepped into the wild orchard, thick with pawpaw trees, and inhaled the cool dampness of the rich soil feeding underneath. Inspecting the green banana-like fruit, not yet hinting shades of yellow and brown and still firm to the touch, she sighed. It was early yet, but she often grew impatient to find one or two had fallen and waiting just for her.

The rare short-season fruit, barely thirty days long, was packed with nutrients and vitamins, according to her *Mountain Foraging* book. A good steward needed to know her environment, and Stella never skipped out on snagging a few books at the yearly library book sale.

But books don't know everything, she mused, fingering a long fruit. This area wasn't common to grow pawpaws, but like birds spreading seeds into unnamed places, so Gott also sprang up bountiful groves where He saw fit. The shady understory of the forest held just the right amount of dampness for pawpaws to thrive unnaturally.

"Kumm, Ellie." Stella motioned her companion forward. At the highest point on the hill, they took a short rest to admire the winding valley below. The crooked creek and the vast farms spread out as far as the eye could see, while a small cluster of Englisch homes hugged the curvy asphalt.

This had been the happy picture of her childhood, the sole reason she had made Walnut Ridge home. She had been desperate to leave behind a life that only treated her harshly, and it was the fields and the forest, this perfect view, and a home where love had resided that made her heart sing just as it had when her grandparents were still living.

Shading her eyes, Stella frowned at the changing landscape. Weeks of timbering the adjoining hills had marred her view. Much of the lush forest was gone, leaving behind space and clutter that only made a rabbit content. She understood the importance of good forest management. She just didn't have to like it. Change had a way of forming a blister on her creature comforts.

Ellie barked, snapping Stella back to the morning at hand. Her friend was right—it was best to get back before their Friday visitors arrived. With that in mind, Stella clutched her basket and aimed for the road that would lead them back in half the time.

Stella reached her front door slightly out of breath. She noted the buggy parked nearby. Her doors were never locked, and by the sound of a crying *boppli*, Grace and Tessie were waiting impatiently inside. Stella smiled and stepped into the house.

"Hiya, Grace, Tess," Stella greeted and quickly slipped out of her shoes before placing her basket on the small kitchen table. Warm weather always made going barefoot a pleasure.

"Out on that hillside again?" Tessie Miller lifted a judgmental brow before looking into the basket filled with late summer blackberries, and her frown relaxed. No one could frown at plump blackberries, especially so late in the season.

"How can I find the best herbs, if I don't go searching for them?" Stella dislodged a small stick clinging to her sleeve and grinned. "And I happen to be a fan of cobbler."

It was no secret the elder found her odd, as did many. Stella smiled broadly and then turned to Grace as she cradled her newest child, who had been suffering terribly with summer's colic burden. Stella remembered the day little Johnathon was born, feeling blessed that it was a quick delivery considering Stella had only begun to accept her unexpected role as the local midwife when Martha retired. She didn't mind, as it kept a person too busy to think about all the things they wished were different. Thankfully Walnut Ridge was a small community, and she seldom had to submit herself to the miracle she would never experience for herself. Having a family was as far off a dream as having a life without hardship.

"I was hoping you still had some catnip for tea. He takes it so well, and I ran out yesterday," Grace said with a tired voice. The shadows under both blue eyes were evidence she had slept little lately. From cradle to rocking chair, dried catnip made into a tea had the powers to sooth stomach issues, help with hives and sleeplessness, ease nervousness, and combat the colic. Stella always made sure to keep plenty on hand, which, this time of year, was freshly picked from her scant yard and scattered garden beds.

"Jah, and I can pick you some fresh," Stella said happily.

"Danke, Dok Stella." Stella nodded at the attached name. She wasn't a doctor, but she never shied away from sharing her vast herbal knowledge, her healing teas, and the occasional help assisting a new mamm on a delivery. Serving others gave her purpose and earned her a level of respect Stella never achieved back in Ohio.

In Ohio she was Sam Schmucker's daughter and was looked upon with the same stern glares as the rest of her family. Her outdoorsy urges and need to read rather than sew her own dresses had been an embarrassment to her mother. Yet it was Stella who felt the heat of embarrassment each time her family had to leave one rented homestead for a more broken-down one. Stella would rather extend a hand than accept one.

Moving to the long, uneven shelves filling up the space of one full wall, Stella began to search for what was needed. On the left, rows of vitamins approved for sale by the federal government, but on the right, herbs grown and foraged and dried. After pouring out the remaining catnip into an envelope, she sought out the wild chamomile, lemon balm, and a heap of rose petals and lavender.

"I hear you told Leon Strolfus you had no time for courting," Tessie announced bluntly. She ran a finger over the clean counter and looked at the imaginary dust there. Tessie Miller's thoughts on how a woman should spend her days had been mentioned plenty yet. Stella aimed to help her elder keep her rheumatism at bay, which earned her some graces in the lecturing department. Today, Tessie must be suffering a little extra, Stella perceived.

"Leon Strolfus needs a fraa, not a date," Stella replied, and Grace chuckled. "And he should be more concerned with his farm than gossiping." Leon Strolfus needed more than that. He needed someone who could sew a few shirts before someone saw right through his.

"Jah, like as not. There're two men now needing wives, kinner needing a mamm, as Gott wants it to be." Tessie Miller was born with the sturdy conviction that if she had a thought, it was God's will that she share it. She came for Stella's tea concoctions and salves, made a living sewing Amish dolls for tourists, and always had advice to offer up without being asked for it.

"Now Aenti Tess, we don't need to be fuss'n when it's Dok Stella who keeps you in such gut health." Grace switched her unsettled boppli into the crook of her other arm and offered Stella a tender *I'm so sorry* smile.

She need not apologize for her elder. Tessie did mean well. Her barking had love attached to it. Stella appreciated a person who spoke their mind rather than one who concealed it. The thin, elderly woman involuntarily huffed before she leaned closer to Stella's fresh herb collection. Adjusting her glasses, she read the tiny print Stella had inked onto the front of each pint jar.

"Any one of them would give you a proper home," Tessie continued. If only her elder knew the small house had been the best home she had lived in yet, she wouldn't be so judgmental.

"One day we'll all wake to find you and this place in the creek below. A woman need not be so stubborn when she can be properly provided for," said the seventy-year-old spinster.

Stella let out a long breath as she spooned dried nettle into the center of the paper and folded it four ways. Not only did Tess suffer from speaking her thoughts but also from inflammation when the air grew humid. Stinging nettle had the power to keep one of those under control. For the other, Stella quickly collected the herbs and flowers required for her special blend of sunshine tea. If ever a woman needed her spirits lifted, it was Tessie Miller.

"It's a gut haus and has much life left to it, I reckon," Stella replied, noting how low she was on lavender. Thankfully she had plenty fragrantly blooming just outside.

There were rules one was to live by being Amish, and Stella wasn't so oblivious to them all, as Tessie was suggesting. Bishop Mast had spouted the same lectures on Mondays when he paid his weekly visit on the importance of her marrying.

Sure, her house wasn't the sturdiest, but time had worn it. Her grandfather had built it with his own two hands. Laughter had lived within these walls. Sitting on the edge of the mountain might scare some, but not Stella. It was just the right amount of space for her and Ellie. She had a good many years left before her first step in the morning would be her last. Only a fool would give up a good house with this view.

And marriage. Stella let out a huff. She had given her heart away once. *Lesson learned.* When Burl Hilty decided he wanted a wife who didn't smile at nettles, he left Stella for Arleta Weaver. They had four kinner now. Stella wasn't counting, and she wasn't staying in Ohio for the rest of her life watching Gott grant them a hundred blessings either.

Although she liked her solitary life, Stella did still long for kinner, for companionship that didn't have four legs and no reply to her thoughts, but she never believed in stewing over the past either. She was doing Gott's work. Helping others was a life of servitude. She didn't need a husband for that. Her life in her little house, dangling or not, was just fine by her. Ellie was all the companionship she needed on the day-to-day, and there were plenty of gatherings and the biweekly service to attend.

She wasn't that lonely.

Stella glanced at Ellie, who could sniff out danger and unwanted pests from a distance, and smiled as she narrowed her teal-blue gaze on Tessie. Even her hund knew when it was best to hold her tongue.

"How will you ever find a husband, keeping to yourself like you do?"

Stella stepped closer to her elder, and the floor underneath groaned at the slight pressure, almost as though it didn't like hearing Tessie's constant complaints any more than Stella did. "I think we best worry about you getting wed first. You are older yet." Stella smiled politely.

"Don't be smart, Stella. Your head will swell, and you'll naet fit through the door," Tessie argued. "I'm concerned for your faith."

Which led to the biggest reason Stella was the oddity of Walnut Ridge. Being baptized didn't drown her stubborn independence. If anything, it made her stand out like a dandelion in the lettuce. One could only rely on self. People. . .they could never be counted on.

She handed Tessie both paper pouches. "Now, it's the same for the morning tea here. One ounce to one quart boiling water and steep thirty minutes." Tessie took both without question. "I have faith that this will keep you young yet."

Tessie deepened her frown. "Gott decides the timing, for all things."

Stella nodded. Of course He did. And sometimes He felt not everyone was born to be a mother or wife. Some were simply better served being useful to others.

"It is no good for you to live here alone," Tessie continued. Like a bluegill on a grub, the woman was determined.

"You live alone," Stella countered. "And I have Ellie." Hearing her name, the silver Labrador barked. Stella knew Ellie appreciated her intervention when the neighbor's dog had a litter of eleven pups and passed suddenly after. Then Ellie barked again. That's when the women realized another visitor was coming. It was probably Adam Zimmerman for his weekly muscle rub salve.

Adam walked with a limp and had a hitch in his right shoulder. Stella remembered the day when he got caught up in the wheels of a grain wagon. She'd worried he might lose a limb when he was taken to the nearby hospital, but Adam had pulled through, all limbs intact. She admired the fact that his deformities didn't slow him down.

Adam's coming only punctuated Stella's point to the importance of her duty. She would be a wasting-away woman in a kitchen all day. Stella was just about to say as much when Grace opened the front door, and there in the doorway stood a man, arm raised to knock.

In the dim shadows of morning and day colliding, she squinted to make out the stranger. The silhouette of a hat told her he was Amish but not Adam Zimmerman. Not standing erect as he was. His straight-up-and-down stature, his sturdy frame, didn't register. He was not one of the *menner* from Walnut Ridge. Stella had seen over a few in the neighboring communities, but less than a handful came all the way for her special teas.

"How do," Stella greeted, happy to welcome a new patron. "Can I help you?"

"If you are the dok fraa, I've kumm to fetch you." It wasn't the first time an anxious father showed up at her door. Stella didn't have a phone shanty or a neighbor close enough for others to reach out to her if necessary. No matter. Folks seemed to find her when a need arose.

Stella lifted a brow as he moved farther into the room and a set of rich blue eyes landed straight on hers. Despite the man having no expression she could easily read and one uneven brow hiked sternly compared to the other, Stella could see the happy creases in the corners of his eyes. Wrinkles told their own stories, and his were proof he'd had many happy moments in life and was clearly excited to welcome another boppli to his lot.

So Stella smiled back.

CHAPTER THREE

The last time Simon had traveled to this end of the county was for Cousin Marion's funeral. That was many years ago, but he knew the area well enough to cotton to Verna's directions for the doktor's house.

The steep hill leading to Walnut Ridge had his horse panting hard. Doves convened in clutches on the side of the road, getting their fill of saffron and milk thistle seeds. Veering left, the road narrowed and turned to gravel and was cloaked heavily with thick-hanging tree branches. Simon welcomed the cool shelter against the heat, and so did his horse after working so hard to get here.

At the mailbox marked SCHMUCKER, Simon tightened his grip on the reins and eased over the slight slope of an uneven drive. The lack of rock was disconcerting, but Simon released a small chuckle while stuck on the name. *Schmucker* meant to coddle and kiss. How many times had the Schmuckers prayed for a different name? Surely it brought with it some amount of jesting.

A small wooden structure came into sight surrounded by bulging flower beds, two large boulders, and tree trunks that had been recycled for growing flowers as opposed to rotting into the earth.

He looked ahead, and barely thirty feet from the front door, the earth fell away, revealing the home was truly on the edge of the hill. Pulling hard on the reins, Simon let the buggy hug the slanting hillside best he could. Appearances meant nothing. He knew that as he set the brake and climbed down from the buggy. Still, putting a person so near the edge of danger didn't sit right with him.

Oddly, flowers poking out of tree trunks made him smile. Upon closer scrutiny, flowers and weeds and vegetables lived rather harmoniously together. Like patches on an unfinished quilt, everything flourished in the sparse landscape in a whimsical fashion. *Mudder* would call it chaotic and crowded, and Simon would agree, but the various scents and buzzing of bees did carry a quaintness about it that he found oddly eye-catching.

Casting a glance behind him, Simon pivoted and took four long steps back, out of instinct. That hillside was entirely too close. That's when his gaze trailed beyond the ending of earth and the beginning of heaven. He blew out a satisfying breath as fat clouds meandered past, gliding along a cornflower-blue sky. His gaze lowered on the yonder of the valley below. The response in his chest was between peaceful and disappointed. Clearly the views at this height were something to admire, if not for all the timbering taking place. Thankfully, Simon had an eye for looking beyond the temporary, imagining it fully restored, and concluded this had to be reason enough someone would dare live in such a precarious spot.

What a magnificent view of Gott's hand.

He had no business staring at clouds as if he wished to lay his head on one. Michael was sick. Turning back to the house, he noted how small it was and sorrowfully tended to. The roof was new, but the wood was old, and no matter how many coats of paint covered it, it did little to mask the need for new boards. Perhaps the husband was unable to see to the upkeep. Who knew what ailed the man. Age? Disability? No matter, Simon could quietly offer his help. He'd been known to use a hammer just as well as his brothers who had all followed their father's trade in carpentry.

Lifting his fist to knock, the door swung wide open, revealing a frail young woman. In her arms, a bawling infant. Simon dropped his fist quickly and swallowed.

"*Guten tag.* I'm looking for the dok fraa who lives here."

"Jah, she is here." With her free hand, she opened the door wider, and Simon stepped cautiously inside.

It was the meadow scent that first took him, like a hundred childhood memories had been trapped here awaiting to be discovered. The shallow interior had sparse furniture. There was a small table centered in the room with a scattering of envelopes, a strange oblong basket, and a mason jar of flower blooms. Shadows moved in the dimness, but his eyes were still adjusting. At this hour, morning light hadn't reached either of the two small windows. Sugar Mountain tended to work the sun harder to reach on this side of the county. It gave the room an eeriness he suspected suited the rest of the teetering-on-the-edge structure.

All but that scent. Like roses bathed in a spring meadow.

Shifting his weight, the floor underneath moaned faintly. Though Simon valued his life, it was Michael and the other ill fallen who mattered, and his knowledge of healing the body could fill his mother's thimble. A doctor was to be had, he'd concluded, so he took another step forward as he closed the door behind himself.

When his vision adjusted, Simon was met with three sets of curious eyes. He hadn't meant to scare anyone in his urgency, and he offered a friendly smile. An older woman, whom Simon recognized as Tessie Miller, a local seamstress who made dolls Verna sold in her store for any passing tourists, stood in the center of the room.

Then Simon's eyes settled on the one standing over a steamy kettle. She was dressed in plain pale gray with a black apron, and he could see she was not elderly but fairly young. *Too young to be a doktor.* Amish doctors must spend generations learning how to heal and bring comfort to others. Simon was expecting an older couple living here.

"Can I help you?"

What a plain question, but Simon was momentarily taken back. Surely this wasn't the dok. "If you are the dok fraa, I've kumm to fetch you."

She tilted her head ever so slightly, a thinly marked brow angled high as eyes examined him from hat to boot. "Dok fraa?" Pale brown eyes and a look that appeared more intrigued than frightened.

Simon blinked, trying not to let the look of her distract him. Suddenly, a threatening sound came from just beyond her. The shadow stalked closer, but Simon didn't flinch. He'd dealt with his share of rowdy colts determined to best him and wouldn't let a silver hund set him uneasy. Simon was curious as to why the critter was inside as opposed to outside where all God's creatures belonged.

"Ellie, he is *freinden*," the pretty one said firmly. As if understanding the words plain enough, the hund sat down. Apparently freinden meant Simon was inedible. The hund's teal eyes remained suspicious of him nonetheless.

"If your fraa is in need, I can be ready in a few minutes, but I'm not. . ." She gave him a sheepish grin as if she already knew what ailed him, and she couldn't be more wrong. Simon quickly cut her off.

"I'm not in need of a midwife," he replied quicker and harsher than he meant to. There would be no more need for such in his life; any reminder of what was lost to him always brought out the sensitive side of his demeanor.

"We have a few that are krank in my community. I'm Simon Graber," he introduced.

"Well, Simon Graber. I should hear their symptoms first. Not every condition requires me to leave my haus."

Simon took offense at her amused tone. "Coughing," he replied. By her lack of interest, coughing apparently was not life-or-death enough to warrant the same attention she was giving whatever cooked on the stove. "It seems to be naet a seasonal kault. Some have weathered it, but it is traveling faster than a spring flood. *Mei* own sohn woke with a fever that hasn't broken yet."

"Coughing can be a sign of little or of much," she said, stirring.

Simon stretched his neck and saw nothing but water in the pot. Her bedside manner needed adjusting.

"Ragweed has been strong this year. They most likely have allergies or a possible sinus infection."

Simon's jaw clenched. Was she even a doktor? "A whole community?"

he returned with equal contempt. "My sohn has no allergies to speak of. There is concern." Enough for him to be here, he wanted to add.

As if something shifted inside her, she turned her attention to the far wall. Simon followed her gaze to what appeared to be her medicinals, though he wasn't sure by all the small-print labels. Like the rest of her home and yard, those shelves looked equally cobbled together. Dangerously so.

"Fevers? Aches? What about breathing issues?" Her voice became tender, like a soft rain on a spring morning, a mist that barely touched the skin. Simon cleared his throat, ignoring the way nearby lamplight glinted off her hair. It was an undetermined shade, made up of many colors. He didn't have time to decide and nodded to all three symptoms. Then she stared at him long and uncomfortably, as if trying to determine what he ate for breakfast. She was making him tense.

"Have you considered seeing the dok in town? Sounds like the flu, and a fever for long can have terrible effects." She turned back to whatever concoction was boiling on the stove. She was pretty, an odd fact that managed to somehow register in his brain. Simon wasn't accustomed to being spoken to so plainly, pretty or not.

Despite her fragile chin that jutted out slightly, aside from her sun-kissed complexion, she had eyes for knowing. Simon knew that look, in horses at least, but sometimes in people too. Hers were pale brown, like muddy water or soft earth, and when they found him again, Simon felt a mosquito prick. As if she knew his every thought, felt his loneliness, and in fact knew he had nothing but cold kaffi for breakfast.

That's why Simon started to sweat.

"And there is dehydration to worry over. You must keep giving him fluids," she continued. "Your fraa should consider broth too."

"Not everyone is trusting of the Englisch." He lowered his gaze and tugged ever so gently at his shirt. The windows were open, but he couldn't feel a breeze. He hoped to not have to explain in further detail. Being Amish, many were accustomed to self-healing, but in dire circumstances, even they sought out professionals. Carl Hooley was a special case indeed.

Simon cut another glance at the shelves lining the wall nearest the door. What a sad state for someone trying to make a living. Her husband clearly had no talent with a hammer, but that was none of Simon's business. There were vitamins, jars of dried flowers, and colorful liquids. He wondered if she had a remedy for the Mary Alice Yoders in the world, then quickly shoved the terrible thought away. Lizzy would tell him he wasn't being a very good bishop with such thoughts, but Simon was human before he was a bishop and still struggling to minister to some of the more stubborn of his flock.

"But none so that they would risk the life of another," she replied sternly as if he found a sore spot to push upon. Simon agreed, but he wasn't just here for Michael. Many were in need of her help.

"That is not my decision to make for everyone. Are you a doktor or not?" He was wasting his time with this woman who seemed more concerned with watching water boil than to his sick son.

"Dok Stella can be of help," the younger woman piped up. "She has a remedy for just about anything."

"Stella? Stella Schmucker?" Simon blinked. In all his hurry, Simon had not inquired about one major detail. *The good dokter's name.* Stella wasn't a common name, and Simon had only once heard it spoken of before. It had been a good many years, but now he recognized it from his youth.

His memory of her had certainly been old, of the fearless child who survived a raging flood. Simon would never forget the name he and the many volunteers had called out to in their search. When word of a small child being swept away reached the four corners of Pleasants County, every man able had come to help. Simon still marveled over the fact that after the many hours of searching, she'd emerged all on her own. Gott gave strength when it was needed, he firmly believed, and before him stood the proof of His mercies.

"Jah, I am Stella, and of course I will come do what I can for your kinner and for any who need me." Stella went to the stove and finger-tested the large pot of water. "But I must see over the water, gather a few things, and then I will be ready."

"I'm sure your water will be fine, but you might want. . .shoes." His voice held an amusement he rarely spent on strangers.

"Nee, water is *verra* important. It cures many of life's ailments. Clean water is the main ingredient for all of life. Shoes can do none of those things," she said with a stubborn chin in the air before slipping out of the room.

"You ready up," Tess Miller hollered behind her. "Grace and I will see to the chores and pick some catnip."

"Clean water?" The hund made a sound in her throat, low but loud enough Simon thought it best not to question the dok.

"Dok Stella boils all her water to be certain nothing harmful is in it. She never makes tea without it."

Perplexed by the idea that water needed to be cleaned, Simon simply nodded as he watched the doktor reappear in a bold blue dress and matching apron. She was also wearing flip-flops. He scowled.

"I will need a few more things too." She began pulling jars and vitamins from her shelf. "Tessie, can you fetch my bag?" Tessie went to the next room and returned with a large brown leather bag.

Simon shifted nervously as the three women worked to ready one. The hund was still studying him intently, and the heat was only growing. The house was small and stuffy and oddly secluded, terribly cramped, and too dark for his liking. More so, it did not match the woman who appeared more earthy, light, and full of quick answers.

"Can your *mann* spare you? We might be all day if you don't mind seeing to a few folks," Simon said. He didn't have all day to spare, considering two colts were waiting for him to continue their training, but people came first over his livelihood. To Simon's shock, a laugh burst out of all three women. Sure, he shared a laugh with others on occasion, but none ever laughed *at* him before.

"Stella is from Ohio and unwed," Tessie said with a hint of chastisement.

The doktor tucked her chin inward, confirming the truth, and Simon's wits scattered like dust on a breeze. He hadn't taken into account that she was not married, pretty as a rose petal, and about to ride in his buggy all the way to Cherry Grove. His hat suddenly felt strangely tight on his head.

"Only 'cause her intended had a change of heart," Grace quickly defended. "Stella would make a fine fraa for any man." Simon didn't need the particulars and frowned at both women before turning his attention back to the doktor. She lowered her head and worried her lip. No one wanted their private matters shared aloud, and he for one knew the feeling.

A woman living alone. He gave the home another scrutiny, only this time with reverent sympathy. Clearly she struggled with the day-to-day all by herself. He looked to the silvery hund again, his eyes still narrowed, and felt the tingle in his sinuses. Yes, now he remembered why he never owned a dog.

"We should be going," he offered and motioned to the door.

With bag in hand, Stella turned to him again. "Can you see to loading those two jugs of water for me?" She pointed to a dark corner, and then she motioned for the hund to follow. "Kumm, Ellie." Who knew doctors were so bossy?

"I assure you there will be water where we are going."

"Not clean water," she countered.

Simon took a deep breath and let it out slowly. There was no time for quarreling. Not when Michael needed something to lower his fever and help him breathe more easily.

"Can you not leave your hund?" Simon had only brought his single-seat buggy. Not much room for a seventy-pound hund and two people, he figured.

Stella turned swiftly, and those pale brown eyes locked onto his firmly. "Nee, I cannot. We are family, and we go everywhere. . .together." With that, both the woman and the hund marched out the door.

"We'll pray for *die krank*, and for your patience with that one, Bishop

Graber," Tessie said as Simon bent to fetch the water. "She even takes that animal to gatherings, of all the stuff," she added with a disapproving tone.

Simon headed out the door, perplexed. Since when did Bishop Mast allow dogs at church?

CHAPTER FOUR

Ellie needed no prodding getting into the buggy. Stella, on the other hand, did. She had never gawked at strangers before. Surely the humidity or perhaps Tess' constant badgering was making her *gegisch*. The sound of voices urged her up into the short buggy seat. Now the three of them would be squashed like stacked pancakes. Cherry Grove wasn't too far, she reminded herself and focused on her inventory. Hopefully she got everything she would need. You never knew what trouble might surface when you least expected it.

"Elder, honey, mullein, stinging nettle, rose hips, and chamomile." She continued to focus. She had snagged a couple bottles of CC-A and FVE-W, favorites with all the same herbs but for those who turned up their nose at tea. She was just about to get her mind straight on her duty when Simon approached carrying her water jugs.

Stella had only ever ridden in a buggy with one man since coming of age, and now her stomach was in knots, foolishly so. He clearly was plainly worried for his son. However, the strange, unsettled feeling in her chest didn't spawn out of sympathy but of shame. Simon Graber was handsome. He was also a daed, and clearly married if his beard was any indicator.

After seating both jugs on the floor at her feet, Simon quietly climbed into the buggy and grunted as he rutted into the crowded seat. By the time he'd gotten comfortable, Ellie was panting hard and leaning heavily into Stella.

"You ready now?" He faced straight ahead, his lips in a firm line. Clearly he didn't like clean water or dogs, but he had come to her, had he not?

"Jah," Stella replied softly. She didn't like making others feel unhappy. Looking down at her exposed toes in flip-flops, she positioned both feet on each side of the water jugs, so as not to let them move about. At least he had reminded her to wear shoes, as addlebrained as she had been.

"It's mighty warm yet for taking your hund along," he quipped as he set the horse in motion.

"I have my bike." Cherry Grove was a good eight miles or so away, but if he insisted, Stella would oblige him.

"I'd rather have you there quicker, considering Michael feels so poorly. A bike is not acceptable for today."

"How old is. . .Michael?" Stella shifted uneasily. She wasn't particularly looking forward to riding around with Simon for long, but she was slightly curious about the man in the seat next to her. Was he a carpenter? Did he work his horses in the fields all day? It was none of her business. Simon was wed, had happy wrinkles, and didn't like hunds riding in his buggy.

"Sixteen, but I hope you can spare the time to see over a few others."

"I'm happy to help, and sixteen is not a child at all," Stella commented and braced herself as the buggy dipped to one side on the slant of the drive so she wouldn't fall out. Well, his discomfort was solely his own. She'd mentioned the bike.

Simon might think her fickle for insisting on Ellie coming along or for boiling water to ensure that it was safe. And unmarriageable, she mentally added and let out a frustrated breath considering Tessie insisted on sharing that too. But he did not know her.

He knew nothing of her strong dedication to others, or how many long hours she spent with the sick or a mother-to-be through the long stretches of labor. He clearly didn't know the sting of heartache she suffered after Burl Hilty had upended her hope for a family of her own.

He didn't know the courage it had taken her to leave one community for another. *To leave my family.* He was just like every other man she knew. He thought he knew it all.

After twenty minutes of nothing but the sound of hooves on the pavement, Stella spoke. "You don't talk much, do ya?"

"Better a handful of quiet than a mouth full of rambling," Simon replied.

Stella stared at him, her jaw slack. Just because he was off limits didn't mean he couldn't carry on a conversation. "You have the right to your opinion." She lifted her chin and stared at the cornfield that dipped with the land.

"In quietness and confidence one shall find strength. It's not my opinion."

Stella quickly faced him. He was too quiet, frustratingly confident, and plenty opinionated. "So you quote Isaiah and don't like clean water," Stella said. "What do you do, for your livelihood?"

Simon turned his head slowly and stared down at her for two blinks before replying. Those eyes were the most beautiful deep blue; it was hard not to look at them.

"I raise horses, among other things," he replied in a rusted-over voice. She liked the sound.

"Do you like that kind of work?"

Up shot that one dominant brow again.

She was rambling, asking questions far too personal for someone she was not tending to. "Sorry, that's none of my business." She waved a hand.

"Nee, I just haven't been asked that before. I do enjoy watching a young colt find its legs, but readying them for their purpose can be a difficult process. It earns me a wage as well as frees me up to see over. . .other things as well." He turned his attention back to the road. "I have a few hats, but I ain't getting any younger and don't know how much longer I'll keep with it."

Stella quickly cleared her throat. "Age is just a number. I don't want to ever get too old to grow herbs and flowers or brew my own teas."

"I admit I had no idea you had grown up to be a healer of sorts," he said as he worked the buggy around a long string of potholes dotting the road.

"Have we met before?" Stella squinted against the sun to get a better look at him. She liked the looks of him and the way his brows forged two sharp arcs that met matching wrinkles at the corners of his eyes, but she found his rigid posture a little overdone. He wore dark blue broadfalls and an overly washed powder-blue shirt rolled up to the elbows.

"Jah." He half-heartedly grinned. Stella had only been to Cherry Grove a few times. Not in one of those memories did she recall him, and he wasn't a man one easily overlooked. His eyes did a funny dance when he grinned, she noticed. His beard did not arrow to a point but rather smoothly rounded the face of a man who spent his time out-doors. His straw hat darkened the thick brown locks of hair, and those wide-set shoulders and massive forearms spoke of a man who labored heavily. No, Stella would have certainly remembered if he had paid her a visit before today.

"I remember you as a child from a flood many years ago. I thought your family moved away after that."

Stella's shoulders dropped at the comment. The reason her folks packed up her family and moved to Ohio was from the embarrassment of that day. She turned to the landscape, shivered at the still-fresh memory, and closed her eyes. She could still hear the roaring waters, feel the remarkable strength and speed of the current. No one knew the truth of that day, and Stella never told. The consequences would have been costly.

Being the youngest, and the only girl in the lot with three pesky older brothers, one would expect some teasing. Only Stella never knew a time when meanness wasn't a part of her life.

Edsel had been the most sympathetic, being the eldest and all, but the first to punch her in the arm if she tattled on any of them. Perhaps that was why the Lord saw fit to gift him a lot of daughters, seeing as he never learned how to treat his own sister.

Matt was the idea maker. His wild imagination gave Stella a love of the outdoors and tended to drag her into more troubles than she could ever find alone. He grew up, mostly. He now owned his own leather shop, but last Stella heard, he was in trouble with the elders for some fancy gadgets he insisted he needed to do his work. Schmuckers tended to make more bishops' heads shake than a car full of *youngies* on *rumspringa*, and though she tried to never sway from the Ordnung or rules set by her elders, Stella gave her bishop a wide berth.

But it was Paul, just a year older than her, who carried a streak of meanness Stella's other siblings never possessed. As a child, she had hoped they would come to like her, love her even, and she did anything they asked of her in exchange for their acceptance. However, she became their every excuse for falling short. Mamm always insisted Stella was the cause for her headaches, which left her powerless to do more than rest in a dark bedroom for most of the day. Daed said he couldn't face his freinden, knowing he raised a child mocked for her many antics.

But Paul. . .

Stella swallowed hard against the memory of words spoken seconds before shoving her into a swollen creek.

"Think you can outswim me?"

Nee, Stella never told, because she knew her punishment for tattling would far exceed any her parents had handed out. So folks thought she jumped, testing her common sense and making a mockery out of her parents for raising a willful child. They thought her weak and foolish, but Stella wasn't either.

She survived. After what felt like hours of fighting to stay afloat, Stella had managed to find a good hold on willow branches and pull herself out. That's when she knew Gott had given her the strength to save herself no matter what others did to her.

Except for that three-year-long moment of weakness, she reminded herself. At the peak of womanhood, she had hoped love and marriage would answer her every prayer, and that's when she met Burl Hilty. He was plain looking but not homely, and the only man who had seen her beyond her humble home and family. She recalled the rainy afternoon he found her walking home from her job at the grocery store. He'd offered her a ride and a smile, and Stella had happily accepted both. Burl talked of the weather and his work on the farm, and asked to drive her home a second time. It was only a week later when he asked to court her, and before Stella knew it, one buggy ride home had turned into three years of getting to know the man who had stars in his eyes. . .for her.

Burl had promised to save her from a life of misery. She in turn promised to love him all the days of her life. Her life was almost normal until he had a change of heart and broke what remained of hers. Though her roots were strong in her faith, her feet had never been planted to stick to a spot where she didn't belong. It was as clear as the freckle on her middle toe that she didn't belong in Ohio any longer.

She'd outlived the life given her, and where better to start over than in the little community that had all rushed to save her all those years ago when her own folks hadn't even made an attempt to find her. Her grandparents welcomed her with open arms, and Stella was blessed to have them for a few short years.

And he was there. She opened her eyes and turned to the man at the reins. Simon remembered that day and was part of the folks looking for her. Her heart warmed at the thought.

"That was a long time ago," Stella replied and waited with a held breath for the questions to start coming. How many times had someone asked her why she did it or wanted to know the details of how she felt fighting to stay above water or if she prayed for Gott to deliver her?

To her surprise, Simon asked nothing. As he held a tight hold on the reins going over the steep incline of Sugar Mountain, Stella watched as he took in the high view of hills and valleys around them. The curvy hillside was painted in summer green as far as one could see. The dry air held barely a waft from the goat farm as they passed.

"Is Michael the only one sick in your family?" she asked, laying to rest a past she didn't want to dredge up any further.

"He is." Simon turned to her, his gaze lingering as if to say more, but he returned his focus to the road again. She shouldn't have asked.

Now he was stiff and bound tighter than a burdock thistle. Or, perhaps like her, Simon Graber relished his privacy too.

They hadn't gotten more than four or so miles when the urge to move grew too strong to resist. Stella wiggled, searching for comfort. Ellie's right shoulder leaned heavily into her as the sun overhead decided to make good on another hot day. The buggy was cramped. She was perspiring, miserable, and they hadn't reached the first sick family yet. Out of habit, Stella kept rambling on and asking dumb questions.

"What is your horse's name?" Part of being a good doktor was asking lots of questions. It was important to know what a person could take, or needed, and questions never found answers if never asked. She rubbed Ellie's paw, now lying on her forearm as water sloshed around in the jugs at her feet.

"David," Simon replied.

"David?" *What an odd name for such a beautiful animal.*

"He was a small colt but grew mighty."

"Like David in the Bible?"

Simon nodded, and there was that wry grin again. The horse was a good seventeen hands tall and very well toned. More Goliath than David. Shifting again, Stella wondered how much longer it would be.

As if Gott knew her thoughts, the buggy came to a stop at the end of the lane as a large truck whizzed by on the main road. Stella gripped her bag with one arm, Ellie with the other, as Simon waited for a string of cars to pass before pulling out onto Route 57. The main road traveling from one end of Pleasants to the center of town always made her nervous, especially this high-grade pullout, giving one little view of the traffic coming and going. Even with lights and reflectors, cars barely slowed for a horse and buggy.

Last year, two local youngies had been struck by a car, twice, simply going to feed calves down the road. *A bike is much safer,* she silently proclaimed.

Simon's grip tightened, and she wondered if he felt the same unease pulling out here as she did. In less than a minute, they were veering onto

Cherry Grove Road. To her left, strings of cars and buggies filled the parking lot of Wickey's Bulk Foods Store at the peak of the hill. The large Englisch church came next. Stella always liked seeing the Christmas nativity scene each year. A group of children played on a wooden ship, Noah's ark–style. "They look to be having fun," Stella commented.

"Jah. It is good to laugh and play. Soon enough it ends," he finished grimly. Perhaps he was a doting father, not wishing to see his kinner grow too quickly, or perhaps Simon Graber grew up too fast too. Having no kinner of her own, Stella did not agree with his thoughts on the subject.

"I hope naet," Stella muttered under her breath. A life without laughter was no life at all. The road curved sharply, and Stella placed a hand over her nostrils from the strong stench.

"Shep Ebersole's hog farm," Simon commented. "It can carry a mighty stench in summer." That was putting it mildly. Hopefully David would pick up the pace before she needed to take a breath.

One left turn and thirty seconds later, they were pulling into a wide circle drive. Stella paid no mind to first impressions, though she preferred to be greeted by flowers or Simon's fraa. Before Simon could set the brake and offer her a hand, Stella stepped down from the buggy, thankful when the fresh air hit her. "Ellie, stay," she ordered, sensing this home would be less accepting of her companion entering inside. Stella quickly glanced about. To her left was a row of young fruit trees—peach and cherry by the shape of the leaves. Stella was a huge fan of both.

Without a word, Simon aimed for a plain front door, the upper half made of glass, the lower gray metal. Lots of Amish homes these days were metal on the outside and built out as opposed to up.

Inside, Stella found the spacious home eerily quiet aside from the sound her own steps made. Beneath her thin-soled flip-flops, the floors were made of hardened concrete, not the wooden planks she was familiar with. Simon closed the door behind her and motioned for her to follow him to a door across the way. Shoes clapping on concrete, she did her best to slow and quiet her steps. The absence of adornments or any sign of dolls or colored pages hanging from the walls struck her as odd. Perhaps his kinner were too old for such, though she found the man young yet. Perhaps he ran his home like he did his conversational skills. To a point.

CHAPTER FIVE

Simon stepped into Michael's room. Late morning light seeped through his single window, casting heavy shadows in the corners. Under a pile of quilts on the bed, tufts of sandy hair peeked out. Simon gave his son a nudge on the shoulder. This end of the house was warmer than the rest, but Michael might appreciate such warmth if he was still chilled.

"Michael, the dok is here to take a look at ya," Simon announced. Stella remained by the door, her oversized leather bag clutched in front of her. Surely it was heavy, and he chided himself for not offering to carry it for her. Her soft brown eyes widened to take in her surroundings in the dim bedroom.

Simon had made most of the furniture himself over a stretch of many years. The tall, salvaged barnwood dresser and the plain desk sat just under the window. At the end of the narrow bed lay a braided rug gifted by the Keim sisters the year they moved to Cherry Grove and became members. Under the wooden pegs with a straw hat and a felt one was the chair. Lizzy had rocked all three of their bopplin in that chair. How many times had Simon found Michael rocking and reading in that chair, he couldn't count. Right now it sported a pair of worn broadfalls and a wrinkled shirt. If he wasn't so far behind on his work this morning as it was, Simon would tackle the dreaded chore of laundry.

Michael rolled onto his back and glanced up at him with glassy eyes and cheeks speckled with heat. Despite the inches Michael had grown in the last year alone, he was thin, like many boys his age. Simon remembered those lanky years and knew hard work and a healthy appetite would soon fill out his boyish frame.

"Hiya, Dok." The welcome encouraged another round of coughing.

"I hear you caught a bug and can't get your chores done," Stella greeted and moved to his side. Noting the bowl and washrag nearby, she dipped, rang out, and placed the cloth to Michael's forehead.

"I wouldn't ask him to chore like this," Simon said defensively. Did she think him some sort of ogre?

"Daed, it was a joke," Michael said in a congested laugh and rose to the sitting position. "Sorry, Dok." Michael leaned closer to the sweet-smelling dok and muttered, "He's not very gut with humor. It's nice to meet you, though I reckon this is not a fine way to meet anyone."

"I got that impression." Stella grinned as she placed a hand to his forehead and then his cheeks. "I meet folks in all kinds of ways. How long have you been feeling poorly?" She slid two thin fingers over his wrist. Simon appreciated her being so thorough and tried to ignore the fact she was unimpressed by him.

"One's never poor as long as he has beans at the supper table."

The dok grinned as she checked Michael's pulse. "Or water," she added. "A person can live months on water alone."

"I reckon I plan to live on love, as long as there's beef and noodles in it for me. There's only so many bowls of oatmeal a man can take before it makes him ill."

"Sohn," Simon said, shooting him a reminder that sick or not, manners were required. Simon admired Michael's easy way. He never met a stranger and often made folks feel better when he left them than before they met. Right now, he was embarrassing his daed.

"This is the second day. I just started feeling cold yesterday, aching all over. And now my throat hurts." Stella pressed and felt about his neck, found a spot on the left, and pressed harder.

"Well, you got a fever, jah, and swollen glands like as not." She dropped the rag in her other hand back into the bowl of cold water. "I think a day in bed and some tea will have you right as rain by morning," Stella said with confidence and floated a smile Simon's way. Simon's shoulders relaxed. Michael had always been a healthy child, but all this talk of fast-catching flu had him worried.

"Tea? Well, that I can drink. Do you know how to make noodles too?"

Stella laughed as she stood. "I'll see what I can do about that. If you have an appetite, I'll certainly see ya do." Michael's brows shot up. Simon knew what his son was thinking. What he was always thinking. Life for him was about eating or spending time with friends.

"The kitchen is this way." Simon motioned her out of the room before shooting Michael a disappointing glare. "You are not so sick to get out of mucking stalls this evening."

"Ach." Michael waved him off and grinned. "I have to stay in bed all day. Dok's orders, and I get tea and noodles. Be nice and she might make some for you too." Michael winked. Simon shook his head and followed Stella into the kitchen.

"Don't fret. Michael will be back to himself in just a couple days. I do need to brew tea if you don't mind." She glanced about the room, searching for what, he wasn't certain.

"All you need is here." He fetched a small pot and coffee cup, suddenly wishing he'd taken the time to tidy up this morning. *Three visitors in one day*, he mentally scoffed. Now the stack of unwashed dishes caused his cheeks to warm.

Sensing his unease, she went straight to work. "As soon as I finish here, we can go see the next family. Is your fraa home? I can teach her how to mix his tea."

The question stopped him as he laid the kaffi cup on the countertop a little harder than he meant to. "She is not." He couldn't speak of Lizzy with a stranger, especially since the mere thought of her only reminded Simon of the other room with two empty beds.

"I will go see to the chores and return shortly." He slipped outside and let the heat of the day bear down on him.

Michael Graber was full of jokes, fast at drinking tea, and could snore a roach out of hiding. He was also the complete opposite of the man to her left. Stella still was uncertain of where Michael's mamm was. Visiting relatives? The sink of dirty dishes and high stack of laundry revealed as much before Simon hurried her along to check on another family. He appeared to carry a load of concern. Surely he wished his fraa was there to see over Michael.

"Your sohn has an appetite. I should have made chicken soup or at least toast and eggs," Stella said, not liking to be rushed. "The tea will help," she assured him further. "The herbs will see him through."

"I'm sure what you gave him is fine, but there are others to see to before the rain comes."

Stella flinched and looked to the wide blue sky overhead. Not a rain cloud in sight, but Simon appeared to know something she didn't. "Jah, it is best we hurry, then," she replied trustingly. The last thing Stella wanted was to be caught in another storm.

Ellie whined and bored her teal eyes on her. "In our hurry, I forgot to feed Ellie. She gets terribly grumpy if neglected," Stella said, glad her faithful companion snapped her back to the present. The past was behind her. Forward, that was her life now.

Simon looked down on Ellie and flattened his lips. Well, he might think Ellie was just a hund, but Stella adored her for how well she watched over kinner, and not one cow had escaped her valley neighbor's farm in months. Mr. Brown must be mighty grateful for her help since he had yet to mend the fence between them.

"I'll see over the hund while you tend to Mark and Sadie's kinner."

"I'm not sure she likes you yet." Ellie was selective of new friends, just as Stella was.

"I might grow on her." Simon smirked.

Stella wasn't sure why, but she hoped he was right. Ellie could always use new friends and, she had a feeling, so could Simon Graber.

CHAPTER SIX

Watching Dok Stella administer to his sohn sent a surprising warmth into Simon's chest he hadn't expected. There were a great many things Simon missed in the last dozen years, but Michael had missed something Simon could never give him back. *His mother.* Verna always tried to fill that role, consoling and loving him alongside her own kinner. Mamm too, but the years had taken a toll on how much she could give him aside from her unfailing love.

But aentis and grandmothers didn't remind Michael to not eat so fast or to be more diligent about washing his hands or to be careful about spending time around folks who might carry a germ. They didn't find his humor as amusing as Dok Stella had either. Dok Stella was nurturing, clever to Michael's wit, yet held nothing back when it came to information. Clearly she knew the ins and outs of motherhood that Simon didn't possess.

It took less than a mile to reach Mark Schwartz's and sicker kinner who could use some of the dok's gentle ways. Simon led the doctor and hund up the long-worn path to the house—the sound of her flip-flops on the pavement annoyingly distracting.

"Nettles!"

Simon turned, half expecting Stella had brushed too close to a few thorny weeds, but instead he found her bent over admiring them.

"Jah, don't touch them or. . ." Simon reached out to stop her.

"I know not to touch them." She smiled while continuing her odd affection of fingering the menacing leaves. "I just wish I had them growing in my yard. Sometimes I have to hike all the way to the creek below to find them."

A tangle of dust and a hot breeze moved over them, Simon could only stare down at her bent head, the slimness of her neck, the fragile shoulders. She was an odd one, for certain sure. Then she smiled up at him again and *ferhoodled* his brain further.

First, she didn't have much of a yard, more like a rock garden with blooms. Second, who wanted weeds, especially those that caused a miserable hurt? And third, why was she smiling like she had just found a fresh hive of honey? All good questions.

"Why would you want to?" It was the first question to come to mind.

"They have many uses. Nettles can help with painful muscles, skin rashes, gout, and even hay fever. They make a great tea to help you focus and are good for the heart."

Stuff and nonsense, he thought skeptically. A weed that cured all types of ailments. Old wives' tales, gossiping yarns. Then her eyes brightened and her lips split into an adorable smile. Both unsteadied him. She really was beautiful, and perhaps smarter than he'd like to admit.

Simon lifted a brow. He should be working colts and seeing over his last mare to foal. Instead, he was standing on Mark Schwartz's walkway, perplexed and completely enamored.

The front door opened, and Simon snapped his attention upward. Last thing he needed was being caught gawking at the dok. He was simply trying to figure out the creature in front of him.

That was all.

Nothing more.

"Hiya," Mark welcomed, and his gaze quickly went to Stella as she stood. "We hoped you'd stop here soon enough. You must be Dok Stella." The Amish grapevine ran faster than Fox Creek in a flood. Simon swallowed back the poor metaphor and motioned Stella inside.

"Jah, I am," Stella replied sweetly and then turned to Simon. She pulled a small container from her leather bag. "You said you would see to feeding her?" He did say that, now didn't he? Accepting the clear plastic container, Simon didn't miss the humor on Mark's face.

"You got him trained," Mark said and burst into laughter as the front door shut.

Simon turned to the hund, her tail thudding on the sidewalk like the ticktock of the old clock hanging on his kitchen wall. He was hungry, so he reckoned the mutt was too.

It didn't look like the dry food he would have presumed one fed such a critter. He popped open the lid, and the scent of stew hit him like a punch. "You get better meals than I do," Simon grumbled. "Kumm, hund," he ordered and moved to the grass so the stew didn't draw any flies to the front door.

The hund remained glued to the spot. Apparently *hund* wasn't the right word.

"Esa?" he tried again in a softer tone. Still, the hund looked bored. Maybe she wasn't hungry.

"Best be getting this now, or I will," Simon threatened. Not Simon's best idea when the hund started growling. What was her name again?

"Kumm, Ellie." And just as quick as a snake striking a field mouse, she bolted, knocked the container from Simon's grasp, and finished the full meal in three gulps. Simon looked down at his hand, the mark already growing to a welt.

"Trained, huh?" He cocked his head. Ellie looked up at him, unamused. Then she licked her mouth in one slow swipe. If Simon wasn't mistaken, she grinned.

Fifteen minutes later Simon stood in the doorway talking about the weather while Stella checked temperatures and pulses, and tickled Mark and Sadie's kinner into instant laughter. The hund watched in curious infatuation, cocking her head left to right. Simon frowned down at his hand. Hopefully she didn't scratch anyone else with those sharp claws of hers.

"It looks to be moving around us. . .again," Mark said, drawing

Simon's attention back to him. Mark had once been as plain as the next man, except now the tall man with a beard as red as autumn maple leaves only showed his youth in the twinkle in his eyes when humored. His carousing days ended after offering Sadie a ride home. One of her siblings—Simon couldn't recall which—had forgotten to pick her up after her job at the millhouse. One buggy ride and Mark knew. One buggy ride and Simon's young cousin had been a goner.

Simon nodded as Mark continued on about something to do with rain and roots, but his gaze was once more on Dok Stella. The woman simply perplexed him. Why was she unwed? Was it her choice in livelihood, or had one man's change of heart been too hard to overcome?

"Jah, roots need rain," Simon muttered, slipping his hands into his pockets.

"Now I will have to get them a hund." Mark chuckled as he ran his hands over the mutt. Sure, she looked friendly right now, but like the woman at the stove with Sadie, the hund had a few layers to uncover yet. Stella had warned him how untrusting Ellie was. She simply forgot to mention she was prone to lashing out. Simon kept a close eye on the mutt. One growl and she was out the door and tied to the buggy no matter what the pretty doctor had to say about it. He was still the bishop, after all.

After learning what symptoms the Schwartz kinner were having, Stella went straight to boiling water and pulling out jars from her leather bag. She did have a thing for clean water, he mused. A whole lot of unnecessary work if you asked him. If folks thought tea made of weeds and flowers made life better, so be it. He wasn't swallowing the stuff.

"I heard they even had a new corn picker. That auction is going to bring in a crowd, for certain sure," Mark said, but Simon wasn't much interested in the upcoming auction just down the road. His focus was on a thin wisp moving in brisk efficiency. Most Amish homes were set up basically the same, his being more a cobbled mess, but Stella knew her way around without Sadie's instruction.

"So if cows give honey and bees are done milking, what do I do about building a new workshop?"

Simon snapped out of his musings. "What?"

"It's a fine thing to see a bishop's ears closed but his eyes opened." Mark leaned close and whispered, a laugh in his voice. "I say you have a good eye." Mark slapped Simon on the back and walked over to the corner where the kinner were tossing a blue plastic ball for the mutt to slobber over.

As if he had a splinter under his nail, Simon winced. He didn't much like folks knowing his thoughts or that his thoughts had become focused on the dok.

"Are you krank, Onkel Simon?" young Gracie asked. As eyes turned his way, Simon felt a heat flush over him.

"Nee, it's just warm in here." *Warmer now,* he wished to add. Simon felt lots of things currently, but being sick wasn't one of them. His duty was to simply buggy the dok to *die* krank, and buggy her back home and be done with it. He had colts to work and Michael to see to. He didn't have time to spend answering foolish questions about cows and bees and shops.

"Rose hips have a lot of vitamin C, as do elderflowers," Stella informed Sadie as she spooned contents from two jars, dried flowers, into cups. It looked like the same concoction she had made Michael. "Just make sure *yer* water boils a full fifteen minutes."

"You really have a thing for boiling water," Simon dared to mention.

"I'm making tea, but jah, clean water is important. You would be surprised how many things are in water." Her gaze left his and wandered to the corner where five-year-old Kaynoshia and four-year-old Henry were giggling and playing with the hund. A smile played around her mouth. Helping others had shown a light on her that Simon found appealing. It wasn't his place to notice such intimate details.

Why hasn't she married? She was barely into her thirties, by his guess. She was plenty young yet. He watched the kinner, listened to high squeals and giggles, and found himself smiling too. He would always ache for Claire and William but shouldn't ignore the fruits of others.

"The elderflowers and rose hips will fight it, and the ginger will be easy on the stomach," Stella continued.

"I can add some honey. Verna sells it locally, and with Kaynoshia's allergies, it has been a must-keep." Sadie added the honey.

"You know you have nettle right outside, and it also—"

"I hope it doesn't taste like medicine," Gracie interrupted before the dok went into another string of herbal information. "Henry is verra picky," she whispered loudly. Stella smiled. Though barely eight, the young girl seemed more concerned with her siblings than herself, and Stella paid her more mind than the younger three, he noticed.

"It will be sweet and warm on your throats," Stella informed. As the dok told Sadie what to watch for, in case one of the kinner was allergic, Simon noted her ease. He admired a woman who was confident in her thoughts, as long as it wasn't Mary Alice Yoder. Simon noticed something else. Stella made fast *freindschaft* with Sadie as the two women mooned over the lot of coughing, sniffling kinner. If she feared catching the flu, it didn't show.

"I can return in a couple days and see how they are faring."

"Danke, Dok Stella. Let me pay you for your troubles." Mark reached for his wallet, but Stella only waved him off.

"Nee, we cannot know when sickness befalls us, but be glad the Lord provides what we need when it does." Be it words or tea, the statement warmed Simon's heart.

"But you must take something. It does not feel right otherwise."

"Is this poison?" six-year-old Enos asked, staring into a murky cup. He was clearly the favorite of his eldest sister if the smile was any indication. Yes, now he could see Stella paying extra mind to the eldest. Was it the efficiency Gracie had seeing over the others that the dok admired? Simon had more questions now to add to the lists he would probably never pull out and use. After today, he would most likely not see her again anyhow.

"Nee, it is tea," Dok Stella replied with a smile.

"Daed says we can't touch poison," Enos continued. Simon should have warned her about this one. Enos always had a question to spare and a habit of offering one up at the worst of times.

"Onkel Ethan said he had poison that went bad."

"Enos, Dok Stella isn't making poison." Sadie gave her son a *be silent* look. Stella was smiling at him, trying her best to conceal a laugh.

"But, Mamm, if poison goes bad, is it still poison?" Simon straightened, as did Mark. Both men stared at the boy. For six, he was either smart for his age or best knew never to try to answer all his own questions.

"Poison is never to be touched. . .ever. Now, go sit with Henry and Kaynoshia and drink your tea."

"If Onkel Simon drinks it, I will too." This time the dok couldn't restrain her amusement and clamped a hand over her mouth quickly, but not before a snort seeped out.

"Jah, sohn, because Onkel Simon should always try new things too," Mark added, a hint of clever in his smirk.

"Let me ready you a cup." Stella moved so quickly, Simon had no time to react before she was placing the warm cup in his hand. The fleeting touch sent a spark of knowing through him. The simple act should not have affected him this strongly.

So that's why Simon drank tea.

He didn't like it and only sipped the cup. It needed more honey, he concluded.

"*Vell?*" Stella asked with a sheepish grin.

"Not poison," Simon informed Enos and figured now was the best time to get the dok on to the next home before he made an even bigger fool of himself. One whiff of the Martin farm would set aside any foolish thinking for sure and certain.

Simon was itching to get this day over and get back to seeing over his newest colt. That, or the hund had fleas, which wouldn't surprise him. It had nothing to do with the woman squashed in the buggy seat, or her kind attention and infectious laugh. It had nothing to do with those flowery concoctions she was serving up to folks, even if they might just yet be the remedy his community needed. Simon had to admit, it didn't taste. . .terrible.

"Gracie is a good schwester," Stella remarked as they moved to the neighboring farm. Storm clouds that had been emptying over areas to the west all day had finally inched closer. *It will be a chore separating young colts from their mamms now,* he thought.

"Jah, family is important to her, as it should be." Aside from Gott, family was what mattered most.

"Jah, but not all siblings are the same. Her family loves her. Young Gracie will make a fine mamm one day." The slight downcast in her tone struck Simon's heart and also his curiosities. All siblings had a duty to love and care for one another. Stella seemed to have a different opinion of family. Families could be hard, it was true, but at least she had one to complain over, thankfully so.

CHAPTER SEVEN

At the top of the hill sat an old greenhouse, its unsecured plastic blowing in the wind. Stella noted the sign marked HOOLEY'S GREENHOUSE. The paint was fading, revealing the weathered wood underneath. She remembered when it had been the best place for heirloom plants after she had moved to Kentucky.

Simon veered into the gravelly drive. To the left, a phone shanty sat in a corner of the property line, its need for fresh paint obvious. Phones weren't permitted in the Old Order Amish, yet Stella knew rules changed from community to community. She had once seen a house with a built-on phone shanty on the back porch, while many had to rely on the kindness of Englisch neighbors to allow for them to be built nearby.

They stopped in front of a white two-story house with freshly installed gutters that pearled in contrast to the worn paint of the home. Simon set the brake, but before he had exited the buggy and rounded to Stella's side, she and Ellie had already bounded out. She need not be assisted at such a simple task. Stella collected her bag as the wind kicked up hot and humid.

"You should know, Carl is a good man but has had a hard couple years. His dochter, Carlee, has been ill as well."

The doktor in her perused Simon's features and the way his brows carried a silent warning. It was the face that told a person's thoughts more than the words they spoke. He had beautiful eyes. Like a summer storm rolling through the valley in the wake of the thunderheads. His height was also something Stella was suddenly more aware of now that he was standing so close. He wasn't the tallest man she knew, but partnered with broad shoulders and a stocky build, she found him a statue of certainty.

A sudden awareness caused her to sway slightly. She had no business noticing the color of his eyes or if he was capable of protecting a person from storms, and she dropped her gaze quickly to the bag in her grasp.

"You need not worry," she said with full confidence. Stella had no delicate nature. If she could muster through her childhood, she could certainly face whatever the day had in store. She'd once delivered twins in an ice storm, and she could bring joy to Tessie Miller with a few herbs. Whatever lay ahead, she would face accordingly.

Stella lifted her chin and was just about to tell Simon such when his focus shifted from her eyes to the rest of her face. The brisk halt to circulation in the atmosphere coupled with the day's humidity was surely the cause for the air to become so thick. Who knew the freckle on her lip was so distracting, or that a man was causing her to chill in the middle of a heat wave.

"I don't doubt it," he said huskily, and Stella hadn't sturdied herself for what came next. It only lasted as long as it took to strike a match for the stove, but it was what it was. Attraction. Shame immediately coursed through her.

"Anyone brave enough to jump into a flood has little fear, but this is not a test of courage, nor a time to be plainspoken," he said sternly. "One must know their place."

And just like that, Stella felt the bubbles in her chest turn to pebbles in her belly. His assessment stung. After all, he was the one who stared at her freckle. With embarrassment coursing through her, she looked away, waiting for a murder of crows to suddenly appear and mock her.

"Bishop Graber!"

From the barn came a lengthy shadow of a man. When his sights set on Simon, Stella felt the ground beneath her slightly shudder. *Did he just call Simon a bishop?* Glancing around, Stella noted no one else about.

"Bishop?" her voice squeaked out as she straightened. "Are you a bishop?" Stella waited another heartbeat for Simon's reply, but his silence was only a confirmation that he was in fact the bishop of Cherry Grove. *Of all the stuff,* she mentally spat. Stella never misjudged tea or remedies before hearing all the symptoms. She took great care to hear details and prodded harshly before treating the sick. How had she missed this very important fact?

Stella shook her head. He sure didn't look like a bishop. Not with those eyes and barely a gray hair showing. Bishops were older, their beards longer and white. Never before had she seen one look so. . .appealing.

"Bishop Graber," the elder greeted a second time as he neared, and Stella took two long steps back on her wobbly legs. It was a proper distance. She turned her attention on the other man, his lanky strides eating up earth faster than most. Dust puffed upward with each boot step, a reminder of how desperately rain was needed in the area.

"Carl," Simon greeted. The men shook hands, but Stella remained glued to the spot, trying to absorb her currently reality.

"This is Dok Stella. She's come to see over Carlee and the many fallen ill."

She would no longer think of him as Simon. She'd simply have to put aside the treachery for now and focus on her reason for being here in the first place.

Carl's sour expression remained stone set. He looked over her to Ellie and then back to her, doubtful. Daed used to look at her the same way anytime she wanted to learn something new, such as harnessing a horse or building her own birdhouse for the cardinals Mamm was so fond of.

"I never asked for no dok."

Stella shivered under his harsh tone and the sound of distant thunder. It wasn't the thought of rain that could birth into a storm. It was the deep-seated frown cemented in place on the man named Carl and a bishop who deceived her by not sharing who he was. If ever she had felt more uncomfortable, she did not remember it.

Absentmindedly, Stella reached down and rested a hand on Ellie's head. Her faithful friend was always at hand, her love unconditional. Ellie also gave an extra sense of safety when safety was sought after. *Dogs don't lie either,* she silently quipped.

"Gott provided for our needs, certain sure, and many have faith in Dok Stella for such," Simon returned. "Michael too has been ill, and she saw to my sohn as well as many today."

Stella tried not to take it personally. The bishop had told her Carl had been given a hard row to hoe for some time. Her heart immediately went out to him, despite his cold welcome. Tightening her grip on her bag handle as a hot last-day-in-July sun beat down on the three of them, she waited for the men to come to an agreement.

It didn't appear to be coming soon.

"My faith is in the Lord, not a woman." Carl darted a glare toward Stella. "Man and woman only disappoint." Carl's eyes traveled grudgingly between the two of them. "We will pray." Two long arms folded over his chest, and his brows gathered in a mulish expression. The men locked each other in a stare as if a thousand words were being tossed back and forth.

"Jah, we will pray. . .while Dok Stella sees in on Carlee," the bishop persuaded more demandingly. Stella wasn't accustomed to anyone defending her, especially one so deceiving.

"She's not from here." Carl's tone held unmistakable displeasure. "I know who you are. You sell those Englisch pills and dried-out flowery concoctions. We have no need for such here." He flattened his palm and motioned a cut through the air.

Stella sucked in a breath. Here she and Simon were offering a helping hand and it felt as if it were being slapped away.

"Then we will pray together, for many prayers reach Gott's ears more quickly."

Carl Hooley's frown deepened as if the bishop asked him to eat week-old oatmeal without even a cup of milk. Most folks would appreciate a bishop being so caring to come fetch her. Stella certainly would have.

"A prayer of faith shall save die krank," Carl added between clenched teeth.

"Jah, then we shall let our requests be made known to God and be thankful He delivered us help."

"Her mudder will see to her. I know what is best for my family. The head shall lead over them. I am not one who would build houses for our young to live among the Englisch."

"All have the freewill to choose the side he sleeps on."

Stella stared at the bishop under that harsh accusation. Clearly this back-and-forth was a raw topic that had some salt rubbed vigorously in it.

"In all your ways acknowledge Him, and He shall direct your paths."

"If we trust in Him with all our hearts, and lean not on our own understanding," the bishop rebutted by speaking at the beginning of the proverb. "One who does not love all does not know the Lord."

Stella was dizzy, darting looks from one man to the other. She had never witnessed a proverbial argument before. The two men weren't discussing the importance of prayer or the long-argued lines of obedience and being separate from the world; they were yanking a doctoral rope in a tug-of-war over matters she had no knowledge of.

There was a story here, but Stella was here to help, and standing under a climbing hot sun while the men decided if they were praying now or later was not helping the sick one bit.

"Those who are well have no need of a physician, but those who are sick." She had memorized the verse years ago and found it was the right time to finally use it. Both men turned to stared at her. Her place was to be quiet and wait for instruction, but Stella had a duty to another.

"I grow my own medicine, and what comes in a bottle is from Utah. I did my research," she defended. "Before the both of you start drawing eyes on you, perhaps you can see to the horse and finish this. . .conversation in the barn. I will go see die krank."

It was an act of rebellion, as sure as the sky was blue, but Stella lifted her chin and ignored the tremble inside her. She squared her shoulders and marched into the house without glancing back. She didn't like being so forward, and she disliked bullies even more than bishops who concealed truths even if they didn't look. . .bishoply. But there were times one had to muster up gumption and use it for the good of others, and it seemed like the perfect time.

CHAPTER EIGHT

Upstairs Stella placed a hand on the young woman's forehead. Her skin was damp and ashen in color, and she wasn't just warm but hot to the touch. Stella knew instantly her fever was dangerously high. Nothing like Michael's had been. The upper bedroom of the Hooley home was exceedingly warm and tight on oxygen. Not a good combination with those symptoms.

"Carlee, how are you feeling?"

"*Ich vays naet*," the young woman replied, her pale eyes glassy in appearance, which was another sign of the temperature raging through her.

"Does your throat hurt, or any of your limbs?"

"Jah, everything hurts."

Her coughs were shallow, doing little to clear the airway. Going on what she knew, Stella thought it best to seek a real doctor, but that was a sore subject with Carl and could cause more hardships on Carlee. The next couple of hours would let her know if she was able to help the girl or if she should go against the bishop's warning and try to change the mind of Carl Hooley, who was sternly watching over Stella's every move.

"Can you help her?" Carlee's mamm asked on a worried breath.

"Gott has the ability to take away a fever and bring comfort to the sick." This earned her some space from Carl as he backed away and settled to loom in the doorway. Stella would not take credit for what

God provided.

"If you have a room downstairs, where it is cooler, we can redd up a bed. That will be best."

"Jah, but she was freezing, and we thought. . ." Carlee's mamm bit her lower lip.

"What a thoughtful mudder," Stella quickly added. Dark dips under the women's eyes showed evidence of her round-the-clock care. "She will be closer yet, making the work lighter for you," Stella insisted and placed two fingers on Carlee's pulse. The fast beats concerned her. Stella ran a soothing hand over the young *maed*'s hair then lowered to listen to her chest. Congestion in the head matched that in her chest. Stella needed to keep her from developing pneumonia.

"We need to get her fever down first," Stella instructed. "Instead of bathing her," because that was a mother's next step Stella had observed over the years, "I will clean her off up here, with warm water and vinegar. It will draw out the heat and room-warm water won't let her pores close." Carlee's mamm cocked her head quizzically. "Cool water traps the heat inside." Stella went to her bag to fetch the jar of vinegar. Folks simply didn't appreciate the many uses vinegar had. Just a spoonful a day had the power to keep a body in good health.

"You sure you know what you're doing?"

"Kumm, Carl, let Dok Stella and Susan tend over her. We will pray Gott sees over the three of them," the bishop said and gave Stella a slight smile. The bishop's words eased the knot between her shoulder blades. As if he truly had faith in her ability to help Carlee when he seemed so skeptical of her before. Between her knowledge and the bishop's prayers, whatever flu was thought to be attacking Carlee had no chance of surviving.

"I'll see a cot set up in your sewing room, Susie. You watch over the dok," Carl ordered before leaving the room.

Stella ignored his fleeting remark, but Carl's distrust was clearly not limited to the Englisch. "I'll need something light to dress her in. The softest and lightest fabric will be best," she said.

"Will you need to brew teas for her? I know you do that for plenty of other folks." Susie retrieved a dishpan from a nearby dresser and set it down nearby.

"Jah, feverfew for the fever and mullein for her lungs, for the next few hours. I hope by morning we can give her broth and elder tea. She will need her strength." Susie nodded, trusting Stella would care for her daughter.

"And we can only use water from the jug I brought with me to bathe her. It is pure and clean." Susie's expression pinched, but she said nothing about the odd request and quickly retrieved a thin gown and fresh towels. Even if Susie wasn't certain of Stella's methods, she wasn't ignoring them either. Most who sought her out seldom questioned her methods, but here in Cherry Grove, Stella felt as uncertain about things as she ever had.

Stella bathed and dressed the young woman before Carl carried her downstairs to the sewing room just to the left of the kitchen. She saw to putting more water on to boil and helped Susie with stripping all the bedding from Carlee's room and giving everything a thorough cleaning. Her knowledge to help others didn't limit her ability to see a chore through.

"The bishop did a kindness, fetching you for us. Carlee is already resting better than she had been. Danke for all your help. A mother can only do so much, and I fear I'm so tired I have been little help to her."

Stella placed a hand on Susie's arm. "I cannot know the burdens or blessings of being a mudder," Stella encouraged. "But I know you must rest now too, while she sleeps. If you grow weak, you might catch this too."

"Oh, we already had it," Susie admitted. "On the last Friday. Carl missed working in his shop, keeping to the bed, but Carlee seems to not overcome it. That's why the bishop worried, I reckon."

"So Carlee has been ill for a week?"

"About six days or so. She first had a sore throat, and a couple days later she grew tired and her cough grew worse. I tried cough syrup and warm honey and lemon, but it seemed to do little to help." Stella began measuring out the right portions for both teas along the cluttered kitchen counter. It was an easy chore, but substance was essential for a weakened body.

As soon as the fever breaks. Broth.

"If the weather holds, I will visit tomorrow and see how she is faring," Stella offered and watched relief waft over Susie's face. "We will have her right as rain in no time."

"Speaking of rain, it seems to be nearing." Both women peered out the large kitchen window where dark clouds eased over the small parcel. A disturbing shiver ran up Stella's spine, and that all-too-familiar worry began building. It didn't look like just a summer rain shower but more like swollen-bellied clouds ready to fill every creek from here to Walnut Ridge.

Please hold off a little longer. She sent up the silent prayer. At the buggy barn nearest the home, Stella noted both men standing. The bishop stood frozen to a spot while Carl spoke with obvious disagreement. She'd give the bishop credit—his frame remained calm as he listened to Carl's words. A bishop who listened and not just spoke was something to be admired. *If only this one wasn't so secretive,* she silently quipped.

"I reckon I should see about getting a ride home before it comes." *Because there is no way I will be caught out in a storm,* she wished to add. "I can call a driver." Karen would be her first choice, as the woman never minded seeing Stella reach those in need no matter the hour. But it was the last of July, which meant she was still out west with the Millers. She could call Mr. Doyle, her neighbor, but he didn't allow dogs to ride in his truck. Stella let out a sigh.

"Ach, Bishop Graber will see you home. If he brought you, surely he won't mind returning you." Susie nodded and smiled. "You are not married, jah?"

Stella blinked. "Nee."

"Then you should know you are the first woman he has ever carted around since Lizzy, aside from Lena, and she's his own mamm," Susie said with a slight hike in amusement. "It wonders me if he doesn't have an eye for you." That would have been laughable if not for being just another shock to her system.

"He is widowed?"

"Jah, many were lost to us that day. A terrible accident it was." Susie clutched her chest, securing the details of the tragedy.

"He never said," Stella stammered. Then again, he never said he was the bishop either.

"He is very private. I see you are curious," Susie said, but before Stella could respond, she continued. "He breeds horses and dabbles in black-smithing. Simon is a gut bishop no matter what mei husband thinks." Susie grinned, revealing answers to questions Stella hadn't dared asking.

"He does what is right and can be trusted." Stella could disagree if she wanted to be rude and interrupt the woman singing the bishop's praises. It was none of her business, she concluded. Even if they'd had an awkward moment, he was a bishop. Bishops and Schmuckers were like oil and vinegar. They simply didn't mix.

Stella began collecting her herbs and carefully placing them inside her leather bag. "He only fetched me out of need, I assure you. In fact, he didn't even tell me he was a bishop!" Then again, Stella hadn't given him much a chance to do so, had she?

"I reckon he wanted to be seen plain as any other." *Which he wasn't,* Stella mentally replied.

"Simon is a humble man, not proud at all, and if he kept such from you, I reckon he wanted to get to know you first. But how can he if you worry over your thoughts so?" Susie continued.

Was that true? Stella liked to think not, but in truth, she would have been much quieter and less demanding if she had known. The bishop had lost his fraa, and suddenly her own sore heart seemed ridiculous to ponder after all these years.

"A man's needs and wants are not so far apart, jah?"

That much Stella could agree with.

CHAPTER NINE

Leaving the Hooleys', Stella inhaled a deep breath of fresh air. Between the stuffy house and Carl's constant insistence that the bishop meddled in his life, it was all Stella could do not to let loose her tongue during the whole stay. Ellie was no happier, pouting as she was. Stella hadn't wanted to tie her to the buggy, but clearly a hund wasn't welcomed in the Hooley household.

"I think Carlee will be on the mend soon, as long as they can get her to eat by morning. I agreed to check in on her tomorrow." Stella stroked Ellie's head, an apology, which was not being accepted currently.

"I can fetch you for that," the bishop offered unexpectedly, and Stella couldn't help but think of Susie's parting words. Then she turned her gaze to the hillside. Any other day she would have been giddy to ride alongside a handsome man with twinkles in his eyes, but not a bishop. No way, no how. Not even for a hundred-dollar donation or a new solar dehydrator.

"You should have told me who you were," she huffed, letting him know she was still sore.

His blue eyes squinted, causing his nose to wrinkle as if he'd caught a whiff of something foul. "I told you who I was."

"You said, 'I'm Simon Graber.'" She shot him a glare. "Not 'Bishop Graber.'"

"I was Simon before I was a minister and longer yet before I became bishop. It should not matter as all men are to be treated the same." He lifted that arched brow in disciplinary accord.

He was right. Stella let out a flustered sigh as they pulled onto asphalt. She didn't know what to make of him. Despite being a woman of thirty-eight, she had only known three bishops in her life.

Bishop Wagler in Ohio had made her ten-year-old heart beat with a mix of fear and excitement when he spoke of the dangers of sin after Paul and Matt robbed his peach trees and sold the fruit on the side of the road.

There was Bishop Schwartz from Miller's Creek. Stella often found the elder full of mischief and humor. The man could tell a story with few words but with more facial expressions than she believed three faces could possess.

And then there was Bishop Mast. Just this past Sunday he spoke of the need for constant prayer despite God never answering his very own. His stern looks were intimidating, yet Stella had learned her first year on Walnut Ridge that they were simply due to his constant state of disappointment. Whether because of her reluctance to marry one of the widowers he had chosen for her or because his son had jumped the fence, Stella hadn't a clue.

One thing Stella did know was that a bishop's duty was constant, considering no community was perfect. Stern looks and firm instruction seemed appropriate to keep a person from getting too close to the edge of the slender line between Plain and worldly.

This one with sweat dotting his temples and a smile crinkled in the corners of his eyes made Stella question her definition of a bishop. What Stella knew about ministering to the soul didn't compare to ministering to the sick. On that sudden knowledge, Stella decided to forgive Bishop Graber's reluctance to introduce himself properly. It was always best to be in good graces with everyone, and it was best if she wanted to do the folks of Cherry Grove any good.

The skies to the west grew darker, which added a rush of humid air ahead of the storm. Stella didn't mind the rain. It fed the earth, washed away germs, pollen, and dust, and simply made everything new. It was when there was too much of it that the hairs on her neck rose upward and she felt a need to return to her hillside home. Growing uneasy as the sky claimed an eerie bruised hue, Stella tried to put her focus elsewhere.

"Susie said you were a widower," Stella remarked.

"Jah." His tone tightened and his back quickly straightened. "Michael and I have seen our share of loss." He gave her a probing glance and quickly changed the subject.

"Did you always want to be Dok Stella?" It wasn't the first time she was asked such, but she suspected the bishop would rather ask questions than answer them. If that be the way of it, he was in for a long day indeed.

"Plain Stella is fine," she replied. A gnat clung to her hand, and Stella tenderly nudged it on its way. "I always liked the outdoors, meeting new people, and helping others."

"Many like those things." He glanced at her hands and then back to the road. "But you chose a different path."

"Or it chose me." She chuckled. "I was never much use with a needle. There are plenty of bakers in Walnut Ridge, and don't make me share how terrible I am at building houses."

A laugh sprang out of him, crinkling the corners of his eyes. "If you say so."

Stella liked the way his eyes glinted in laughter and the deep sound of his voice when he wasn't being all authoritarian. He had fine features, a strong chin, and a thick lower lip. His nose suited the shape of his face, not too big, not too thin. The very idea that she was thinking too much about his appearance forced her to look elsewhere. Tessie Miller was right. Stella was spending far too much time foraging and brewing tea than being with others. She made the decision then and there to attend the next frolic no matter if it was a cleaning, canning, or quilting one.

"I reckon there are many things a woman could do that are less. . .demanding."

"Maybe so." She shrugged, thinking on how Carl Hooley surely

71

held the same opinion. "I simply dropped possibilities into a straw hat and pulled out doktor." She made a motion with her hands as if she had actually chosen to be a doctor by chance. It had taken her years, all her life really, to learn what little she had. From her very first walk into the woods with her *dawdi* to her first infected scab, to accidentally visiting Frannie Weaver on the day her boppli decided to come, God had directed her path to be more than what her parents saw ahead of her.

"God directs our paths, but I guess that works too." The bishop smirked. Maybe he did have an amusing side like his sohn. It wasn't her fault she was rambling again. She was nervous, a little sore, and plenty uneasy.

Because you're not just with a bishop but with an unwed man who smells like horseflesh, sunshine, and sanctuary.

"And thankfully so. For Carlee and Tessie Miller's crooked fingers," she continued. Anything to keep the bishop smiling and the storm edging closer out of mind. "I found early on I was no good at cherry farming, and raising *katz* wasn't for me." She took a long breath, felt the hairs on her arms lift. The air was electrifying.

"Does Cherry Grove have an orchard? Like a cherry orchard?" Oh how she wished she wasn't a nervous chatterer. Ellie squirmed at her feet. She too was no fan of foul weather.

"Nee, Cherry Grove has no cherry orchards," he replied.

"I remember cherry picking with a dear friend in Ohio. Cherry Grove should have cherries, don't you think?" She shot him a look. "It would make a fine livelihood, jah?" Really, who named roads in this county? That's what she'd like to know.

"I suppose it would."

"Couldn't you just imagine an ocean of perfectly pink blossoms like snow over the hilly landscape?" She took a deep breath and immediately felt more relaxed.

"I normally don't have much of an imagination, but I guess I can see how some things could be, given time. Why are you not married?" It was an abrupt question, a tad forward, but Stella had addressed his widowed state, had she not?

"Men never much care for someone who'd rather read about wild herbs than make a meat loaf." It wasn't altogether true. Men also didn't like courting a Schmucker when they met the family. Burl had kept a safe distance from her bruders' teasing, but in the end, he too knew he was better off dealing with a *maedel* from a more respected family.

"How did you learn to make. . ." The bishop swallowed as if something salty caught in his throat. "Who taught you to make teas for fevers and colds?"

"My *grossmammi* taught me to grow many things, and Dawdi loved walking. After his heart condition came about, he said walking was the best medicine. When I was verra young, he would take me on long walks and teach me about many plants and trees and berries. I'd spend weeks with them after we were forced to move. It came in handy because I was the only girl, and mei bruders were always getting into scrapes or catching something. And I like the library."

"Forced to move?" The bishop shot her a concerned look.

Stella clamped her lips tight as embarrassment ran hot and cold over her. When would she simply just let the silence have its turn?

"I remember Elmer Schmucker. He used to build houses in the area."

"Jah, that was my dawdi," she said with a hint of pride, thankful the bishop was good at moving past touchy topics. "I moved in to tend to them, and when they passed, I inherited the place." A place all her own.

Stella had worked so hard to earn the love she felt all kinner should be given, the kind all her friends seemed to receive, but it was her grandparents who taught her that love wasn't a chore. It was a gift, easily given and purposefully made. Why her own parents had not inherited the same knowledge eluded her. Had marriage and starting a family really been so difficult for them to enjoy?

Thinking of the two people who loved her unconditionally, Stella finally grew quiet. The *clippity-clop* of the horse's hooves on asphalt helped slow the unease in her chest. She had a terrible habit of inviting the past in at the most inopportune times. Perhaps it was the impending storm. Those often drew her into scurrying places. It made her think of her family.

There was never a time Mamm wasn't miserable, and more often than not, she expected everyone else to be miserable too. Daed had a habit of starting a great many good ideas but never the spark to finish them. He would spend hours planning the next opportunity, and all those hours sitting gave him little ambition to see if they would work. How many times had the elders and ministers visited their home, she couldn't count. Stella wasn't the only one affected either. Paul struggled to fit in with boys his age, and given a long leash, he found that mischief-making earned him more attention than being obedient ever did.

It was Stella's dream come true that Burl stumbled into her life with his eagerness to settle down and raise a family. They joined the church together. It had been a cold spring day, but she didn't mind sitting with him late into the evening as they planned a life together. How wonderful it felt to be chosen; yet how familiar it was to be set aside.

Simon didn't know it was so much work carting a doctor around, but he had to admit, it wasn't that much of a hardship either. Her nervous chatter filled the quiet and made him smile, as did the rest of her. Evening had gained some ground and it was nearly suppertime by the time they left the Millers'. Simon worried over Michael, but then again, he also knew Verna would be there despite his instruction not to be. She was a terrible fusser, yet he could always depend on her.

Stealing a sidelong glance over the mutt's head, Simon could see that Dok Stella took her duty seriously. He'd watched firsthand as she gently moved a soft damp cloth over Mahone Miller's forehead just an hour ago—and how she ignored his feverish tone, his cigarette-induced hacking and coughing, and his insistence that he didn't need to be ministered to like a child.

Simon grinned recalling just how quickly Stella had quieted Carl. Simon had been struggling for seven long years to help the broken father, and yet Dok Stella reminded him in one fast scripture of her purpose. Her fluency to administer to one's health was not like ministering to one's soul and mind, but the two did follow the same creek bed heading for big water. She was a book full of long chapters, and she smiled at hunds and nettles. There was always something new under the sun to make a man see the world through another set of eyes. Simon didn't like to admit it, but today had been the most interesting day he'd had in years.

The humidity thickened, a push of rain narrowing closer. Flashes of lightning off to the west caused the dok to jolt in the seat beside him.

"We should hurry," she insisted, her voice carrying a tremble.

She need not worry. He always kept an umbrella in the buggy for Mamm. "Hurry or naet, I reckon we are both to get wet." Simon reached down into the narrowed floorboard and produced the umbrella for her. As hot as it had been all day, he didn't mind a little rain, but a woman with a wet kapp tended to fret more than one with a dry one.

Ignoring his gift, she eyed the heavens and hugged her leather bag tightly as a parade of shivers rode over her like a colt standing alone for the first time. She lived alone, in a home dangerously edging on disaster, with a hund. So why did she look like she could crawl under the seat for the rest of the ride home? She didn't strike him as one who feared a few raindrops.

"You might better take it." He offered again. The doctor jerked ramrod straight, finally accepting the umbrella. She tried to look collected, but Simon saw past her forged independence.

A sheet of heavy rain in the backdrop of Farrows Creek had Simon urging David to move faster. He might be able to outrun the rain to Walnut Ridge, or maybe not. One thing was for certain, Stella Schmucker was afraid of storms. He knew the look, the body language.

"Perhaps I can call a driver. We aren't going to make it in time." The urgency in her voice pierced him.

"It will take longer to call and find one willing to fetch you at this hour than to just keep going." Which was true.

"I want to call a driver." Thunder cracked behind her desperate plea.

The hund lifted her head and looked to her owner with what Simon could only see as sympathy. Animals had a way of knowing things few folks ever did. Even her dog could see she was struggling internally.

That's why he made a spur-of-the-moment decision. It was best to get Stella safe under roof before she bounded out of the seat and sought shelter herself. The fear in her eyes as she studied the raging heavens, the tremble of her bottom lip, and the tight grip on her bag all bore deep into his protective nature.

"We can't outrun it. You will stay with Mamm tonight." It was a simple act of charity, of kindness. That was all. Any bishop would offer the same given the circumstances. It had nothing to do with the panic of her breath or anxiety riddling over her. It wasn't the way the terror in her eyes set off alarms he didn't know he could hear.

"Danke, but I don't want to be a burden." Such a thought forced him to frown. She needed to be seen after, and if he was being honest, Simon couldn't ignore the fact he wanted to know her better. He was nothing like Mark, who could fall in love in a day, but after one day with Stella, Simon was. . .curious.

"You are no burden, Stella Schmucker," he said, making a mental note to stop saying her last name aloud. The last thing Simon needed to be thinking about was kissing and coddling. "We cannot have the dok getting a kault now too," he said matter-of-factly.

"Sadie said I should see the Lengachers, and Michael will need more tea. Maybe so, I can. . ." Her shoulders remained stiff, her body tense, but her breath seemed to even out as she struggled with the growing winds against the umbrella.

"I appreciate you seeing over him, and after morning chores, I'll see you to the Lengachers' before taking you home." She nodded and he felt his own concerns vanish. He'd sleep better knowing she was safe nearby and not in a house that might slide over a hillside. All it would take was one mighty wind, like the one kicking up now, and her home might blow right over.

It was a short ride, but by the time they reached the farm, the hund was half on the doctor's lap, and half sitting on her feet. The umbrella was a task to keep over them. Neither had kept her dry, but it was closed eyes and whispered prayers that worried him most. Simon set the brake and hopped out of the buggy. He didn't take the time to pull the vinyl covering over the seat when it became clear Dok Stella wasn't budging from the seat on her own, her own panic nailing her to the spot.

Thunder cracked, lightning flashed, and rain drilled into weeks of dust and dirt. Simon scooped up the doctor into his arms and rushed around the side of the house to his mamm's front door.

It was the right thing to do.

CHAPTER TEN

Stella carefully folded the omelet as Lena buttered biscuits freshly pulled out of the oven. Simon's mother had been wonderfully welcoming despite the late hour. She took to Ellie swiftly too, happily offering to let her sleep on the floor instead of out in the storm. If Stella wasn't mistaken, Lena Graber liked hunds. Thankfully, she didn't mind soaked-to-the-bone women either.

She turned off the burner, the events of yesterday still fresh in her head. From Simon appearing at her haus, to meeting Sadie and her delightful kinner, to the terrible storm that left her frozen in fear—how could a single day be so filled with yanking emotions?

She gave her dress another adjustment. Stella appreciated Lena lending it to her while Stella's hung to dry, but her elder was a mite smaller, leaving Stella to feel like a wrapped boppli in a blanket.

"That dress suits you. Brings out the hickory shades in your eyes," Lena said.

Stella had never had her eyes compared to hickory nuts before and found she liked the comparison. "Danke for letting me borrow it. I'm sorry to be such trouble. If not for the storm. . ."

"Ach, it has been collecting dust too long." Lena waved a hand in the air. "Storms can bring a mess, for certain sure, but they can also carry in a fresh new day. Don't fret over landing here. Michael will be all the better for it. I have plenty more of Lizzy's things you can wear. Shoes too." Lena glanced down at Stella's bare feet. She had no idea where her one flip-flop had gone. Somewhere between struggling to stay dry and being carried to shelter by a bishop. The memory caused her face to flush, and she quickly gave the omelet two flat pats with the spatula.

"It has been some time since I've had a visitor, aside from the grandchildren. Gott knows company feeds the soul and sharpens the skills." Stella liked the elder instantly. "I hope the couch was comfy. Kinner can sleep on a hard floor and not slow a step, but we know better." Lena winked a frosty pale eye before moving toward the icebox standing tall in one corner.

The small *dawdi haus* held all the amenities a home required, but few still used an icebox anymore. If one didn't have a refrigerator, then an icehouse often served a family better. Then again, Stella remembered, Lena and Simon had both lost their spouses, with only Michael to raise yet.

There was a short countertop with a sink. Three sturdy cabinets hung low on the left. In the absence of curtains she had seen hanging in many of the nearby Amish homes, Stella smiled. Who wanted the view of the outdoors hidden?

Curtains, like tight dresses, only made Stella uncomfortable.

"I'm no youngie, for certain sure," Stella jested, "but it was comfy, danke." She opened the front door to let Ellie out.

A brush of warm, damp air wafted over her. The world was calm now, nothing like the gnashing and growling of last night. It was just rain, she had tried schooling herself, but that truth never stuck when rain carried on in buckets instead of sprinkles. Looking down, Stella noted a pair of black-soled shoes just in the doorway. They didn't look worn. She bent to retrieve them, noting they were dry.

"I found these." She lifted them up for her elder to see.

"Jah, Simon must have fetched them for ya," Lena said as if it were nothing. Then again, the bishop had frowned at her flip-flops, and she couldn't very well go visit the Lengachers barefoot. It hadn't escaped Stella either that, like the dress, the shoes most likely also belonged to the bishop's late fraa.

"I like her," Lena said. "Yer Ellie. She is verra well behaved and doesn't bark or pester. Mei eldest sohn, Ervin, raises shepherds, and they can stir noise faster than a kitchen full of women."

Stella chuckled. "She knows her place. I take her everywhere, so she is used to folks."

"I hear you own a small shop, selling medicines?" She lifted a brow.

"A very small shop," Stella added, closing the door. Ellie never wandered far and would let her know when she was ready to come back in. "Jah, in my home. I sell a few Nature's Sun products and many dried herbs for teas. I like tea." Stella shrugged modestly.

"A worthy livelihood, indeed. Much to keep one awful busy. Best you remember there is much to life, and it's not all work."

Stella flinched. Her life was routine. She woke, gathered, welcomed those in need, and, after a modest supper, went to bed so she could do it all again the next day.

"My free time is usually spent gathering herbs or helping new bopplin into the world. I like what I do. It does not feel much like work but. . .having a purpose."

"Jah, I reckon many are thankful for your dedication." Lena was kindly encouraging.

Stella lifted the omelet onto a plate. "Few Englisch dare try the teas or homemade salves I create since Merle Weaver went to jail for poor labeling." He'd gotten six years because a woman broke out in hives using his chickweed salve. It was why Stella asked so many questions before offering remedies, for fear of what could come of it. Then again, she would have happily stopped selling chickweed salve or changing the label to avoid such chastisement too.

For it is better, if it is God's will, to suffer for doing right than for doing wrong.

"You sell to the Englisch too?"

"Our bishop allows it." Stella bit her lower lip, wondering if Lena was much like Carl Hooley when it came to doing business with outsiders. "Not everyone wants to swallow a pill, and they understand their health is worth some effort." She meant the words wholeheartedly, but as Lena stilled and looked at her, Stella worried that she had been delivered to a community of old thinking. Much like the one she had fled from years ago.

"Jah, and your bishop would be correct. Gott says to care for all; He didn't say help only those who plowed his field on this side of the fence."

Stella smiled at her elder. She was making yet another fast friend. Lena began humming a familiar tune as if joy was in her heart as the sun burst into the east-facing window. Sweet-natured Lena had a spring in her step and a smile that filled her whole face.

Stella hurried, adding a pinch of salt and a healthy shake of pepper to the omelet she had divided equally for two people. She wasn't accustomed to starting her day so late. As she stared down at the concoction, at the pretty colors of perfectly beaten eggs, sausage, tomatoes, wild garlic, and nettle, she couldn't help but hear Mamm's voice call out what an odd child she was.

Mamm was seven years and over two hundred miles away, yet Stella could still hear her. Stella took in a deep breath and let it out slowly. The storm was over, Lena was humming, and the omelet looked beautiful.

"While I fetch jam, be a dear and go fetch Simon and Michael," Lena said.

Stella set the hot skillet into the shallow sink and swallowed. "You want them to join us?" Stella's thoughts scrambled faster than a dropped egg basket. True, she needed to see how Michael was feeling this morning, but thoughts of seeing the bishop again suddenly stole her appetite.

"Look at all this food. Mei Simon is no cook, and Michael is due a fine meal," Lena said sorrowfully. So Michael was his only child.

"I didn't do it alone," Stella reminded her.

"Nee, but you collected those greens, picked the tomato, and I know it took you a while to ready that tea I'm eager to try." The aromas had filled the little space with a minty smell. "Simon never eats early. He must tend to his colts first, but a working man deserves a hearty start." Lena grinned, a row of perfectly fake teeth and two sunken jaws. It was easy to see joy radiating around Simon's mother, which was why Ellie had been so quick to saddle with her. It was also evident Lena Graber didn't tolerate any waffling as she waved Stella to be quick about it.

So that was why Stella helped cook breakfast at seven in the morning and had a sudden urge to run all the way back to Walnut Ridge barefoot. Lena wanted her to share the same table with the bishop.

Stella glanced out the kitchen window as day spilled over the landscape. At the barn, the bishop led two colts out to pasture. It was a shame he had no more sons seeing to other chores or any dochters out collecting fresh eggs. Was he lonely with no young kinner at his side or fraa waiting for him?

He caressed and whispered to the colt. One, a dark mare no more than a year old, tried following him back to the barn. Lena said he was separating colts to stand on their own two feet. She imagined it wasn't easy work, but it was the way of things. Stella's heart felt for both of them. They would miss their mamm.

Not like she had. The memory of that day found her. The day when words grew loud but she was no longer willing to hear them anymore. She'd collected a small bag, shoved her spare dress inside along with her notebook filled with notes she had collected over the years, a copy of *Rosemary Gladstar's Medicinal Herbs*, and the worn-out Bible her aenti Florence sent her on her seventeenth birthday. Stella had walked away without looking back.

What would the bishop think of her if he knew she had no real love for the people who raised her?

"I see him heading toward the house now," Lena announced, glancing out the kitchen window. "You go on and catch him before he slithers off to his shop and we don't see him again until Sunday services."

Stella made her way outside, wondering if there was anything she could do to help a lonely bishop and his sohn. Then again, she knew tea, not people, so probably not.

———————— ❧ ————————

Simon tracked back to the house, his right shoulder already aching. The storms rolling over last night had unsettled the colt as much as it had the pretty doctor. Replacing a few boards on the stall wouldn't be much trouble, but getting the animal back on track would take a little more time than Simon wanted to spare. Separating mares and colts was a delicate process that was best not interrupted. One could gain head, form a new routine, and suddenly with one skipped lesson, all was back to the beginning.

He rubbed the place on his shoulder. Critter surely could sneak a bite on a man not paying attention. It was already starting out to be a long day, and Simon hadn't even made oatmeal yet. Michael would surely be hungry this morning.

As he strolled past the dawdi haus, Simon thought of the dok. Like the skittish colt, she too had a way of making a bishop shake his head. Both looked healthy, strong, and capable of doing as they were created to do, yet one thrash of lightning across a dark sky, and both found themselves sinking and grappling for purchase.

He couldn't help but recall last night, carrying her to shelter. She'd clung to him like a life raft in a river running wild. He was strong yet, despite his years, and hadn't forgotten what it felt like to hold a woman.

Stop it, Simon, he preached to himself as he stomped past a weedy pumpkin patch and overly crowded vegetable garden. A bishop with scarce a minute to himself had no business entertaining fanciful thoughts. A smarter man would have taken Pricilla as a fraa already and been done with it. Michael could use a woman's hand—he saw that with his own eyes—and a man could never be lonely with Mary Alice for a mother-in-law.

Remarrying made sense. Meals would be less. . .burnt, for one. Mamm was getting older, a fact that had not escaped him, and seeing to the garden simply reminded him how a helpmate could bring much to his lonely life. But his heart could not commit to someone he simply didn't love.

Pushing aside silly notions of adding another responsibility to his already full life, Simon reached the front porch. He took the first of three steps in usual stride but stopped midstep before reaching the top. Lifting one brow, he homed in his glare at the heap of brown fur blocking his front door. Usually his farm pests kept to themselves, burrowing deep under his knife shop, but today it seemed this fat fella wanted to pay a visit.

Simon groaned. "You don't live here," he said sternly. The critter didn't move. For a second he hoped the brave fellow didn't have rabies.

"Tired of living under the knife shop, are ya?" He stomped to scare the animal, but it never so much as flinched. *Well, it's not rabid.* Taking the toe of his boot, Simon nudged it cautiously. It wasn't just a groundhog but a dead groundhog.

"There you are."

Simon turned at the sound of the pretty dok. He should probably start thinking of her as Dok Stella, but then his breath caught in his throat as he noticed her shape in the snug-fitting dress. She was no taller than the rosebush hugging the side of the house, and she stuck out like a violet among gravel. *A violet with shoes,* he noted. There was no reason Lizzy's things needed to sit collecting dust, not when they could be of use to another. Nee, there was a reason Simon hadn't considered remarrying before. None had stolen his breath away like this before.

"Lena asked that I fetch you and Michael for breakfast." The lazy sun found a spark of energy, rising just above the hillside in time to land directly on her. In a burst of morning light, she looked to have gained back her smile and forward-moving stride. Nothing like the frightened child he carried to safety. A chill rolled over his flesh.

"Your ears are closed, but your eyes open." Mark's words mocked him currently.

"We'll be along shortly." He turned away from her.

"Danke for the shoes," she said modestly. "I'll see them returned as soon as I can."

Simon simply nodded.

"I know I should not question a bishop." Yet she was doing that now. "But Lena made you a fine meal, and it's getting cold. It's nearly eight o'clock." Simon shifted again, giving her his full attention. He wasn't accustomed to being told when to eat. Even Mamm knew patience, and he knew full on what his mudder did for him daily. She would understand if he was a little late. He'd never met a woman so independently determined and forward speaking, aside from Mary Alice Yoder.

Stella crossed both arms in front of her, impatiently so. It was not a becoming trait in a woman to be short on patience. Then again, persistence had its rewards. He had worked hard to overcome his stutter. Few folks even remembered that it had once plagued him, but right now he was finding that he might have a new disability to overcome.

"What is that?" Finally spotting the ball of fluff blocking his doorway, Stella pointed.

"It's a groundhog." He kicked it with the tip of his boot again. Yep, dead. "Old fellow must have had a heart attack." He should focus on getting it tended to, yet the meadow scent that moved near him held him hostage. She smelled of summer and spring and. . .his favorite chewing gum. Simon clenched his jaw.

"Jah, and a big one too," she said, moving closer.

He couldn't help but feel a grin sneak up, noting the way her lower jaw jutted out when she was focusing hard on something.

"You have troubles with them, I noticed. That shop might just fall into a heap yet."

"The shop is sturdy." She need not point out what he could see plainly. Right then the silver hund marched straight past him and sat down next to the fur heap. Simon didn't think animals capable of smirks or grins, but one looked to be proudly smeared across Ellie's face. Simon narrowed his glare.

"Well, it would seem Ellie tended to your groundhog problem." Sure enough, the hund looked to Simon, lifted a brow, and waited for her reward.

"I don't much like having dead animals on my porch."

"Nee, I reckon naet, but you should be happy Ellie stopped this one from digging further under that shop. She might have saved you plenty in repairs. You should thank her. Perhaps she thinks you are freinden after all."

Her smile wasn't convincing him to thank a mutt. "Thank her? It's a dead groundhog. . . on my porch." He motioned toward the fur heap.

"Rather I train her to catch 'em so you can name 'em?"

Simon was momentarily speechless. "You always this. . .plainspoken?"

"Nee, sometimes I like to sit in the quiet and watch others figure out stuff themselves, especially those who fail to tell me who they are properly." And with that, Simon could do no more than groan. She still had a bee in her bonnet about that.

"We already went over that," he said and turned to the fur ball on the porch again. "This is why I don't have pets. No cats, no mice, no hunds, nothing."

"What kind of life is that, I would not want to know. Kumm, Ellie, he will soon learn your worth." Simon watched her march away, the mutt following.

"Well, I like her," Michael said from an open sitting room window. Simon rolled his eyes. For a quiet fella, Michael seldom missed much.

"Get dressed. Mammi made breakfast."

"Good, I'm starved."

CHAPTER ELEVEN

The small house wasn't roomy enough for four people and one large dog, and Stella fumbled to fetch butter from the icebox, nearly dropping the dish on the floor. Lena was all smiles and not being very discreet, slipping a sausage patty under the table. Simon's frown was evidence he was still not over Ellie doing him a kindness, but Michael looked to have tackled the worst of his illness and was staring at the humble meal greedily.

Setting the butter closer to the bishop, Stella quickly took a seat. She'd never shared a meal with an elder before aside from the biweekly fellowship meal, and sitting this close, Stella suddenly knew how a caged rabbit felt. Heads bowed for the silent prayer. Stella prayed breakfast would be swiftly eaten. She was going to see the Lengachers today, and hopefully another visit with Sadie and Carlee. Then she would be back home where she need not worry about being plainspoken or fidgety any longer.

Heads lifted and forks immediately began moving. Michael needed no nudging to eat. The bishop, on the other hand, poked at his plate with a quizzical brow.

"Are these garlicky things from my yard?" His expression creased. His hands were leathered and large. The knuckles on his three middle fingers calloused. Without his hat, strands of dark hair had fallen over his ears. Stella noticed the thinning spot in his beard. Had it been from a scar?

Stella quickly swallowed her mouthful. There was no reason for her to be unsettled. Mammi had always encouraged Stella to ignore whatever others thought, for that was none of her business, and just be herself. "You'd be surprised what one could eat from right out the front door." Mentioning his front door was probably not the best idea. She quickly forked up a second bite to prove the omelet wasn't dangerous.

"It's the best thing I've eaten in weeks," Michael added, shooting her a kind smile. "Better than. . ."

"Oatmeal," the bishop grumbled. "I know." The father and son looked as different as night and day, and Stella couldn't help but hold back a giggle at Michael's over-trusting appetite compared to his father's untrusting one.

Bishop Graber examined the tea next, swirling his glass around. The lavender blooms she'd plucked at daybreak from outside Lena's porch step began spinning. Early blooms were best, and Stella couldn't help but add them once she'd discovered them on her early morning forage.

His face pinched as if the tea might kill him yet. Michael caught her gaze, and they both tried not to laugh at his gruff expression. Where was the bishop's faith in all the good things God provided?

"Stella, this is delicious," Lena said. "You know, there's a canning frolic planned kumm the first of the week for the Martins."

Stella had met and liked the older couple instantly, as Cecil reminded her so much of her own dawdi with his meandering pace and sweet smile.

Michael was on his second helping of sausage and biscuits, already having devoured his portion of the omelet, when Bishop Graber surrendered to his fears and finished off his plate.

So he isn't picky, just cautious. Or starving. She didn't think it was the latter, even if Lena had mentioned three times already how poorly the two ate.

"There was a quilting frolic planned just this day at Cathreen's," Lena continued, "but with so many sick, it will be some time yet." Lena shook her head. "Perhaps you can get them right again and join us."

"Mammi will have you moved in and married in a week if you say yes," Michael said, earning him a stern look from his father. Stella had no interest in moving or getting married, but the invitation to be included warmed her heart. She wasn't the best at quilting but always enjoyed the fellowship and meeting new women. Perhaps Sadie would be there too. Stella immediately sat up at the thought. Sadie showed a lot of interest in rose hips and tea. It would take so little effort to become fast friends with Sadie, as sweet as she was.

"I haven't attended a quilting frolic for some time. Most of the women on Walnut Ridge prefer quilting alone, but during canning season no one turns down help and a chance to gossip."

Bishop Graber frowned. Any mention of gossip was like gnats to the ear of a bishop. At least he looked full and satisfied as he pushed his plate to the side.

"Another cup of Stella's special tea?" Lena offered her son.

"I could stand another, jah."

He liked her tea. The thought bubbled up inside her.

"I'll get it." Stella dropped her fork and hustled to refill his glass. It sloshed over the side and down her fingers. Thankfully, Bishop Graber accepted the glass without a word to the stickiness, gulping down nearly the whole full glass.

Stella knew better than to put too much stock in trying to please others like she did, but nothing made a person feel more a part of something than being useful. A person who served a purpose earned a place at the table. Had that not been what her father spouted all her growing-up years?

She pushed aside the voices always plaguing her, always ruining a day, and focused on the man at the head of the table right now. This was not her father. This was a bishop enjoying her cooking and sticky tea, and that spoke volumes to drowning out old thoughts.

Stella resumed eating, taking stock of the man. His rolled-up sleeves revealed muscles and dark hair and tanned flesh. Arms that could run carrying a woman yet not squeeze her too tight. Under all those stern looks and lingering gazes was a man who tended to all his flock, not just the ones he preferred, and raised a child alone. She swallowed her well-chewed-up mouthful and let out a sigh.

"Danke for the meal. It was. . .good."

Mercy me. Despite knowing they were as opposite as the moon and the sun, Stella was filling up on omelets and all kinds of flights of fancy. She quickly stood to clear the table. With shaking hands, she grabbed his plate and moved to the small sink.

"After we make our visits today, I can make a meatloaf for supper if you all would like. Before I leave, that is." He had been kind to help her. It was only right to return it, and Michael could use the extra nourishment. Growing *buwe* needed plenty to eat, did they not? Aside from the occasional dish for a gathering, when was the last time Stella cooked for more than herself and Ellie?

"Can you make herbed chicken and mashed potatoes?" Michael quickly put in. Stella chuckled at the request.

"That isn't necessary." Bishop Graber locked gazes with her. He would be the first man she knew who didn't like meatloaf.

"I'll gather more herbs for meadow tea too." Lena spoke, forcing Stella's gaze away. "Lizzy planted a peppermint plant years ago, and now it covers one side of the house."

Stella loved peppermint and had a whole chorus of it growing near her coneflowers and lemon balm, but at the mention of his late wife's name, the bishop's jaw clenched tighter. If Lena noticed, she didn't seem to care that speaking of his late wife might disturb him. Stella instantly regretted her offering of meat loaf. What if it only reminded him of his late wife?

"I'm sure whatever you make would be *wunderbaar*, Dok Stella. Danke for offering," Michael said. What a kind young man he was.

"And I could sure use help with blackberry jam after you've checked over folks. If Michael feels up to it, we can have the last of them picked by the time you return. Ellie can stay with me and Michael." Lena stood slowly, her age having some effect on her swiftness. Stella could happily help pick the berries for her and save her elder the hardship.

"She can keep me company while I take a nap." Michael began scratching the place behind Ellie's left ear she liked so well.

It seemed all was settled until Stella looked to the bishop. It was uncertainty his face wore. It had to be terribly hard to live without his wife. Stella had never been married. She never knew the responsibility of raising fine kinner, but she did know heartache and disappointment sure enough. *It's having something and losing it,* she told herself. Simon had love, and he lost it. Michael had a mamm, and she was gone. Her heart ached for them and for the emptiness she saw in the bishop's eyes that she feared she had no remedy for.

"Michael needs to rest, and Dok Stella came to see over the ill. I'll be returning her back to Walnut Ridge once she's seen to a few more folks," Simon announced, expressionless. "I'll have Verna send Laura over to help with the jam making."

"Laura will eat more berries than make it into a jam jar," Michael muttered.

"Whatever you think best," Lena said without a quarrel.

The bishop's remark struck Stella like a knot on an apron. Of course she needed to get home. There was lavender to harvest, dock leaves to dry, and soon elderberries and ginseng would be ready to harvest. But Stella had wanted to repay Lena for her kindness, not be an eat-and-run visitor. Still, it was best not to question the bishop.

After a quick change, Stella collected her leather bag and bonnet and tied on her borrowed shoes. A dismal ache wafted over her. How had she grown attached so quickly to the little haus and Lena in just one day? Lifting her chin, she left a silent prayer behind. *Gott, watch over Simon, Michael, and Lena.*

Stella sat quietly in the buggy seat next to Simon as the landscape shifted from rolling to flat to rolling again. Cherry Grove was a postcard in spring and in winter when the pines and cedars were heavy in snow, but even in late summer when leaves were losing some of their luster, it appealed to her all the same.

Homes here were often gray metal single story, with a scant few of the two-story white houses that were signature of the Amish. A blue cloudless sky filled overhead, white with the streaks and lines of jets crossing it in fading arrows. Her valley view had once been precious to her, but it would take a good many years for it to regain its brilliance from all the timbering. It was good to see beauty in other places, she liked to think. She wasn't uptight.

"I didn't realize Cherry Grove was so big," Stella said as they took a graveled road and veered off the beaten path to venture into a shadowy lane. "Walnut Ridge is a small area and still spacious enough for more families."

"Growth is good, even if we will soon decide to split it for the well-being of all," the bishop said. Many communities divided once they outgrew fitting into one house on a church Sunday, though Stella couldn't imagine Walnut Ridge ever splitting with as few families as it had.

"But there is always room for more," he added as he pulled into a long drive with a FOR SALE sign at the beginning of it.

At the first house, Stella worried over young Jacob Lemmon's deep cough. His lungs were working hard to clear his pathways. A healthy broth and protein diet along with mullein, elderberry, and honey tea, and Stella felt confident he would be fast mending. He was only twenty-four, living alone with no fraa or parents to tend to him. Stella had a terrible habit of worrying too much. Jacob had been living alone for better on two years now, had he not?

"So why is Jacob selling his farm? Surely he hopes to marry soon and have kinner," she said as the bishop buggied her on to the next house. If a man was blessed with land to steward, why sell it?

"Not everyone marries so young." He glanced her way in an isolated expression. Those eyes were forlorn. It was hard to fathom—a bishop, surrounded by so many yet seeming so desolate.

"Jacob has been working for the Englisch at the animal rescue down the road. The owner fears it has become more than she can handle alone."

"So he is buying an animal sanctuary?" *What an idea*, Stella thought.

"Nee, I spoke to her about letting Jacob take over, run the farm for her. He likes the work, and she has a little place out back that we intend to fix up for him."

Stella stared in awe at him. Despite his many duties, he was helping a young man find his footing.

The Lengachers had six kinner ranging between seven and seventeen. Eldest daughter Hilly bit her own lip to the point that it drew blood when they first arrived. Stella suspected an unexpected visit from a church elder the reason. This household had been struck with the same flu as the previous ones. Stella ministered teas and advice, and she laughed when fifteen-year-old Ellen revealed she'd been wearing onion slices in her socks for two days to keep from getting the worst of it. If life hadn't changed its course on her, would Stella have had daughters the same ages as Mirium Lengacher's girls?

At the last homestead, Stella met Matthias Martin. The fish farmer. His unusual livelihood piqued her interest. The man clearly had a head for thinking, and Stella wanted to hear more about his plans for organic cows and windmills and why a man didn't favor chocolate pudding, but Simon had cut short that conversation as the clock hanging in Matthias' kitchen announced the noon hour.

Stella didn't normally linger, but getting to know the faces of Cherry Grove, even at their worst, had her looking forward to her next visit. With her bike, of course. Traveling with a bishop tended to make most people uncomfortable. Mirium Lengacher wanted to learn more about the power of herbs and how to make her own drawing salves. An accident-prone husband, she claimed. Stella also wanted to hear more about Matthias' plans to build windmills to aerate his stock ponds. It was a brilliant idea, because the one thing Cherry Grove had in abundance, aside from fast friends, was wind.

Working a few loose strands of plain brown hair back into her kapp, the idea of returning soon bloomed in her heart.

CHAPTER TWELVE

Simon stood by watching Stella nurture and care for his friends and neighbors. Her easy way with others warmed him, and her smile charmed him. He wasn't the only one, if the smitten look on young Jacob Lemmon was any indication of its power. She didn't just brew tea and spoon out cough syrups, but the dok got to know each person she was administering to. Simon couldn't help but grin as her brown eyes widened while Matthias Martin went on and on about catfish and windmills. For a woman who boiled weeds and water and ate grass, she'd been mouth open in awe of the concept.

And she loves chocolate pudding.

Simon aimed the buggy northeast. If he didn't return the pretty dok soon, he'd be tempted to find out what else she liked. He had no time for that. Michael needed him. Mamm needed him. His community needed him. There were the horses and colts waiting to resume training. He had knives to forge. The store had already sent word that they'd nearly sold out of everything Simon sent last time. And what of Mahone Miller? How many packs of cigarettes had he swindled Driver Dan into fetching for him this week? Jah, Simon had much to do, and spending more time with Dok Stella was clouding his thoughts.

Casting a sidelong glance, he saw that Stella was staring at the sky. Her chin pointed upward by the slight underbite of her jaw. Her late-spun honey eyes closed as the wind blew her kapp strings behind her. It was contentment he was seeing. Content in doing something for others, and he was immediately wishing he had a dose of it. Did she never tackle bouts of loneliness? Was she truly content with not having a husband, a family? Suddenly a smile split her face, and she jerked her gaze to him.

"A fish farm." An abrupt laugh bubbled out of her, awakening the closed-off door in his chest. He should focus on the road, not on the urge to push those strands of hair back under her kapp for her.

"I just can't stop thinking on it," she apologized and suddenly looked embarrassed.

"Jah," Simon quickly cleared his head. "I told the fella it was a strange living," Simon said before the look on her face became another question. "His folks always struggled with making something of the land there. Too much clay and lack of nutrients. Matthias always said it made a better mudhole than pasture. He felt it was time to try something new." The young man was risking a lot.

"I think it's wunderbaar," Stella added. "He said he already had a market with two restaurants in the next county and the grocery in town." Simon flattened his lips. He'd missed that part of the conversation. Perhaps it was when he was trying to make out all the changes on the Martin farm or that moment Stella explained the benefits of herbs. Who knew weeds had so many good uses?

"I am always amazed how some find new ways to make a living." She let out a pleasant sigh. He liked talking to her.

"The Englisch make a living just talking about making a living," Simon said all too quickly. Clearing his throat, he added, "We are Plain and have no need to reach beyond the necessary." Her brows gathered in disappointment. If Matthias wasn't successful, then his family would be out a great deal of money he had invested. With his parents aging as they were, Simon understood they might have to rely on the church to help see them through.

"I just find it wunderbaar that one uses what he has to make a go of it. Walnut Ridge has buggy makers and the bakery and a cheese shop." She began counting on her hand. "A blacksmith, but most worked in construction before the accident in town. Furniture makers, doll makers, and. . ." She paused, thinking.

"A doktor," Simon added and watched her face ignite with appreciation. She truly loved her work, and it showed in the way her eyes twinkled.

"Jah, but it's nothing like fish farming or windmill builders or organic cattle."

"Nee, it's not," Simon replied. Now that he considered it, Cherry Grove did have a few who liked to think outside of the ordinary. Even if the community split, all would do well, thankfully, in providing for themselves. The bishop in him knew the fear of the elders too. For the more into the world they became, the more chance others could be lost to them. It was a constant worry that robbed Simon of much sleep.

"We have a bed-and-breakfast," Simon put in. Gabriel Fender had reached an age where he no longer could farm his parcel, and having no sons, he'd turned the large home into a respite for others. Visiting families always had a warm place to stay when needs arose, and Simon knew firsthand that Erma was the epitome of hospitality.

"That's good for weddings," Stella said, shifting in her seat.

Her attention, as well as her interest in his community, surprised him. Perhaps she wasn't so attached to her single life on a cliff after all.

"Joe Shetler plans to open an archery business, and if our newcomer has his way about it, a tree farm and nursery soon enough. Jacob will soon be running the animal rescue for all kinds of critters, and. . ." Simon pulled back on the reins to guide David to the side of the road to let a car pass by.

"And a fish farm with windmills," Stella finished with a widespread grin. "You have a large and interesting community, Bishop Graber."

"It can be both, to those looking in," he said and shifted uneasily. She wouldn't be smiling like that if she knew three young men had already jumped the fence since he'd become bishop. Simon wished she would call him by his Christian name. Something about the way she said it, he liked.

It was true Cherry Grove had many members, and each did their part, but there was one thing Cherry Grove didn't have. He glanced her way once more.

"We don't have a doktor," he said and watched her flinch in surprise.

"Walnut Ridge isn't so far," she replied and flapped a hand in the air. Her reply was simple, but as they returned to pick up Stella's four-legged companion, Simon suddenly wished he had a doktor. Or better yet, that his community did, because of course, it was the community that mattered. Not him.

Ellie's warm body leaned into her as Stella considered the bishop's words. Cherry Grove would benefit having a dok. She never liked to see folks at their worst, but it had been an interesting couple of days. Getting to know Simon was no hardship. He had an important role in his community, and if Stella wasn't mistaken, he wasn't opposed to catfish farming. Those worried lines between his brows spoke of a man who only wanted the best for everyone.

Like seeing that they had someone to help them in times of sickness.

As the buggy veered over her steep drive, Stella's concerns for others turned to concern over the debris scattered about. Limbs sprinkled her muddy driveway and scant yard. Flowers were stripped bare of blooms. There was no burst of life, of nature's colors welcoming her home. Cora Mast had once told Stella she would never grow a thing in rocks and roots. It had taken hard work, sweat, and a stubborn will, but Stella had proved that life could flow abundantly anywhere if one put their heart into it.

"Storm looks to have reached out this way as well." The bishop set the brake.

"Jah," Stella muttered as she took in the chaos. Climbing down from the buggy, Ellie right after, Stella was certain she could hear Cora Mast's words as if she were standing at her left. There were no lavender blooms to harvest. No daisies or coneflowers boldly danced on the late summer breeze. Foxgloves lay limp, battered under a pile of leaves and twigs. Erosion and heavy rains had cut deep streams into the earth. The strong winds and heavy rain had taken a toll.

Stella sucked in a breath and found her mint garden still thriving. Brambles still held firm despite what they'd endured.

"I promised Lena some mint to plant outside her doorway." Stella leaned over to inspect the thick bounty. She plucked a spearmint leaf, rubbed it gently between finger and thumb, and brought the delightful scent to her nostrils. At least some of the rocky gardens still had life in them. She was thankful for that.

"Dok Stella," Simon said in a low, warning tone.

Rising to stand, Stella turned. That's when she saw it. It was a fresh crack to her heart. The house her grandfather had built, the sanctuary offered to her as a child and again later when she was thirty-two and filled with a new hope and a second chance, destroyed. It was clear the problem wasn't with a few drowned plants or uprooted flowers but by the way the front porch dipped. She took a couple more steps toward the front and clutched her heart as a gasp slipped out of her.

"Oh no!"

"The storm must have felled it." The large oak on the east side, once providing a cool respite, had fallen over the heart of her home. The front door was shut, but limbs protruded out her two front windows. A sudden panic swelled up in her chest, making it awfully hard to breathe. Clearly this was nothing easily fixed. It was devastation all over again. Grasping her middle, Stella swallowed back the hard rock in her throat. *Seven long years of joy gone in one storm.*

"Stella," the bishop said.

No way could she fall apart in front of him. Despite the need to run into the tree line where tears could fall in private, Stella would face the day as it came, even if she was nauseous. It was that same gut-twirling ache she'd felt the day she walked out of her parents' house. How many times she had schooled herself that she was doing the right thing by running away, doing what God wanted her to do. But running now would not help the situation.

Lifting her chin, Stella inched closer. Had not life taught her to take the good with the bad? She had picked up and started from scratch before, and she would do it again. She'd keep on keeping on, just as she always had, and she'd start with a cup of tea. Nothing helped sort one's thoughts better than a cup of hibiscus tea with a couple of peppermint leaves.

"It will be a task, for certain sure. Oh, what a mess." She turned to the bishop. "Danke for delivering me home, but as you can see"—she pushed up her midlength sleeves—"I have much work to do today too."

"You can't think to go inside." The bishop put out a hand to stop her.

"It's my home," she replied. He was not her bishop, and she was not his concern.

"I'll see if it's safe first," he said in a voice of concern.

Suddenly the thought of all those limbs tangled up among her things sent a second dose of nausea through her. All her herbs, her dishes, and the tea set. *Mammi's tea set.* Her heart leaped into her throat.

"Stella." The sound of her name jerked her to attention. "Wait here."

Helpless to do more than nod, Stella watched the bishop force the door open with his shoulder. Wrangling her lip, she waited with a held breath. Beside her, Ellie sat watching the doorway, waiting too. Aside from one leather bag, all either of them possessed was just on the other side of that door.

A Cooper's hawk screeched overhead. It had lived there nearly as long as she had. Stella bent her head back, watching it dart into the tree line and disappear. Time ticked in heartbeats. She was desperate to know what had become of her things. What of her precious tea set? It had been the only thing left after Stella was forced to sell all of Dawdi's furniture to start her modest shop. Mammi said a good cup of tea tasted better in one of those cups than any other, and she had been right about that.

The bishop emerged from the house and gave his trousers a brushing. "There's too much damage. I'm sorry, but you cannot stay here. I can see to speaking with your bishop, getting a few men from the area to help clear the mess, covering the hole for now, but. . ." He removed his hat, giving the outside a second scrutiny.

"It's Gott's will," she muttered. Tears sprang up completely unbidden.

Bishop Mast would say such before insisting she marry now that she had nothing left to cling to. *Leon Strolfus, most likely.* Her stomach roiled at the thought. She hadn't yet met a woman who wanted to marry for shelter and safety over love.

"I think it best you decide where I can take you. This will take some time to remedy." He stepped closer. "We cannot know His will, but we must face each day as it comes."

Stella peeled her gaze from the house to the man. She didn't trust herself to decide right now, not with her livelihood crumbled before her. What was she to do? She didn't want to think about Bishop Mast or Leon Strolfus currently.

"Stella, I cannot know what you are thinking unless you tell me." Sincerity replaced the seriousness, and she felt she might melt into the dirt.

"I'm afraid of storms," she blurted out. "And now you can see why. They destroy everything."

"Jah, and they can clear the way for a fresh day too. He knows what is best for us"—

Simon glanced back briefly before turning to her again—"even if we cannot understand it."

"So He wanted me to lose my haus?" She clamped a hand over her mouth. What a terrible thing to say.

"I'm certain that was the storm, but no matter, you cannot stay here."

The last thing Stella wanted was to once again be at the mercy of her community. Had she not separated herself from being like her parents? She looked to the house once more. It was limbs and wood and work, but it was all mendable.

"We have to stay here," she replied. She appreciated his concern, understood it even, but it wasn't just her that was homeless. She looked down at her faithful companion, the one friend who would never leave her.

"I thought you to be a smart woman." His deep, graveled tone held correction.

"Nowhere in our Ordnung does it say I can't live in my own haus. We are not in Cherry Grove, Bishop."

"Your roof is gone." He tilted his head, but his tone remained level. "I cannot leave you here. What if another storm comes?"

Stella's gaze shot directly to the sky. Was there a storm coming?

"Let's see what can be saved, and I'll take you back with me."

"With you?"

"You can see over the sick and Michael until I can speak to your elders." He looked at the little house, the befallen roof and destroyed eastern wall. "Bishop Mast probably has a better solution of what is best."

"Jah, he'll marry me to one of the widowers in less time than it takes to mend the roof." She hadn't meant to spout the words aloud, but the truth was sometimes hardest to harness.

"The Bible makes it clear. Gott intends for each to marry, but you will not be married today, Stella Schmucker," he assured her with a crooked grin. "Let's fetch what we can and be on our way."

"Why are you helping me?" Stella stood firm to the spot. "You have helped plenty, but this is not your community."

"Gott has but one church, and it has a duty to extend a hand to others beyond any lines we've drawn on a map."

That was true. Stella herself didn't let lines and confines keep her from ministering to others. How did one argue a point they agreed with? "Okay," Stella replied and prayed silently that Bishop Mast wouldn't use her current situation to persuade her into a life not fit for her. She didn't need anyone meddling. She'd find a way to preserve her life, the safety it covered her with, as soon as Gott revealed the next step to her.

CHAPTER THIRTEEN

Stella wasn't sure who Lena was happier to see, her or Ellie. After the day she had endured, Stella was happy to be close to the elder who emitted sunshine. She and the bishop had salvaged most of her books and two dresses that were now washed and hanging to dry along with a few quilts Mammi had stitched together. Those, Stella would never sell no matter how dire her circumstances. Michael cleared space in the barn for her books and totes of Nature's Sun products to be stowed away without being subject to mice or weather until her home was mended.

Evening fell fast over the Graber farm, and Stella welcomed helping Lena in the kitchen. There was no use in dwelling on the day's events right now, and tomorrow was Sunday church and the fellowship meal. Stella always found baking a great time to sort one's thoughts.

"I have been craving lemon sponge cake," Lena said as Stella pulled a cookie tray of violet shortbread cookies from the oven. The pleasant scents filled the kitchen with wonderful aromas. Stella almost forgot she was temporarily homeless. Baking with Lena had been just the remedy she needed.

"I can make you one," Stella said and quickly flipped through Lena's little box of treasured recipes. It was the least she could do for Lena letting her continue to sleep on her couch. Once everything was baked, cooled, and stored up for morning, Stella prepared herself a cup of tea, tidied the kitchen, and bid Lena good night when she slipped into her room and closed the door.

Despite the overly warm house, Stella finished the full cup before slipping into her gown and putting her hair into the common braid she wore each night. Curling into the worn cushions, Stella found a spot that suited her and said a prayer.

She yawned and rolled onto her left side as Ellie chased imaginary groundhogs in her sleep by the door. Stella envisioned the man with one high-arched brow. She liked how his smile made her pulse race and how he'd lift a stiff shoulder as if nursing an old wound. She also liked the way he could take charge of a situation, despite her wishing he didn't. Simon Graber had many layers. Stella would have considered them all if sleep hadn't finally found her.

She rode along the narrow blacktop, a vast cloudless sky lying gently over the hilly landscape. Beside her Ellie lapped at air as the buggy picked up speed. Stella wasn't scared, as racing hooves clomped ahead. In fact, she liked the feel of the wind in her hair. It had been so long since she had taken it down for longer than a good drying.

Four large horses, their heads bobbing as they plod belly-deep over a patchwork string of rolling landscapes, were at her left. Were they planting wheat for winter, or spring corn? She wasn't certain, but as she drifted deeper into the dream, a warm sensation filled her.

She was wearing deep blue, the dress Lena had first let her borrow. Only now it didn't fit at all, as if she had somehow shrunk. The buggy hit a rut, bouncing her high in the seat. A laugh spilled out of her, landing on the wind and traveling back to where she'd come from.

She could smell Lena's cobbler, the sweet scent of summer, and peppermint. A song sprang up, an older woman's voice, cracking a thunderhead, darkening the already tragic tune. Stella never liked the old music of woe and heartache.

In a yard just ahead, a man tossed a small boy into the air. As the buggy whizzed past, Stella looked but didn't see the catch. It was as if the boy hadn't been there at all. The buggy hit another hole, this time forcing her to turn around and take a better hold.

"We're going too fast," she shouted. But no driver sat behind the reins,

and Ellie no longer sat beside her. An immediate panic swelled up inside her. Stella searched frantically behind her. Her companion gone, and the buggy was only going faster and faster.

The skies darkened like a quilt over her head. That's when she heard it. The sudden rush of roaring water filling her ears and nostrils. It was no longer a pleasant Sunday drive through Cherry Grove, and there was no one waiting to help her as the buggy plummeted into the swollen creek.

On instinct she took a deep breath before the cold consumed her. The last thing she saw before the murky water filled her eyes was the bishop watching her get swept away.

Tossing and turning, Simon simply couldn't get any sleep, not with the image of the dok still filling his thoughts. Her home had suffered so much damage. Surely her bishop would see it tended to swiftly. It was not for him to concern himself with. He'd given her shelter, and in turn she could help his community. Still, the idea of her returning to the hillside troubled his conscience about as much as knowing she slept nearby did.

With sleep far off, Simon got out of bed. He could read awhile. A man could never read his Bible enough. He turned on the propane-powered light overhead and made his way to the stove. Filling his kettle a quarter of the way, he placed it on the stove and turned on the gas burner. Warm milk always did well for nights when sleep was far away.

It was then Simon heard the scream. He was half into his boots when Michael emerged from his room.

"I heard that," Michael said, searching for his own boots, but Simon was already out the door and turning the corner.

"Stella," Mamm called out, giving her a shake. Simon could see no threat about, but clearly something had gotten ahold of the dok.

"She's having a nightmare," Mamm said just as the dok opened her eyes to see three worried faces. Simon had bad dreams, often those of the family no longer with him, but never before had he cried out that he could remember.

"I'm so sorry," Stella said with a sob in her throat. Her face was soaked in tears, her blanket twisted at her feet, and her hair. . . Simon turned to the hund. Jah, even she knew it wasn't proper for him or Michael to be here.

"I was going so fast and the water was so strong and the boy disappeared. I don't know who was singing, but it was *seltsam*, Lena, just terrible."

"*Du arma kleina ding*," Mamm whispered.

Simon still knew so little about Stella, but he did know she was fearful. Was she remembering the flood or simply dealing with the recent damage to her home? Simon recalled when Joe Shetler suffered for a time after his fall that left him paralyzed. Simon dug back into his memory. Had not John and Linda seen to having a therapist to help him accept that he would no longer walk again?

"You two get on now. She will be fine. . .eventually." Mamm waved for them to leave, and Simon ushered Michael out the door. Mamm was wise and seemed to know what Stella needed right now. Simon simply had to trust, for she was in good hands tonight.

"Think she'll be all right?" Michael asked as they weaved around the side of the house.

"I think she will be. Some folks go through things we cannot understand. Sometimes no matter how hard you try to let the past go, it tends to show itself."

"I hope whatever it is wasn't too bad. You'll talk to her, right? You are the bishop, and talking to folks is kind of what you do a lot," Michael said.

"I do more than that, sohn, but I will if need be. Sometimes a person doesn't need a bishop, but a friend."

"Then we can be both. Nightmares can sometimes be so real you think it's really happening."

"Do you have nightmares?" Simon asked as he opened the front door. He had never known Michael to so much as snore, as quiet as he was, but if he was having dreams about his mamm, Simon wanted to know.

"Nee, but I do dream pretty vividly." Michael grinned playfully.

Simon immediately missed the little boy and wasn't ready to face the teenager.

"Get to bed, sohn." Simon playfully shoved him on inside.

CHAPTER FOURTEEN

Sunday dawned with a cloud-filled sky. Stella sat at the little kitchen table sipping weak kaffi and taking in her temporary situation. She needed to put the embarrassment of last night behind her. It wasn't the first time her nightmares woke her, but it had been the first time she'd woken others.

Lena had been kind, and seeing both Michael and Simon standing over her with worry-filled eyes surprised her. Was a traumatic childhood to blame? Lena thought it was so and tried to coax Stella into talking. Was it the flood she had survived as a child? Stella didn't know what spawned this nightmare, but she did know she'd not likely drink sleepy tea again.

And Stella didn't want to talk about it. She could never share her nightmares with another. They'd think her *narrisch*, dreaming about boppli disappearing, runaway buggies, and hearing woeful songs.

"Excuse me." Stella stood and slipped into Lena's room to ready for church while everyone finished the nutty french toast bake and bacon. It was already past eight. If they didn't hurry, they'd be late for the biweekly service. This would be the third time in her life she'd be attending as a newcomer. She expected some uneasiness. Being a fresh face always came with a few looks and curious questions, but as they climbed into the buggy, Stella had to admit she was eager to sit among fresh faces too.

"Whatever you do, don't drink Betty Marie's lemonade," Michael shared over one shoulder as they made their way out of the driveway. In his black hat, he looked more grown than the boy who had just scarfed down three plates of breakfast. "Not without adding a heap of sugar and water to it first."

Stella appreciated his humor and the warning. She liked a person who'd rather find joy in the day than frown.

"Sohn," the bishop scolded, "it's not proper to insult Betty Marie."

"She insulted lemons by never adding water and sugar to them," Michael replied playfully.

Pothole after pothole, Stella worked to keep the lemon sponge cake from spilling out of her lap while Lena announced each house along the drive. Buttermilk Branch was as narrow as a fine-tipped pen, but the scent of a sly fog and damp earth was a familiar welcoming.

August had slid in quietly on the heels of July. Stella always counted the fogs of August, just as her mammi taught her. It was the best way to prepare for winter, seeing as the same number would tell a person how many snows to expect. August was also a busy time for harvesting the last summer herbs. It would be some time yet before she could do that, though Simon insisted it wouldn't take the men from her community long to see to mending the roof.

A waft of pine soap reached her, pulling her attention forward. The bishop looked handsome dressed in his best clothes and *muszer* jacket. Taking in his rigid posture, she worried that he was still sore over the small, dusty paw print on his trousers leg, which Ellie had kindly given him moments before they left the house. He clearly had no appreciation for pest control, but Stella was confident that the man and dog would warm to one another soon enough. Ellie was wonderfully keen on good folks after a few sniffs.

The sound of buggies traveling behind them soon filled the quiet morning. Stella's focus had been on the canopy of trees overhead when the buggy suddenly dropped. The drive ran straight through a shallow creek bed. She let out an involuntary gasp as Simon maneuvered through it.

"Are you all right?" He swiveled his head to see for himself.

Stella nodded, clutching the cake tightly as they bounced over rock and water.

Up the embankment and into the wide drive they drove, and her fingers relaxed. A half dozen buggies were already aligned along the fence. Teenage boys were seeing horses out to pasture. This home was also the shape of a rectangle, with a gray metal, high-pitched roof, and it was terribly close to the creek.

Do they not fear a chance flood?

Once stopped, Michael offered Lena a hand. Not giving the bishop a chance to bestow his good manners on her in front of others, Stella climbed down herself.

Michael skidded off to where youngies stood at the fence while Simon quietly disappeared into a sea of black hats at the barn. Stella touched her kapp and bonnet for straightness, collected the lemon sponge cake, and followed Lena into the house.

"*Wilkum,* Dok Stella." Sadie was the first familiar face Stella recognized. "We're blessed to have ya, and you brought *kuche* and *kichlin*." Sadie's smile widened as she reached for the cake and handed it over to a young girl. "Edna, see to this and those kichlin too, but don't you be testing them yet," she said before turning back to Stella. "You can hang your bonnet there." Sadie pointed.

"Sadie has been singing praises about the dok who can fix one up with a cup of tea." A larger woman laughed. Her smile sunk her dark eyes but sprang up nearly a half dozen happy wrinkles. "I'm Judy. It's gut to have fresh faces join us." Her raspy voice was a strong indicator she had been overcoming the recent sickness as well.

"Judy is Deacon Burkholder's fraa," Lena leaned in and whispered.

"Danke." Stella barely got out her next words when a woman rushed by on the tails of two young boys. The spacious kitchen filled with women split into infectious laughter.

"Ida will never gain a pound as long as those two keep running." Judy clicked her tongue. Stella watched Ida continue to chase down her sons and wondered if she had always looked so. . .pale. Perhaps she should suggest a diet of plantain or a routine of peppermint tea.

"We heard about what the storm did to your haus."The young woman reached out a hand. "I'm Betty Marie. Would you like some lemonade before we head to the barn to gather?"

"Nee, I am fine, danke," Stella declined with an amused grin. She appreciated Michael's earlier warning but was warmed by the friendly welcome here.

"It was kind of Lena to offer you a place to stay. I reckon you will be a busy bee in our community for some time yet." Always positive, Sadie was, but Stella detected she was referring to more than Stella's duty, and that brought heat to her cheeks.

"Many have seen Bishop Graber taking you about," another woman said and ducked her head. It appeared Stella had become the current chatter.

"I heard many of your belongings were destroyed," a tall woman of Stella's age said with gentle concern. Her hair was dark and her eyes curious. She was very beautiful. Stella imagined in her younger years she had turned many heads.

"I had little to lose." Stella shrugged. She tried not to think of her grandmother's teacups or the herbs and broken jars that would take time to replace. She at least had her Sunday dress, proper shoes, plenty of vitamins still worthy to sell, and her favorite books. It was more than she had started out with not so long ago.

"A home is not a roof over one's head but a solid foundation under his feet," Lena quickly inserted. "Mei sohn sees over all, just as he will see Stella through this bend in the road."

Mother and son were of the same mindset, Stella mused.

Half past eight, men began making their way into the barn. Stella joined the women as they made their way out of the house. It was true, a foundation was important. Trouble was, Stella had never really stood solid anywhere, and each time she gained her footing, in blew another storm.

The patriarch led the procession across the lawn. Stella hadn't missed how Lena conveyed that Stella was one of them. She wasn't. She had come to help others, not to linger in praise. She would enjoy her time here, but in the end, her place was on the hill with Ellie. That was home.

Warm weather always made Sunday gatherings more to her liking, as then they could be outdoors. Winter was hard when services and the fellowship meal were both held indoors. Stoves warmed efficiently, but when a couple dozen families cramped into one house, removable walls and an open window did little to help.

Stale air greeted Stella as she stepped into the barn. She hesitated briefly. There were at least forty families already crowding the large space. Barely a bench not consumed. Perhaps the community *would* benefit in being divided after all.

"Wilkum." An older gentleman nodded her way.

"That is my mann, Freeman," Judy said. "You best find a seat quick, or he'll be preaching that two are always better than one." Judy winked. "It's his favorite sermon." She brushed by Stella to take up a seat on the first bench.

"You may sit here." Lena pointed as women instantly moved down a few spaces, and so Stella sat. She noted kapps touching and whispers rising as she cautiously lowered onto the end of the bench. She focused on the center of the room, ignoring the curious looks.

To the right of the wide room, the bishop sat. Despite three other men at his side, Simon appeared deep in thought. Perhaps considering his sermon today? Sensing her, his head turned, locking eyes on her. Then she saw it, the emptiness there. *A man carrying the weight of many, but who carries the weight of his loneliness?* How could one be lonely in Cherry Grove?

Then again, Stella knew a person could be surrounded by many people and still feel completely and utterly alone. It was also as plain as the freckle on her middle toe that he missed his fraa. It must have been hard when he lent Stella the shoes and dress. How blessed Lizzy must have been. Stella would never have someone who would love her despite her flaws and unusual livelihood. Someone who could love her without a change of heart.

With that thought, Stella sat straighter. She was a healer, was she not? Her tender heart wanted to help. Offer freindschaft. Bishop Graber wasn't alone.

———————— ⚓ ————————

Simon felt the hairs on the back of his neck bristle as eyes watched his arrival. He should have offered to carry the lemon sponge cake and treats for the kinner, but he knew tongues would be waggling if he did. Instead, Simon went straightaway for the men gathered under the barn eve. His eldest bruder, Ervin, was the hosting family today.

"Bishop Graber?"

Simon slowed his steps. His duty was to always be there when called, but Mary Alice's voice sent a seed of dread into his gut.

"Pricilla and I noticed you have a visitor," Mary Alice prodded. Simon glanced over her shoulder to Pricilla and her eldest daughter, both shaking their heads. When was Mary Alice gonna let go of the idea he and Pricilla were a match? Thankfully Simon had never known the embarrassment of a mother's interference.

"Is she family?" Mary Alice inquired with two faintly lifted brows.

"Nee, she is the doktor seeing over die krank."

"That is the healer of Walnut Ridge," Mary Alice said and cleared her throat. "How kind of you and Lena to invite her today." Her smile was forced.

"All are welcome to hear the Lord's instruction." With a quick nod, he moved into the barn. Simon quickly gave his trousers another brush. The dirty paw print was embedded. He let out a frustrated breath. The hund was a nuisance.

"Got you a fresh face yet," Deacon Freeman said with a grin tugging at the corner of his mouth.

"She's the dok seeing over die krank," Simon repeated and knew it wouldn't be the last time he would do so today.

"I heard she lost her home. The wind blew it right over a hill and dropped it in a creek on its head." Freeman was a dandy deacon, always first to help instruct young members and see that funds were distributed fairly, but he was terrible about taking gossip and sharing it as fact.

"Storm blew a tree on it, but it will soon be remedied, according to her bishop." The storm had done more than that. Simon recalled Stella's heartbreak when discovering her stock and dishes destroyed. Perhaps he could see to replacing a few of the cups that seemed sentimental to her. Verna sold some pretty ones at the bulk store.

"So"—Freeman stroked his long, wide beard—"she's just passing through. Too bad. We could use fresh faces." The burden of his duty as elder coupled with a few young men leaving, always on the deacon's mind.

"We are already dividing, certain sure," Ervin grumbled. It was no secret that the line would be drawn at the hill of Cherry Grove, putting Ervin's eldest in the new community.

"You know just because we divide does not mean we are apart," Simon reminded him. When a district split, each attended his own church, but gatherings were still for all who gathered. A youth gathering often brought about youngies from three districts. "I've been working hard on adding to the flock, divide or naet. I got a call from a young man just the other day. Seems he has been taken with one of our own and hopes to make a go of it here."

"Jah, gut news. Gut news." Freeman's face split into a wide smile. "Yet I'm sure your dok may find a better roof to settle under. Plenty here who could use a wife." Simon followed his gaze to Stella as she made her way toward the barn. Head down and smiling, she stood out among the others. The parade exited the house, chatting and laughing. The scene warmed him unexpectedly.

"Two are always better than one." Freeman's signature statement always sounded more like a personal point to Simon.

Simon nodded in agreement, but his stomach roiled at the despairing thought. It was true Cherry Grove sported a few men Stella's age who had not yet married, as well as two widowers.

Three, he added. But a bishop had no time for romance or flowering a pretty doktor into his heart and home. As eyes lingered her way, Simon hoped the rest of the men in Cherry Grove didn't either.

CHAPTER FIFTEEN

As the song leader began the first verse of the familiar hymn, Simon and three older men stood and quietly exited the barn. Stella lifted her voice into song while the elders decided who would preach today. She always favored this part of the service, hearing each note sung slowly and meaningfully. A kneeling prayer, followed by the second song, the Lob Lied.

To her right, Michael sat with young, clean-shaven men, listening. Despite his playful banter, he was surprisingly attentive compared to the young man sitting next to him who was more focused on a young maed across the room. Young love was blossoming.

A round, jolly man whom Stella suspected smiled at rain clouds stepped to the center of the room. He glanced over the full barn, his gaze lingering in a far corner.

"It is not good that man should be alone." The minister began reading from the beginning of creation but eventually found his footing with Paul. For the next half hour, Stella tried not to squirm through the short sermon, but the message from Paul struck a particular nerve within her heart.

At Paul's first defense, none supported him. She knew how that felt, and like Paul, Stella always forgave, until forgiving became a repetitive act and no longer sincere in her heart. The Lord wasn't a fan of repetition any more than He was with a lie Bishop Mast once preached. Growing up in a home with little food and even less love had taught her the importance of being independent. It had also taught her forgiveness was harder to do than preached.

It was only when the bishop moved to the center of the barn that her attention returned. Suddenly the man who'd been challenging her independence with his kindness had all eyes on him.

"Gut mariye, and wilkum all." He gazed toward the children. Young boys straightened, and little girls stowed away tiny cubby dolls, tucking them inside pockets and under dress skirts. The faceless dolls were great quiet distractions during weddings, church, and many social gatherings.

"My heart is full seeing our children content to sit, ears ready to hear. They are our future, but we must guide them according to God's Word." His voice cracked, and he cleared his throat before continuing. Stella suspected it had to be difficult for him, a widower with only one child.

"Fathers, I hope you know what a blessing you have been given. Our world today has forgotten the gift given to them. Many a young man falls to the wayside, and young women forget their roles as nurturers, teachers. We are to accept God's blessings and honor them." Stella's heart rate moved a little quicker. The bishop was addressing parents and their duty.

"When the commandments are not followed, nor taught and placed as the center of our homes, we fail." His gaze landed on her, and Stella sucked in a quick breath.

"Marriages have taken a back seat in the world. The model of husband and wife is broken down and torn apart. Envy and distrust follow a familiar path where two are not of the same mind."

Stella felt her sinuses tingle. How many times had she listened to her parents quarrel over such? How could he possibly know all the scratches and dents inside her?

"A broken-down path is good enough for a short walk, but a road paved in faith, in community, with the same heart and like minds, is a road worth traveling. We must honor our wives, love our children endlessly, and be an example to all who see us. Though we are to be separate, we are not invisible." Stella's shoulders sunk a little lower.

"The world has no role models to point them in the right direction, and they have forgotten what the Creator and Savior and loving Father already established. In Psalm 68:6 it reads, 'God sets the solitary in families; He brings out those who are bound into prosperity: but the rebellious dwell in a dry land.' God created the family to be the keystone of society, of community. We all have fallen short, made mistakes, but He offers forgiveness." Again Simon looked her way as a tear refused to stay put.

"One cannot simply run from a problem, hide it under a basket, only to hope it will not be seen. For God sees all, knows all." Apparently so did bishops. "Each of us has free will; the choice is ours, but we must choose wisely." The sound of a bench scraping the floor had all eyes turning to a row of benches near four long stalls.

Carl Hooley stood and stepped out of the barn. Stella's heart ached and her eyes went straight to the bishop again. He took a deep breath but continued without letting Carl's abrupt departure affect his message.

"Many chase after more, yet what do we need that is not already given to us? As a community, we too are like a family. The elders and onkels overseeing the flock, the mothers and sisters nurturing the next generation. Brothers and men providing for and protecting each of you. You are all important, designed by His hand, for His purpose, and if one of you falls. . .we all fall with you."

Normally Stella felt uncomfortable when talk of family and community rose to the rafters, but Simon's words arrowed straight into her chest. Clearly he understood her nightmares better than she did.

Community is family. Tears fell unbidden as she sat on the hard, backless bench.

When Simon Graber stood in the center of a room, something special happened. Stella felt a sense of hope. Hope and love, through a faith she had already committed to. Dwelling on the past had only hardened her own heart, and it was time she focused on healing.

As the sermon concluded, Stella wiped dampness from her face as she prayed. *I have worked so hard to depend on no one; but You, Lord, have been my strength. You alone gave me the will to keep moving forward, to walk away from what aimed to destroy my soul. Forgive me for my stubborn pride, my anxious heart. Danke for showing me all the ways I have fallen short. Help me to forgive and to forget.*

With a new perspective, Stella left the confines of the barn while men flipped benches into tables. Everyone was eager for the fellowship meal, but Stella was suddenly starved for something else. Peace of mind. Just because her family had been short on love and their harsh words still echoed in her mind, that didn't mean she had to carry this yoke around her neck forever. Trouble was, how did one simply let go of a past that wouldn't stay gone?

After Minister Gabriel delivered the short sermon, Simon stood and cleared his throat. His gaze immediately found Stella sitting next to Mamm in the center of the crowded barn. Her crisp kapp haloed hair he still had no name for, but just the look of her had him pondering about family and community. She clearly was struggling with both, and he sensed there was more to the woman than what showed on the surface.

Pulling his attention to the rest of the lot, he gazed over the children. Some sat on parents' laps while many took up their seats next to siblings. Each one was a blessing. A brief vision of William and Claire filled his mind and heart. Oh, how he still longed to look out and see them there.

As his words drifted to God's divine love, his gaze continued to be pulled to the dok. Her interest in the lesson inspired him to continue the words he had studied long into the night in hopes that some part of his words would offer a balm to the struggle she wrestled with internally. He might not reach Carl's ears, but the dok was listening to his every word.

"We shall let none fall by the wayside without offering them a hand. How good and pleasant it is when we can all dwell in unity." Not one sleeping eye drifted, but a few grins lifted, and he suddenly began to perspire under their scrutiny.

He quickly averted his gaze to Ervin and was immediately greeted with amusement. That's why he stuttered his next words. Lizzy would be so disappointed right now. He took a slow breath and stared at Verna. She'd always been a good rock for him in the past. Her soft eyes told him all he needed to know. God's Word could be delivered even in a stutter if one had an Aaron near him.

"For if one of us falls, then so we all fall with them." It was not by his own will that he looked to Stella again. The lesson had reached her as he hoped. She sat poised on the fourth bench, intent on hearing. If she minded his stutter, it didn't show, but Simon was almost certain that Stella Schmucker had tears in her eyes. He didn't like to think he had driven her to tears, but the newcomer was in need of a renewed faith and healing doctrine. His duty was not always easy, but it was always necessary.

As soon as he could, Simon slipped out by the way of the side door, escaping into the warm summer air and bright sunlight. He had never felt more convicted, not even when Carl rose from his bench and exited the barn, a man still haunted in the absence of his only son.

"Mighty fine day for a buggy ride." Ervin maneuvered beside him and stared up to the sun.

"I'm certain Beth would love that. One should not stop courting his fraa just because he's an old man." Simon smiled as he watched a few young maedels set out cups and plates. The teenagers were always eager for the meal, and to hurry through it so they could pair off for Sunday buggy rides or long walks over the vast property.

"Jah, I agree." Ervin stretched and crossed his arms. "But I live here." Ervin chuckled. "And you are only six years younger, little bruder."

Simon felt a hundred most days. Oddly, as he watched Stella bustle out of the house, a tray of kichlin in her hands, he was feeling a tad younger than the man he was three days ago. Something else Simon noticed was how quickly Stella had fit in. She had seen many at their worst and didn't show a fear of catching the flu herself. She was making fast freinden here, easygoing as she was.

Are we friends?

The idea burrowed a few roots. A man could never have too many friends. Like sugar kichlin with violets on top. You might feel full, but there was always one more waiting to be eaten.

"I reckon a man with such deep thoughts could use some help on what comes next." Ervin broke his thoughts.

"Next?"

Ervin chuckled and gave him a pat on the back before leaning close. "Michael says she makes you stutter, and we both know you only do that when you're nervous."

"Michael is a bu and should not share his thoughts with his onkel." Simon frowned. Perhaps Simon shouldn't have agreed for his son to work under Ervin.

"I love all my nephews, but yours holds a place close. I trust his thoughts, so I will see him and Mamm home after we eat. The Lord has better plans for you this day, but you'd best hurry before someone else tries courting her."

"Courting?" Simon stuttered.

"Jah, and I think her a good match, if you want my thoughts on it. It's time, bruder." Simon always expected a dose of his bruder's wisdom but wished it came in a smaller bottle some days. Simon was just about to inform Ervin he didn't want his thoughts when Freeman sidled up next to them.

"I reckon you heard about Driver Dan," Freeman said. Driver Dan had been a driver of the Amish for six years or more, and many would rather pay him ten cents more a mile than any other for as friendly as he was.

"Nee," Ervin said.

"Wrecked the van after dropping off the Shetlers, who'd been visiting family down in Tennessee. He's all right," Freeman added. "Say his pride is mighty sore, though."

"What happened?" Simon inquired.

"Just a prank, I reckon. Some kids with too few chores. They pulled up a handful of cornstalks by the roots and planted them across the road to confuse folks."

"Of all the stuff." Simon shook his head. It seemed kinner had too much time on their hands these days. An innocent prank could have easily caused an even worse accident. "It's good he's all right, but that cannot be tolerated. He could have been hurt."

"Agreed. My bet's on Rob's sohns. You know how Leroy and Zane like to pull tricks and such." Freeman looked over the clusters of young men. Marcus Hostetler's lot of boys glanced their way briefly before pretending to be deep in conversation. Simon wasn't the only one to see the guilt on their faces. "Those Hostetler boys live nearby. I reckon Judy is making rounds now to find out." The deacon's helpmate was key in helping find out much that eluded the elders.

"We'll know soon enough," Simon said just as Nelson Beechy stopped Stella and held out his hand. Simon's brows alerted to what the widower was doing. Widowed for more than a dozen years himself, Simon could tell that Nelson was eager to get to know the dok.

"You're staring, bruder," Ervin muttered in Simon's left ear. "You know her name means. . ."

"I know," Simon whispered in reply and hoped Nelson wasn't thinking the same thought.

"Nelson Beechy," Ervin said with a laugh.

"I see," Simon replied. Alan Beechy's father was already making acquaintances. Though they were of marrying age, his kinner still lived at home. A wedding would leave his home empty, certain sure. Simon shifted uneasily. He should be happy to see Stella smile as she was, but he wasn't. Simon shoulder-bumped Ervin as if they were still boys pestering one another, before taking a step forward and aiming toward the house.

"And where do you think you're going? We eat soon." Ervin lifted a brow.

"Don't you know, bruder?" Simon shot him a wry grin. "Save your bishop a seat. I won't be long." All this talk of courting was making Simon itchy. He didn't need to rescue the dok. She could visit with as many folks as she wanted, but Ervin's words propelled him forward. Was it possible a woman as smart as Dok Stella could be interested in him?

CHAPTER SIXTEEN

"Hiya, Dok," an older man greeted. With kind eyes and rugged hands, he reminded Stella of most doting grandfathers who'd spent years behind a plow to feed a family.

"I'm Nelson. Nelson Beechy. I want to thank you for helping our many neighbors."

"You're wilkum. They have been kind to accept my help."

"Mei dochter wanted me to ask you for supper. She can set a fine table."

Stella blinked in surprise. Was Nelson asking her to dinner, or his dochter? "Perhaps another time," Stella replied kindly. "I'm verra busy seeing over die krank right now." Nelson nodded and smiled but lingered as if to say more. Yep, he was asking, and Stella scurried away before he tried persuading her further.

"Whoa!" a voice called out as Stella nearly ran over a small dark-haired woman.

"Hiya. I'm Verna," she announced with a laugh. "I see Nelson is hoping to get your attention." She offered a hand. "Lena is my mudder." She carried a tray of various cheeses and a smile much like Lena's.

"I'm Stella. I'm sorry for bumping into you. I was just. . ."

"Jah, I know. It takes no time for word to travel full circle. Mamm dotes on you plenty. She has been enjoying spending time with you, and many are here today because of your remedies."

"I just make the tea, spoon the medicine. Gott sees over the rest. I did not see Susie." Stella glanced about in search of Carl's timid fraa.

"Nee, Carl surely has her seeing over Carlee yet. Mei sohn delivered a few things to them just yesterday. I own the bulk store at the mouth of Cherry Grove."

"Carlee is not getting better?" Alarms set off in Stella's head.

"Nee, last we heard she is only getting worse." Stella frowned at that bit of information. If she was getting worse, Stella would have to insist on paying the less-than-welcoming house another visit.

"I hope you'll join us for supper soon, for all your kindness."

"You don't have to do that."

"And why would I not?" Verna said with a forged frown. "I suspect Nelson already did as much, and you will be receiving much the same before this day ends, and rightly so. I also suggest that if you want to make a living, you must accept a proper payment for it." The gossips worked faster here than they did in Walnut Ridge.

"It seems wrong to charge one who suffers unexpectedly, but I never turn down donations."

Verna stared at her for an uncomfortable second. "Vell, I reckon we can sell a few of your things at my shop." Verna winked.

"That is verra kind of you." A potential future income was sorely needed if she was to get things back as they were.

"We can discuss the particulars when you kumm for supper. Simon knows the way." Verna winked a second time, causing Stella to flinch. Was she suggesting Simon bring her to supper. . .with him?

"I guess we'd best stop dallying and get this on a table before mei Willis starts looking put out."

Stella set cookies on the table and returned to the house to fetch bowls of pickles next. Verna was nice and a little straightforward. Bustling by a table where women readied bowls of macaroni salad, baked beans, and fresh cucumbers with sweet-and-sour dressing, a bird-small woman glared in Stella's direction. Stella paid no mind. Some folks were simply weary of newcomers. Younger maedels spread tablecloths over the lined-up tables, while a few of the menner worked benches into tables.

"Hiya. I'm Pricilla," the beautiful dark-haired woman whom Stella had noted when she arrived said cheerfully. "I see you came with Bishop Graber and Michael. Lena speaks well of you."

Stella should tell Lena there was no need to talk her up to others. "She is verra kind to do so."

"Many are hopeful you are here for more than helping die krank." Pricilla laughed.

Stella flinched at the comment. What other reason would she be here? "I'm only here to help."

"But you are staying at the bishop's haus, jah?"

"Nee, that would be improper," Stella said, frowning. "I am staying with Lena, and only until my roof is mended."

"Ach, well, Bishop Graber seems verra comfortable with you. It is good to see he has taken to you." Her sly expression and half-suppressed smile made Stella stop with one hand in the air.

"I. . .I. . ."

"He watches you and probably speaks to you more than he has to me in the last year."

A sudden chill ran up Stella's arm at that, but Pricilla's smile remained. She didn't seem like a woman upset, but one happy the bishop spared a word on her. A sudden vision of their first encounter filled her mind. The way the bishop's gaze made her head dizzy. It was a ridiculous notion to have stored up, and Stella quickly swept it into a corner.

"I assure you, I will be leaving soon enough."

"You misunderstand me. All want the best for him. He is a good man. My own man passed a few years ago, and I know how he feels after such a loss."

"I'm sorry."

"Danke." Pricilla glanced around the yard and lowered her voice. "I only speak forward to say because of our losses, my mudder tends to think we make a match. For certain sure she will be seeking you out soon enough. You know how mudders can be. Always trying to match us with their idea of a perfect husband."

Stella didn't. At least not the way Pricilla was insinuating.

"Ach!" Stella didn't want to be questioned by Pricilla's mother for simply being here. "I have no interest in your bishop. I think you are blessed to have caught his eye and wish you both the best."

"Simon has no interest in me, nor I him." Her matter-of-fact tone was quick and sharp like a surprising nettle burr. "I never thought Gott would give me a second chance, but He has. I crossed paths with an old friend just last week. Mudder never had much of a care for him when we were youngies, but we found ourselves talking of old times." Pricilla smiled, and a blush darkened her soft ivory cheeks. "We picked up where we left off."

"Then your mamm will be happy to hear it." Was that not the goal her mamm was trying to accomplish?

"Nee, like I said. She never had a care for Shep, and I have no plans of telling her until I know what Gott feels is best for us."

Stella wasn't following. Usually her perception of others was on point, but Pricilla seemed to need to share too much private chatter with someone she just met.

"It would make things easier if Mudder thinks the bishop already has a special friend." Pricilla glanced about again. This sort of talk was not acceptable, and right before sitting for the fellowship meal, at that.

"*Thinks* he has a special friend?"

"Well, you are unwed, are you not?"

"I am, but. . ." The woman must be ill. Who'd conceive a bishop finding her. . .interesting? That was too laughable for words. Aside from the obvious, who'd court a bishop? That's what she'd like to know. To always be in the bishop's eye would be unsettling.

"I cannot see if Shep and me are matched if she is constantly pushing me onto another."

"But I don't even know him," Stella stumbled to say. It wasn't as if the thought of Simon hadn't piqued her interest, but reality seldom gifted thoughts made in private. Stella would give no illusions that she had an interest in Bishop Graber, even if he did make her palms sweat.

There was no denying the attraction, and now Pricilla was suggesting that Stella court the bishop to prevent love from being interfered with in her own life. It was laughable. Not to mention wrong. Bishop Graber would not think to court her. He didn't like Ellie, and Stella was fairly certain he didn't even like tea. And she was a Schmucker. What kind of match was that?

"He would never ask such of me," Stella added. "I'm sure your mamm will be. . ."

"There you are, Pricilla." Just then the frowning woman from before appeared. *This must be Pricilla's mudder.* She looked frustrated and out of breath, and her glare was still intact. "You should be serving, not chatting with visitors."

"I was getting to know Dok Stella. She is a newcomer, after all, and it is expected. Bishop Graber has yet to introduce us properly, but Lena has been all smiles for us to meet. Stella, this is my mamm, Mary Alice Yoder." Stella felt heat rush up her neck.

"Where is your mann?" Mary Alice Yoder was a petite woman in her late sixties, but her sharp gaze was as penetrable as a Cooper's hawk's with an empty belly.

"I am not wed," Stella replied uncomfortably and watched her elder's jaw go slack.

"Not yet." Pricilla winked.

Stella needed to say something before Mary Alice got the wrong idea. It wasn't proper to make folks think a falsehood.

"So you will be wed soon?"

"Mamm, that is private. Let's not scare her off before she can get settled."

Stella tried again to correct Pricilla, but between mother and daughter, it was mighty hard to get a word in.

"And you choose to be a doktor still?"

"It's meaningful work." Stella was practiced in defending her passion. "Gott calls us all to serve differently."

"Well, then it's good you are under the watchful eye of the bishop."

Mary Alice lifted her chin. "Pricilla understands a man in his position."

The beautiful woman behind her rolled her eyes.

Stella wasn't sure which was worse, that Mary Alice Yoder clearly didn't approve of her, or that Pricilla was determined to make others think she and the bishop were. . .courting. The latter made her stomach swirl.

"Dok Stella and I were discussing the importance of change. I hear you made a lemon sponge cake?"

"Lena said it would go well today," Stella replied carefully. It felt as if Pricilla wasn't done shining a lamp on her yet.

"Ach, Lena asked you to make a lemon sponge cake?" Mary Alice's face contorted into a mix of displeasure and astonishment. Apparently lemon sponge cake wasn't Mary Alice acceptable.

"Of course she would, Mamm. What woman wouldn't want the bishop to have one of his favorites? You know speaking of such things isn't proper."

Stella managed not to gasp at the revelation. Suddenly Lena's request last night was not because she had a hankering for lemon sponge cake.

Courting her. . .It was laughable, but Stella reprimanded herself. He didn't just preach well on a Sunday but lived out the words on a practical level the rest of the week. If he was ready to marry again, he'd have no trouble doing so. But not with her. Stella had no interest. Absolutely not.

Pricilla's pleading eyes begged for mercy. *Mercy*. When God sent her here, Stella didn't think it was to help one dealing with an overbearing mother.

"Jah, I have kumm to learn he is not verra fond of meatloaf but loves a good lemonade over kaffi." And with that, Mary Alice huffed, very unladylike, as if someone bumped into her too hard. Her face pinched tightly with the same disdain Stella had received from Carl Hooley. Mary Alice turned on one foot and marched back toward the house.

"Danke, Stella. Mamm has a terrible habit of pushing her thoughts onto others."

Stella blinked twice. That might be true, but Stella was also learning that the apple didn't fall far from the tree.

"Pricilla, I'm not courting the bishop."

"But you could. It's clear to see he has stars for you. He looked at you all through his preaching."

Had he? Stella shook her head. That wasn't the point. Stella had been swept into another flood, and now she feared this one might be rougher than the last.

Simon came to an abrupt halt at the sound of his name. At the corner of the house, Pricilla, Stella, and Mary Alice stood talking, and Simon's itch suddenly grew fierce by Mary Alice's stance. It was best he intervened, knowing Mary Alice as he did. Perhaps his next sermon should focus more on how parents should see their adult children more as a brothers and sisters in Christ, no longer needing instruction.

Simon flinched at the mention of a lemon sponge cake. Disappointment coursed through him to think Mamm had asked Stella to bake his favorite cake. He had other favorites, but Stella had done plenty already. Soon he realized Pricilla was putting Stella in a spot. Here Simon thought Pricilla an upright woman, incapable of pulling the wool over her mamm's eyes.

Simon was just about to step forward, assuring all parties he had no qualms about meatloaf but did have qualms about women who fabricated falsehoods, when Mary Alice stomped away without a word and Pricilla thanked Stella for helping her. Stella liked being helpful, but this was going beyond helpful.

"I'm not courting the bishop, and I fear we have only made matters worse for him. It isn't right making others think we are courting."

"We are not responsible for what others think," Pricilla continued and waved a hand in the air. Simon deepened his frown. "Besides, Simon might ask to court you yet."

"I'm not worthy of a man such as him."

That's why Simon couldn't move. How could a woman like Stella Schmucker, a name meant for kissing and coddling, think herself unworthy of him? Courting her would be an honor. She was smart, kind, and capable. A little overly concerned with water and not concerned enough about groundhog-fetching hunds, but a man could spend a lifetime dissecting all she was.

Simon raised his hand to rub away the prickle on his neck. Why was he thinking as if he was interested? What if he was. . .interested? She had him drinking tea, eating weeds, and thinking about a future. The truth of his own thoughts jolted him. Dok Stella was a perfect blend of wild things, brewed and steeped to heal whatever ailed him, and he in turn wanted to help her with the things that plagued her.

Courting, he silently whispered. He wasn't sure she meant the words she said for Pricilla's benefit, but the idea had been planted.

All it needed now was to be watered.

CHAPTER SEVENTEEN

Wednesday evening, Stella stood in Verna Wickey's kitchen admiring a brightly polished shelf of teacups. She gently traced each rim as she studied the various floral prints, from roses to peonies, on the delicate cups.

Life was so uncertain. Just last week she'd been drinking rose hip tea from her own cup and watching Ellie turn a simple stick into toothpicks on the floor. Now she was standing in Simon's sister's kitchen, missing her habitat and her own teacups, and expecting Mary Alice Yoder to show up anytime now to declare her falsehood publicly.

"I hope Mamm isn't feeling poor," Verna commented.

"Nee." Stella smiled. "She is healthier than you or me, for certain sure, but Lena insisted she had to finish knitting three hats, though it is the peak of summer." Lena's love for knitting was displayed in her worn fingertips and bright smile. "She asked if she could knit something for Ellie. It wonders me if she isn't trying to sweeten my hund up."

"She has a thing for cold heads." Verna chuckled. "And Mamm always loved animals but married a man who built things instead of raising livestock. She will indeed spoil your hund yet." Verna glanced into the next room as Verna's son, Alan, and Michael set a checkerboard out to keep them occupied while supper was finishing cooking. Michael had perked up quickly. Further proof the Grabers had a very healthy bloodline.

"I tell ya, if this heat doesn't run its course soon, I'll be a puddle on the floor." Verna stirred a pot of fresh green beans on the stove. Even in the comforts of the brick home with the basement door ajar, Stella had to admit it was rather muggy today. It was on days like this, when one couldn't escape the elements, that she found solace at the veins of her hillside as they poured into the valley creek below.

"I miss the stream near my home," Stella muttered. "Nothing like dipping my toes in the water when it gets hot." In the next room, the bishop was watching her, a look of concern on his face. Stella let her fingers drop quickly from the fragile tea set. Hopefully he didn't think she was mourning teacups.

"Simon has a creek below the pasture if you're feeling homesick."

Stella perked at that information. Ellie would love a run in the creek. All Stella had seen so far was the slight garden of tomatoes and a rather large patch of oddly shaped pumpkins. She had taken great care to weed this morning. It was the least she could do for all their help.

If only there was more she could do. In the last three days her time had been mostly spent on visiting the ill fallen.

"Simon says they removed the tree and have started mending the roof on your haus."

"Jah, all will come out right," Stella said convincingly as she moved to help ready supper. Verna's eldest daughter, Elizabeth, began slicing fresh tomatoes and cucumbers. Stella inserted herself in the preparation. No sense dreaming over teacups when there was work to be done.

"This apple pie looks *appedilich*," Verna said. "Willis is making ice cream later, and I always found the two to be a good match."

"Jah, they are," Stella agreed, anticipating freshly churned ice cream.

"Do you like vanilla or strawberry ice cream?"

"I like food," Stella replied amusingly. "I have yet to find a dish I didn't like." Stella loved cooking as much as she did eating, but cooking for one left one with fewer options.

"Michael says you eat grass." This was Laura, the youngest, barely a teenager and already as pretty as a sundrop. Soon she'd be attending the youth gatherings and would no doubt catch some young man's eye. Stella smiled at her wrinkled expression.

"Gott has provided all this food for us," Stella said. "The dandelion and violet make salads prettier while making us healthier. Below the surface, one can find roots that cure a bushel of maladies and give us great kaffi." She winked.

"Many are healing because of the weeds—I mean herbs—Stella has harvested," Verna put in.

"Zeb stopped by the store today and said they have managed to avoid it," Elizabeth said as she mixed mayo, sugar, olive oil, vinegar, and spices. After giving the sweet-and-sour concoction a healthy stirring, she poured it over the cucumbers and tossed them gently.

"You know how Kathy tends to clean the paint off the walls more than not," Verna jested before turning to Stella. "It's no secret that Kathy does not tolerate dirt and germs."

Stella giggled, recalling the woman who scrubbed all the fellowship tables before and after Sunday's meal.

"Is there a root or weed I can sneak into Zack Miller's lunch?" Laura said, unsmiling. "He and Samuel Schwartz cut Edna's kapp strings and put a dead fish in my buggy." Her pale brows lifted. Stella admired her refusal to tolerate a bully, but in good conscience, Stella couldn't condone anything vengeful.

Simon's gaze traveled into the kitchen again. Ever observant, or merely hoping Stella was enjoying her visit with his family, she wasn't sure. He had a wonderful family. The kind of family Stella had always longed to have. She offered him a timid smile in return.

"You will pay no mind to foolish buwe with not enough chores to do," Verna scolded. The young maed would soon learn how much trouble buwe were.

With supper laid out, Verna directed Stella into a seat between Simon and Michael. Heads bowed for the silent prayer, and Stella thanked God for the people who had come into her life, the friends she was making. Soon her time with them would end, aside from a spare visit when she was called upon. Lifting her head, Stella felt her insides flutter as Simon looked down at her.

"I was told you replaced Martha as a midwife when she left." Verna offered up a basket of fresh rolls.

"I have seen a handful of first smiles, jah." Stella loved being a part of something so special, but more times than not, seeing the look on a new mother's face as she cradled the bundle she worked so hard for only reminded Stella that she would never be given the chance.

"So you're a midwife too?" Michael asked. "Do you know how to make sweet rolls?" Michael scooped up two rolls from Verna's basket.

"Michael always thinks with his stomach," Verna jested. Stella had learned that soon on too.

"I do, and Martha was kind enough to take me under her wing when I moved to Walnut Ridge. We were close nochbers."

Verna shot her husband a coy grin. "Joel and Rachel will be glad to hear this. The Englischer who often came to see over such retired last year."

"I agreed to be a helper. But when Martha left, I was called upon plenty. The Englisch midwife never liked coming to Walnut Ridge, so there were few choices for new mamms aside from going all the way to the next county." Mostly because bopplin came in the worst weather conditions, and the hill leading to the mountain was dangerously steep in a vehicle.

"That's because that hill was where she became a widow," Willis said from the head of the table. He accepted a healthy helping of pot roast and then spooned extra gravy over it and a mound of potatoes on top. The calamity looked delicious, but when her turn came, Stella accepted a more modest portion. The roast smelled heavenly, but she wanted to save room for ice cream.

"Ach, that is terrible. I didn't know."

"Lots of folks have died on that hill," Simon informed. Something in the way he said that sounded a lot like anger.

"Cars are too dangerous," Michael muttered and set down his fork with an unfinished plate. The room fell instantly still as a great sadness overwhelmed the house and remained there until the meal was over.

"Sorry," Verna said later as Stella helped her tidy the kitchen. "It is a tender subject for young Michael and for Simon."

"It must be hard to lose your fraa, and I'm sure Michael has missed his mamm something terrible." Stella's heart went out to Michael as she watched him move a black checker over the board and jump two red ones.

"And William and Claire," Verna added as she lifted the stack of clean plates into a cabinet. "To lose a fraa is a hard row to hoe, but to lose kinner, harder yet."

Stella gasped at the new knowledge. "Simon lost two kinner?" Why had no one thought to mention that to her?

"Ach. I thought you knew." Verna touched Stella's sleeve. "It was a terrible accident. Many lives were changed that day." Verna glanced into the next room with a sorrowful expression. "Kumm sit." She motioned to a chair. After filling two cups with kaffi that Stella found tasteless, Verna sat.

"A few women were heading to Ohio for the quilting fair. Lizzy was traveling with her sister who had been visiting from Ohio. Mary Lemmon was just twenty-two, and Helen Lapp was my dear friend. None came home to us."

Stella could see how hard this was for Verna to share. "I'm so sorry."

"Many have felt the ache of that day." Verna sniffed back her emotions. "Michael was just four."

Stella held Verna's hand and felt as if she was the worst person in the history of people. How many years had she worked to forget her own family when Simon and Michael had lost theirs? This time when her gaze ventured into the next room, the man who had been interrupting her treasured life and private thoughts suddenly filled the empty recesses of her heart.

As evening waned, Elizabeth and Laura tried beating her at a third game of checkers at the family picnic table just under the shade of oak and persimmon trees. Willis, Michael, and Simon took turns cranking ice cream on the porch. Both girls would not have beaten her if she could have kept her focus on the game and not the bishop, but his loss explained so much about the man, and now Stella was seeing Simon

Graber in a fresh light.

He removed his hat, swiped his brow. His muscles strained under the overly washed pale shirt, and sparrows filled her belly. Her feelings were growing, an infatuation with a man who was the epitome of faith and strength. No matter what life churned his way, he did not run from it.

Laughter sprang up as lightning bugs appeared. Stella surprisingly ate two bowls of strawberry ice cream and thought of Ellie. She sorely loved ice cream.

"*Danke schon, geb mich sum meh.*" Alan politely held out his bowl for a third helping of vanilla ice cream. Stella wondered where the youngie had put all that food. He was nothing but skin and bone and taller than her by five inches already.

"Jake said you jumped into a river during a flood," Laura said, wiping her mouth with her sleeve.

"We should not be listeners of gossip," Simon instructed his forward-speaking niece.

"I couldn't help but listen. . . . I have ears, onkel, but I asked because I didn't believe them." Laura turned to Stella. "You don't look as crazy as Zack or Jake. I reckon they are fibbing on you."

"Or repeating another's gossip." Verna shot Simon a look. "You'd be surprised what folks will share with others."

"The bishop is right. One should never listen to gossip, because. . ." Stella cleared her throat and set down her bowl. She had learned something tonight that would forever change her thoughts of family. Not all families were alike. "I did not jump."

Stella stood, collected a few empty bowls, and slipped quietly into the kitchen.

"You let them beat you at checkers," Michael teased as they rode toward the orange sunset. Humidity hung heavy in the air, and Stella wished desperately for a bath. Michael had jumped in the back seat, on purpose she thought, leaving Stella to ride next to the bishop back to his farm.

"You don't know me well enough to think so. I am terrible at checkers." She gave him a playful grin. "Laura mentioned a Zack and Samuel today."

Simon lifted a crooked brow, questioning.

"I reckon they are no different than any buwe, but I think they have been pranking the girls, cutting kapp strings, leaving *fisch* in buggies."

"Laura once left a bucket of rotten apples in my buggy," Michael put in. "Yellow jackets are not easy to reckon with."

Stella remembered her bruders playing such pranks on each other, but she didn't like to think of Laura being bullied.

"Boys will be boys." Simon smirked. It was the same response her father once had for such behavior.

"And you were once a boy," she replied, frustrated. Did he not understand the results from such pranks?

"Jah, a good many years ago. Laura failed to mention she rubbed poison ivy all over their hats. Zack had to go to the hospital and get a shot for it," he said in a disappointed tone.

Stella sucked in a surprising breath. "She did fail to mention that." She should work up some jewelweed salve for the Millers, just in case there was a second incident. By Laura's determined spirit, Stella feared there would be.

"She's a fast tattler too," Michael muttered and pulled his straw hat over his eyes.

"Sometimes a tattler is telling to keep bad things from happening." That earned her another one of those penetrating looks from the bishop.

"That is true, but sometimes they are only stirring the pot. There are often two sides to every story, and I assure you, I do listen to both," Simon reminded her.

Stella believed him, even if she didn't agree with his brushing off of Laura's account of the teasing boys. "It must be worrisome to care over so many."

"Do you not do the same?" the bishop asked.

It was not the same. What Stella knew about caring for the souls of others could fit under a nettle leaf. "Helping someone be rid of an infection or clear a kault quickly is not as important as a person's faith."

"A man who sleeps well rises early and is ready for the day. What you do is important to many."

"I reckon that is true. I never gave it much thought." She was simply doing her job, being useful.

"You should. If you did not know how to do those things, would you not still help others?" It was an honest question.

"I would, but even if our hearts are pure and we do all we can do, it sometimes doesn't help." Stella couldn't ignore the trespasses scratched over her heart. She could forgive, but forgetting was terrifically hard.

"Every little thing is a big thing. . .to God. All we know is little compared to what Gott knows. But we do it anyway." He winked.

"Jah, we do. Even when it feels like we are hanging laundry without any pins to hold it in place."

"And some days are windier than others."

Stella stared at the man. She couldn't begin to fathom the grief he had endured in the loss of his family, but his faith was intact. If only she had a faith as sound as his.

When they reached the farm, Michael worked quickly to unharness David. Lighting a lamp hanging just inside the barn, Michael disappeared inside. It was time to come clean about what happened with Pricilla. The guilt was setting a terrible ache in her gut, especially knowing what he and Michael had gone through. It was wrong to start a friendship on deception, and Stella wanted to be his friend. A man who lost so much needed friends, did he not?

"Bishop, there is something I must tell you." Wrangling her lip, Stella dug deep within to pull out the words as she followed him toward the main house.

"I have something to say as well," he said, but his long strides didn't slow. Stella quickened her steps to catch up.

"Mamm is going to visit her schwester in the morning."

"I should see about returning to Walnut Ridge then." Stella slowed. Perhaps Tessie Miller wouldn't mind letting her stay a few days.

"Your haus is not ready. You may stay in the dawdi haus," he said flatly and kept walking. He'd soon change his mind, she knew.

"Bishop, I did something. . ."

Simon drew to a sudden stop, his eyes fixed on the front of the house. He turned, revealing a sour expression. "Not again."

Stella peered around him. Her confession would have to wait, for right now she had another matter to deal with.

"It's another groundhog." He pointed, but she could see that.

Stella tried not to smile. Ellie was a good rodent remover. "You should thank her. I reckon she will have all your problems remedied in no time."

"I'm not thanking a dog," he said stubbornly.

"How will she know she did well if you don't?" Stella didn't find his scowl intimidating any longer. What she found was a man who didn't know a blessing when he saw one.

"Some help and never are appreciated." For a bishop, he was blind to simple gifts in life. Stella stood firm. "God knows what we need even if we don't," she said before turning and walking away. Her confession would wait until he was in a better mood. When her house was ready, he was sure gonna miss Ellie's help.

CHAPTER EIGHTEEN

He was dreaming. The strong smell of kaffi and the beckoning aroma of bacon said he had to be. Then a third aroma drifted lazily into his room.

Wet dog.

"The hund," Simon grumbled as he donned fresh work clothes. He had disposed of yet another critter and was no closer to thanking a hund than he was the day she arrived. It was a ridiculous thought, thanking a dog.

"Oh, you're up."

The dok was in his kitchen. . .cooking. Maybe she wasn't still sore at him.

"I wasn't sure what you liked, but Lena is packing for her visit, so I offered to ready breakfast."

"*Ach vell,* Mamm enjoys her visits with Elsie, but you didn't have to. . ."

"She has clothes everywhere." Stella's brows crinkled. "It's just one night, but she insisted that I cook in here so she could decide what to pack."

"Ach." Simon lumbered farther into the room. *Blessed Mamm,* he silently mused. She had pushed Stella out of her kitchen and into his. . .purposefully. Simon had to admit, he didn't mind waking up to the smell of bacon and a pretty woman in his house.

"She also said you'd eat anything but not to cook anything with beans or with oatmeal." Amusement lifted her voice.

"Mudder says much," he replied, raking his hands through his hair. He quickly rolled both suspenders over his shoulders and slipped into his seat. Stella offered him kaffi, though at this point Simon suspected she'd sneaked a few of her weeds in there too.

"Smells good," he said honestly.

"Danke," Stella replied, quickly turning back to the stove but not before Simon saw the flush of her cheeks at the comment. Her bare feet moved over the floor so lightly crickets probably couldn't hear her. She was a beautiful unwed woman in his kitchen. Simon normally frowned on such things, but he couldn't very well tell her not to cook now that she was finishing up. Sipping strong kaffi, Simon kept his eye trained on the doctor.

Courting didn't seem so far-fetched now, but Simon should come forward about eavesdropping. He heard firsthand how Pricilla had painted a picture that they were more than two people working to help others. Part of him liked knowing there'd be no unexpected visitors carrying a dish at his door today. Simon dreaded Thursdays more than he did going to the dentist.

"I made omelets since you seemed to like those?" It came out like a question.

"A man who complains about a warm meal has never been verra hungry," he replied.

"Lena says the bacon is the last of what she put up." Being Amish, one could can about anything, and Mamm always had seen to put up plenty of sausage patties and bacon, for which he was thankful. Mamm was getting older and the chore harder, and Simon knew her hands had been giving her fits of late. A woman who served her family well deserved rest. If she had only chosen to live with Verna instead of him, her needs would have been better met. Perhaps it was a conversation he should revisit with her.

"I came just in time." Lena strolled into the kitchen, the hund right behind her. "It smells wunderbaar in here," she added. "I heard Michael leave already. He sure missed a fine table this morning."

"He had toast and eggs, but I saw to it he has a full lunch," Stella revealed. How had he slept through all of that? More importantly, Stella had seen to his son, had cooked him breakfast, and was making him think selfishly for himself. It was his duty to help her, not the other way around.

When heads bowed, Simon glanced to his right briefly. She would soon leave, and suddenly the idea of the months ahead concerned him. Who would see that Stella had wood? Just one bad run of ice and that hill would be dangerous to travel. She was a doctor, and sickness came all hours and in the worst conditions. She didn't even own a horse!

Worry seemed to be his yoke today. Perhaps the dok had a tea for that too, he mused before closing his eyes and whispering his own prayer. Gott knew the answers and heard his concerns, and now Simon would just have to wait for a reply.

Lord, if it is Your will. Amen.

Something nudged Simon's leg. He wasn't one for dramatics, but he cautiously leaned down to spot Ellie under the kitchen table. Lifting her head, she presented a judging brow.

She smelled.

"It's too hot out there for her," Lena said, as if knowing Simon's next thoughts.

"I have to deliver colts today," Simon said before taking a large forkful of omelet. A man had to choose his battles, and his stomach was making the decision for him this morning. The hund could stay.

Stella poked at her omelet. He didn't blame her. Whatever those new green things were, they looked suspicious and were a bit crunchy.

"Ervin has the driver coming for me around nine." Lena popped a forkful in her mouth and began chewing. Simon hadn't considered how Stella might feel on the farm all day. . .alone. Well, not alone. She had that hund to keep her company. Hopefully the critter didn't leave any more surprises on his doorstep.

"Will you be all right. . .here?"

"I have lived alone over seven years now, since my grandparents passed, and I took care of myself for the thirty or so before it." The comment struck Simon hard.

"A woman who knows how to see to herself and doesn't need much is a treasure to her husband," Lena sang.

Or she simply doesn't trust anyone, Simon thought. He had yet to determine the true cause of her nightmares, and Mamm insisted it was best not to prod too quickly.

"I don't mind being alone, as long as I have Ellie," Stella quickly inserted. "I will see to tidying up, but Ellie and I are walking up to the Hooleys' today. Carlee isn't doing well, I hear." It tore at her, he could see. It wore on the crease between her perfectly aligned brows.

"It would be best if I went with you." He didn't like her going alone, even if she had proved herself plenty capable. Carl was a man one took in small doses. His heartbreak clouded his words and bittered his tones, and Simon didn't want anything to trigger another nightmare.

"But you have colts to deliver, and I hear the truck coming now. Besides, it has been plenty long enough. I'm sure she is hanging laundry and hoping Gabe stops by to see her. Maybe he will bring her flowers."

"Women still like those?" He grinned and caught the surprise flickering over her expression.

"Some do, I suppose." Stella stood, lifted her plate, and tried to pretend the comment hadn't affected her. "I tend to pick my own, so I wouldn't know." With that, she turned to the sink. A horn honked outside, but Simon didn't miss the grin smeared on Mamm's face as he made his way to the door. Perhaps flirting was best kept out of the eye of his watchful mother.

He wanted to pick her flowers or gift her teacups with flowers on them and a shelf worthy of holding them. Yeah, he was in trouble.

Simon pulled the gate shut and watched both colts inspect the small space with anxiousness. Behind him, the truck and horse trailer lumbered down the long gravel drive, stirring up a cloud of white dust.

"Nice looking but a mite skittish yet," Silas commented as he leaned beside him. Not only did Simon's cousin share his love for horses, but they also shared a birthday. As far as Simon was concerned, no man knew horses better. Many sought out Silas for help with troubled horses, and Simon appreciated how efficient he was in breaking new colts to pull a buggy, shortening the time between birth and the sale of an animal and giving Simon more time in his knife shop.

Resting his arms on the top of the fence, Simon watched the bay and spotted colts kick and fuss and snort in hopes their mamms would suddenly appear. After a few minutes, both settled, lowering their heads. They were alone and far from home, and Simon couldn't help but think of the dok with borrowed shoes and a leather bag.

"Well, let's give them a look." Silas slipped through the gate, Simon following.

"This one is near impossible to work with. She likes to bite too," Simon warned as Silas neared and cautiously snapped the line to her bridle. Just as he expected, Silas merely chuckled at the fact.

"That means she has spirit and gumption. It takes a special hand, jah, but I admire both traits, for certain sure. I also like the challenge of harnessing them." Silas' eyes trailed to his fraa in the garden, not the colt at the end of Simon's rope.

"Spirit and gumption, huh?" Simon teased. "I know one like that too." Stella was spirit, gumption, and beauty all wrapped up in one package.

"I heard you had a dok staying at your place." Silas wiggled his brows playfully. Like Ervin, he had always teased Simon in their younger years. They both had no qualms with courting, whereas Simon was particular. Lizzy had been the one who fit his very description of a fraa. So why was he now attracted to a woman so completely different in every way? Why could he not go more than a few moments without Stella consuming his thoughts?

"Mamm is enjoying the company, and she gets so few visitors. Michael likes her cooking, but she's here to help the sick. . .mostly," Simon clarified.

"We had a bout of it but weathered through. Seems like one thing leaves and another comes." Silas took the rope in hand and whispered soft murmurs as he led the colt around. "You should bring her about."

"You said you were well now." Simon lifted a brow.

"Jah, but Lydia enjoys female company, and with the new one coming, it might be good to have a dok close when her time comes." Simon shook his head. How could he have forgotten Silas was near to welcoming his sixth? The cousins were only a couple of years apart, and Silas was still building a family.

"Heard she doesn't own a buggy and lost her house over a mountain. Lydia says she sells wild herbs. Nelson stopped by yesterday to see about a saddlebred for his eldest and said she sells roots and things too." The colt reared, but Silas kept calm, giving him time to adjust.

Simon chuckled. "She can do many things, I'm discovering." She could deliver bopplin, heal the sick, bake a fine pie, and brew a surprisingly good tea. Training a dog, she couldn't do, but Simon didn't want to think of the mutt that was probably digging under his knife shop right now.

"Whoa now, fella. It's gonna go a lot easier if you just give in to me," Silas said as the colt pranced left, shaking his head. "Is she *schee*?"

"What?"

"The dok? She's got a look to her?"

One that kept Simon awake more than his bad knee did. "Jah, she has a look, all right, and likes clean water and eating weeds." When the second colt looked to want to intervene, Simon quickly stepped in and put a hand to him.

"Let me get him to pasture until you want to give him a go-over." Simon held firm to the spotted colt's bridle and aimed for the pasture gate leading to the back side of Silas' home.

"Nee, they have to learn, just as men do. Even when it feels uncomfortable, like Gott's testing you and you wanna just run." Silas stroked the spotted colt, his words caressing the nervous animal. "We must trust."

Stella needs to trust, Simon mentally noted. Had she not learned that Gott would never forsake her?

"You must trust Gott too, cousin, even if it looks impossible." Silas stroked the colt's shoulder. Like a gift given without asking, the animal leaned into his hand. The animal was young and strong but sought comfort nonetheless.

"I trust in Gott plenty. Thought we were talking about horseflesh."

"You are a man, not just a bishop. All things need love, even gumption. Does this doktor have feelings for you?"

And he was caught. Silas had led him right into the heart of the matter like a colt to harness.

"We just met." His cousin continued to stare unconvincingly. "I don't think so, but she did let Mary Alice think we were secretly courting."

"Did she now?" Silas chuckled. "Well, Mary Alice has been pestering you long enough. Lydia and I laugh every time she cooks a meatloaf." Silas made a face.

"Funny, cousin. Such behavior is frowned upon."

"You were my cousin first, and I remember the day we both hid all the cherries Mamm picked because we couldn't stomach eating another fry pie."

"Jah. Stella likes cherries and thinks Carl Hooley should start a cherry farm," Simon shared, thinking back to the conversation.

"Sounds like someone who thinks of others first. Carl could use something to do instead of blaming you for all his troubles. Don't look so serious. We all have a choice, and that bu made his."

Simon removed his hat and raked his hand through his hair. "It was three boys," he reminded Silas.

"You can't look at yesterday. It'll make ya old." Silas had strange advice that oddly made perfect sense. "You need someone who will keep you looking ahead. Perhaps this dok can remind you that you're not too old yet." Silas winked playfully.

"I feel old." He worked the colt to the pole closest to the road. Getting used to vehicles of all sizes was a fast rule in a good buggy horse. "She's fast talking, resourceful, and has a hund that might one day take my leg off. She fits in and is nothing like Lizzy at all. She's also younger than me. A lot younger, I think."

"Sounds just right. . .for a bishop."

Simon shot him a narrowed look. "For a bishop?"

"Well, I don't know how you do it, visiting folks and sorting out troubles, but it can't be easy alone. Lydia sure listens to me on hard days, as I do her. A helpmate is just that, and you've been alone for some time. I know a thing about that. That stubborn streak runs thick in some of us, but Gott put me in my place for sure. Nothing wrong with a younger fraa, either. Lydia has added blessings I never thought I'd have. Michael will soon be courting. Do you want to be alone, cousin, when you could have a second chance?"

Simon didn't want to think of Michael courting yet, but Silas was right. "I wasn't so good at courting the first time." Simon shook his head.

"I remember, but as Driver Dan always says, we can only get better with age." Silas winked, spurring a laugh out of Simon. Hopefully that was true.

CHAPTER NINETEEN

"You've just never had someone give you the right kind of flowers before," Lena remarked as Stella finished drying the last of the dishes. Her words pierced like a splinter under the nail, and Stella winced. It was true, Burl had never given her flowers. What he gave her was better than flowers. He gave her hope and then, in the blink of an eye, severed it with a dull slice to her future.

"My Aaron used to pick me roses, until my own mamm grew tired of him stripping all her bushes clean." Lena laughed.

"Aaron sounds like a man worthy of your heart." *Unlike Burl Hilty in every way.*

"Like my sohns, he was worthy of all I could give him."

Stella couldn't disagree. The bishop was deserving of all one could give him. Stella couldn't pretend her feelings were her own anymore, not with her elder looking at her in such a way. Simon exuded safety, commitment, and hope. All the things Stella had lived without. If only they didn't live in two separate communities, Stella could get to know him better.

"We should fetch your suitcase. Your driver will be here soon," Stella said, leaving the whole idea of courting Simon Graber before she began believing such a silly idea was possible.

An hour later Stella handed Ervin Lena's suitcase. It wasn't even heavy, so why had she insisted on taking up the whole little dawdi haus this morning?

"You keep our Ellie fed, and don't forget to take her to the creek. A hund like that needs water," Lena said as she slid into the passenger seat.

"Tell Elsie we all said hello," Ervin said. Like Simon, he had a serious look about him, but there was a soft twinkle in his eyes that displayed the same sweet affection for his mother. Guilt pinched her hard for not sharing the same notions with her own.

"Mei schwester may soon grow tired of my visits and come see you all soon for herself." Lena maneuvered into a comfortable spot. "And, Stella, you should think on it while you have the day to yourself. A shop here would do well for all. Folks need you. Some a lot more than others." Lena patted Ellie's head tenderly.

"I have a shop." Stella wouldn't give false hope when she had a home waiting on her, though Stella had often wondered about opening one that didn't involve temporary shelving and letting all kinds of folks right inside her home. She had barely the room or the funds to build one, especially once she repaid those mending her roof.

"Not right now," Lena reminded her. "Pray on it. Gott might see fit to plant you elsewhere, and one can make a living anywhere, if she has the heart for it. I know our bishop would approve." Lena chuckled. Clever, indeed.

Stella was growing fond of Lena and Michael. Living here would be wonderful, but Stella could never leave her small hillside home. It had been the only place she ever knew love, the kind so many took for granted each and every day. The kind only grandparents could give you. She might have nursed them through their last days, but they had given her a lifetime of love to hold on to. Every hike on the hillside, every pot of tea created allowed her to reminisce in the warm memories of the only love she had ever known.

Ervin closed the door, and the van disappeared up the lane. Ellie gave a whine. Just as Stella suspected, her best friend had fallen for the family matriarch. Of course Stella believed bribery was involved—Lena's habit of sneaking treats to Ellie when she thought Stella wasn't looking.

"I should get back to work," Ervin said. Much like Simon, Ervin was a solid man with dark hair and eyes as blue as a late summer sky. His beard was less tame, which gave him a more rugged look, but just like all of Lena's kinner she'd met so far, he too had a twinkle in his eye that couldn't be missed.

"Do you need me to hitch up a buggy for you? Mamm mentioned you wanted to see over a few folks today."

"Nee. That is kind of you, but it's a nice day. I like walking." She smiled.

"Very well, then." He made a motion to leave before turning back to her. In the silence of his stare, Stella knew something was troubling him.

"Is Beth well?" Stella asked.

"Jah, but she has been feeling a little different for a spell now."

The scant description did little to help Stella know what Ervin was hinting at. Beth was almost fifty. Stella hadn't observed anything notable about her that would indicate a deeper health issue. Only one thought came to mind.

"Hot sweats?"

"Jah." He blushed, clearly not accustomed to such talk with another. "Dok in town gave her something, but it makes her. . ." He rubbed his neck and stared at the dirt.

"Emotional?" Why doctors continued to give herbs like St. John's wort for women going through the change was beyond her. That was better for folks suffering daily with blue moods.

"Tell her red clover tea, but I will fix a special blend up and send it over soon," Stella offered. It would help with some of the symptoms of the change, but putting together a tea of red clover, stinging nettle, and raspberry leaf would be best.

"Danke," Ervin said with a sigh of relief. "Mamm and Michael are fond of you."

"I am fond of them too," Stella replied. She could see Ervin had something more on his mind.

"You'd fit in, if you want my thoughts on it. And I like that you make him happy again." With nothing more, Simon's bruder climbed into the buggy and soon left a cloud of gravelly dust in his wake.

Did she really make Simon happy? Sweet hope lifted the corners of her mouth into an impenetrable smile, but as she walked along the busy roadway of Cherry Grove with Ellie at her side, those corners slacked step by step, leaving nothing but two flat lips in place. If the storm hadn't come, she wouldn't be here. There was no such thing as a happily-ever-after after the storm.

At the top of the lane. Stella motioned for Ellie to sit as a buggy came her way. Instead of passing on, the driver stopped, a fair-haired youngie with a smile as pert as honey lemonade.

"You Dok Stella?"

"I am," Stella replied, lifting her hand to blot out the sun.

"I was just aiming your way. Heard you were courting Bishop Graber." The young maed suppressed a giggle. Before Stella could correct her, the maedel continued, "My *schwestern* are plenty sick, and I can give you a lift. It's too hot for walking dogs anyhow."

———————— ⚜ ————————

If a person could be called whimsy, it was Chrissy Keim. Stella had never met her and her spinster sisters before, but after today, she would not soon forget them.

Chrissy was the youngest, barely twenty-six, and taller than most women. She was as slim as a lily stem and moved much like a cat chasing grasshoppers. Even her laugh carried a mix of playful cunning and foolish fancies. If she had a serious bone in her body, Stella hadn't found it as she spoke with all three women who claimed the dry weather was the cause of their respiratory issues.

"I cannot miss the next gathering," Chrissy said with a pout before falling into a fit of deep-chested coughs.

"We will if it's best for others. Levi Shetler will just have to take Delilah Glick home. . . again," Leah said, shooting her sister a knowing look.

Stella seconded the first comment. It wasn't worth the risk of making others sick. The second comment was clearly a sore subject in the sisterly household. All three sisters looked near in age, but years divided them in maturity. Leah was more standoffish, the shy kitten of the litter. Her reddened cheeks and need for so many layers in August were just one more telltale sign of the flu.

Stella washed her hands a third time and handed over a bottle of her best flu defense. The Keims wanted no part in natural healing or having a well-behaved dog inside their home. But the eldest, Iolene, welcomed the trusted elixir, paid Stella, and all three went back to the busyness of braiding strips of material into rugs, without so much as a so-long.

Stella admired the sisters' dedication to one another and their fine talent of rug braiding. By Iolene's instruction, Stella stopped by the next house, a small cottage home at the bottom of a hill. Gemma Shetler and her husband, Lester, both seemed happier to have visitors, four-legged included, than they did a warm cup of tea.

"First I felt a little hoarse; then I felt a little buggy." Lester slapped his leg in wild humor. His jokes were corny, but Stella immediately loved them both. Gemma spoke fondly of her eight kinner and thirty-six *grosskinner* but had lost count after that.

Stella's heart tugged for the older pair that had been holed up for nearly two weeks, hoping not to spread germs to their family. It was smart, Stella measured, but as far as she could tell, both had weathered the storm, and their dry spout of loneliness could finally be quenched.

At the top of the ridge where blue sky touched newly mowed fields, Stella took a long breath before lifting her hand to knock on the Hooleys' door. The hairs at the base of Ellie's neck lifted in warning. Stella swallowed when she heard the thud of heavy stomps moving closer.

The door swung open, and the dark shadow towering over her groaned. Perhaps the bishop was right and coming here wasn't such a good idea after all.

CHAPTER TWENTY

Simon listened to the messages on his answering machine. He was dirty and tired, and he needed a bath after handling horses all day. Two more messages revealed Mamm had made it to Elsie's safely and that Mary Alice thought tomorrow was the best time for Simon to pay a visit to her daughter, for she was surely lonely and in need of counsel considering it was coming up on the anniversary of Nathan's passing. She also instructed Simon to remind Carl Hooley his fence lines needed to be weeded.

Simon leaned against the phone shanty wall and let out a weary breath. He had a duty to minister to all, but Pricilla didn't like to talk about Nathan—although she did like strong-arming innocent newcomers into her plight. Where there was no counsel, folks failed miserably. Maybe a visit with Pricilla and her mother wasn't such a bad idea after all.

At the final message, Simon knew the bath would have to wait. Surprisingly his nephew didn't sound worried or rushed. Then again, Joel had always displayed an air of calm. Joel stated in the message that it was only a little after three and that Rachel's pains were weak. Simon remembered how quickly that could change. With Claire, Lizzy thought she had all day. That's why she insisted on planting the garden. But no sooner had she dropped the first handful of seeds did Claire decide she was ready to come into the world. Simon hurried back to the buggy and aimed for the barn.

Nearing the house, Simon saw nothing of the dok or the hund. Disappointment ran through him, and he set the brake and got out of the buggy. He missed her. It was completely unnatural how quickly that happened. Suddenly fetching help was beginning to look a lot like a second chance, just as Silas said.

The freshly swept sidewalk revealed she'd stayed close by today. He wasn't sure she would heed his warning about Carl. Knowing she was here was a relief. Carl tended to poke at others' sensitivities.

Perched on the open gate leading to his back pasture sat a male rose-breasted grosbeak. He looked lonely sitting there, calling out. Lizzy had loved bird-watching, and Simon had learned a thing or two from their conversations about birds. Grosbeaks remained with their mates for life. But did they search out new mates when left alone?

Before Simon could give his next thought much consideration, the hund emerged around the corner of the barn. In her mouth was a limb four times her size. Simon clenched his jaw in frustration with the mongrel. That young peach tree had only been planted in May, and it didn't have a chance. Not with that animal around.

"Give me that," he scolded and pulled the sapling from her sharp-toothed clutch. "Don't be bouncing around like that. I ain't playing fetch with you. This is my tree. Go get your own." The hund dropped to her haunches and cocked her head. If there had been any roots, the critter had chewed them off.

"Where's your owner?" Simon looked about again. Usually where one was, the other wasn't far. An odd pairing that now brought a smile to his lips.

The hund barked in reply and took off through the open gate. Simon, not one for understanding the language of mutts, followed blindly. Through the dry grass and sea of milkweed plumes floating on a warm August wind, he caught a glimpse of the white prayer covering just ahead. Below the surface of a tall mingle of timothy and alfalfa, there was just enough hint of robin's-egg blue for him to know it was her.

He approached slowly, taking in the scene with curious amusement.

She was on bended knees, her bare feet keeping purchase of her balance as she yanked and pulled on a wild cornflower stalk. It was quite the spectacle, a woman battling a helpless weed.

At her right was a spoon caked in rich earth and a basket already sporting a handful of long, narrow, dirty roots. She was an odd duck, but Simon considered that too was part of her charm.

With a hard tug and a feminine grunt, the stalk pulled free, displaying another long root. She twisted and snapped off the stalk and turned to drop the root in the basket when their gazes collided.

And that's when Simon saw the tears.

"You're hurt." He quickly knelt beside her and took up both of her hands to inspect for wounds. His fingers migrated from one callus to another. How could something so rough feel so soft?

"I'm not hurt," she muttered, pulling a hand free and swiping her midlength sleeve under her nose. Now she had dirt on her face. She was a complete disaster, and Simon's heart was taken. She was unlike any woman he had ever known. She was stubbornly independent, terribly fragile, and nurtured by sunshine and earth.

"Carl won't let me see Carlee," Stella blurted out and quickly hid her face in her hands, now crying more earnestly.

The wind rushed out of him. There was no telling what harsh words Carl had spat. "I thought we agreed you would wait for me." He offered her a worn handkerchief.

"It's not *your* duty to see me do mine." She snatched the handkerchief from his hand. "He wouldn't even tell me if she was feeling better. He said I sold tea and flowers to the Englisch and had no place in his haus." Her voice clipped with anger.

"Carl can be stubborn, sure." Simon removed his hat. He swiped his damp brow and placed it back on his head. "I'm sure she is well, as all the others have been." He tried to sound positive, but deep inside, Simon was beginning to worry if Carl was possibly neglecting his daughter's own health out of his distrust of others. He would have to focus on that later. For now, it was Joel and Rachel who needed help. What busy lives they both had, he suddenly realized.

"But how can I know? Susie looked at me with such worry on her face. She was practically begging." He could see the worry on hers. Ellie darted after a squirrel. If the squirrel knew what was good for it, it would shimmy up a tree quickly.

Simon plopped down beside her. A grasshopper landed on his knee then took off for a better place to sit and munch on leaves. "I cannot know all the answers, but no matter what we think, we must trust Gott to see over Carlee. Some things we cannot fix; you know this."

"But we *can* fix this, and—"

He held up a hand. "Stella, I know he will do the right thing if she worsens. She is his child. A father would do anything for his kinner. He loves her more than his troubles with the outside world."

She sniffed and looked up to him. "Not all fathers do." Her doubt was clear, and Simon knew it stemmed from beyond whatever Carl had said to her.

Brown eyes, the color of weak tea, glistened and tugged every string of his heart. "If it makes you feel better, I'll pay them a visit first thing tomorrow." She relaxed at that, revealing that he was gaining her trust.

"Now"—Simon reached for the basket and spoon—"wanna tell me what these are?"

"The little white flowers are yarrow, which are used to bring down a fever or stopping blood where there's too much of it." She dabbed at her nose with the handkerchief and sniffed a couple of times before reaching into the basket to show him her bounty. "And these are chicory roots. They have many uses. Cleaning the liver, helping the heart. And chicory makes a great kaffi without giving you all the jitters." She flushed at the admittance. It was true she wasn't a fan of his kaffi, and he already suspected she had been flowering it. It was one thing that she had managed to get him to drink tea made of thorns and weeds, but kaffi need not to be altered.

Sparing her his thoughts on the matter considering her current state, Simon stood and offered Stella a hand. "You have enough energy for three women already. Makes sense." He grinned.

"A person should always use what is ready about them." She smiled sheepishly.

"You eat weeds and drink about everything around you," he teased playfully as he pulled her to her feet.

"When you grow up with little, you learn quick the difference between what you can forage and what can kill you." It was another slip of her past. Another page in her story being revealed. A picture was forming. Stella would not be the first to be raised in a home with little, but under all that knowledge, Simon suspected Stella went to bed with less than a full belly every night. Simon had questions, but Stella was not a woman you prodded to get answers. She deserved a patient hand and a safe place. He could provide both.

"I'm sorry that past was not easy, but today is a fresh day."

Stella flinched and stared up at him. "The past is never far away."

"Nee, it's not," Simon replied. He couldn't school her on letting go when not a day went by that he hadn't thought of the family now gone from him. "But looking back keeps us from seeing what's ahead. I'm thankful Gott saw you safe and brought you here." Simon took a breath as his words riddled over her features. He wanted to soothe her, hold her as he had the day of the storm, but today a new member of the community was about to make their arrival, and Simon had to get the dok over there to see that welcome came safely.

"I'm wondering if you might want to take a ride with me."

"A ride?" Her eyes widened. "I told Lena I would see over a few things before she returns tomorrow," she stuttered out, "and. . .and folks might get the wrong idea." His gaze locked onto hers, and Simon could see the embarrassment of her part in Pricilla's deception.

"You mean they might think us to be courting," he quickly said.

Stella blinked twice before ducking her head. "Simon, I. . ."

"I hear we are all the gossip, but I don't concern myself with what others think, Stella, only what Gott does, and I don't think He would object to me courting you at all. In fact, I wouldn't mind getting to know you better." He brushed his thumb across her cheek where dirt resided. "But since Rachel needs you right now, we best speak of that later. I'll wait for you in the buggy. Don't be long. One can never know when a boppli is ready." He turned and left her there, mouth agape.

There is a time for everything under the sun, Stella considered as she removed her prayer covering and pinned the dark blue kerchief over her head. She tried not to think about that place on her cheek where Simon's thumb had brushed earlier. His touch ran like a spark of solar fencing down her arms and straight to her toes. For a man who didn't say much, he said plenty.

As a hot sun dipped closer to the hillside, Stella set aside thoughts of the bishop and the fact that his gaze could render her speechless. It was Rachel's time, and new life was coming today.

The small home was neat and tidy, as if just recently cleaned from floor to ceiling for hosting a Sunday service. Martha had called this "nesting," the way a woman simply knew when to ready her home before giving birth. Right now, Stella wished Dok Martha was here. The elder had coached her through many labors, but even now that Stella had assisted with more than twenty births, she felt a tinge of nervousness. She always hoped she made the right decision if one had to be made, and that she could muster through a difficult birth without her mentor beside her.

Without Martha, Stella stole her courage from the soon-to-be father. He was unnervingly calm. Joel had accepted the weak raspberry leaf tea and slipped inside the shared bedroom more than an hour ago. The tea would help move things along. Not all first-time mothers were blessed with a quick delivery.

"I do not have my birthing bag," Stella mumbled to Rachel's mamm as she dusted spotless countertops while giving the young couple time alone. It was probably still under the rain-soaked bed and the little house she hadn't thought about in two days.

"No worries, Dok Stella. After helping mei last grandchild into the world, I readied a few things early on for Rachel's special time," Rachel's mamm assured her, moving to open a small plastic tote filled with all the necessities required. Even the sterile wrapped bulb and scissors had been placed inside. Stella felt some of her concerns float away. "I'm glad you are here to help see all goes well."

"Me too," Stella said and once again considered Lena's parting words about opening a shop nearby where more folks would benefit. There seemed to be an even greater need for her in Cherry Grove than she suspected, and Cherry Grove also had something that was beginning to appeal to her more than nettle leaves and chicory blooms. It had the bishop. What was growing between them could no longer be swept aside, not with his intentions now mentioned. Her cheeks warmed once more.

"There is talk you may never return to Walnut Ridge. I'm happy to know you are close to Rachel if needed, and you won't be too far to fetch if we need you." Rachel's mamm winked. Her face looked larger by the lack of a hairline. Too many years twisting a tight knot into a bun had destroyed her roots. Stella had been researching the benefits of rosemary and wondered if the elder would consider it.

"I'll be returning home as soon as the roof is done." Why did returning not feel as wonderful as it had before? Stella looked up just as Simon stepped inside the house. He'd disappeared not long after they arrived, insisting he needed to see over Joel's evening chores. Stella suspected his absence had more to do with the delicate nature of the day than with feeding a few hogs and chickens. When their gazes locked, she felt a hand wrap around her heart and give it a gentle squeeze. Would today only remind him of all he had lost? Stella gave him a half-hearted smile.

"But Bishop Mast said your house is. . ." A cry of labor filled the house. Stella wanted to know the end of that sentence, but Rachel needed her.

"Let's get more water boiling," Stella said and tried not to notice the color draining from Simon's face. While Rachel's mamm began collecting linens, Stella set the water to boil.

"Can you see over this and perhaps—" Both turned toward the door at the sound of buggies spilling into the driveway.

"That would be Verna and the kinner," Simon said with a shrug. "I'm surprised she didn't beat us here." Lines of concern crinkled his forehead. If only she could be a comfort for him as he had been for her just hours ago.

Simon looked to the stove then to the bedroom door. "I'm not sure being here is best. There is much I haven't told you." His sorrowful tone pulled at her heartstrings. Stella didn't miss the grief hidden there. As difficult as it was to accept she'd never know the blessings of mother-hood, it was harder still for Simon. Reaching out, she placed a tender touch to his forearm.

"That too can wait," she assured him. "We cannot know what each day will bring." His jaw tightened as he looked down on her. "Gott will give you the words and the strength to find joy in this day despite what is lost to you, just as He sees fit to let me be a part of something I can never have."

Simon's brows gathered in a sorrowful expression. "Is that how you feel, Stella?"

"I don't mean to question Gott's will." She lowered her head. It wasn't about her, but the ache of motherhood she would always thirst for. "But I see how hard this is for you."

"I miss them," he admitted. "It felt as if I had no time at all. I should feel glad for the time I did have them. I should feel. . ." His lips tightened, keeping his next words contained.

"You are just a man, like any other. I reckon you feel a great many things."

A flicker of life rekindled in his deep blue gaze. A mutual under-standing of what collected in both their hearts reached the surface. Simon had lost so much, but he still had Michael. Stella would never have children, but she did have a role in so many lives. Life had joy in it, regardless of how many trials and aches it pressed upon a person. One simply had to seek the joy and set aside the haunts of yesterday.

"Jah, and we must lean not unto our own understanding." He nodded and lifted his shoulders. "You are a smart woman, Stella Schmucker."

His lips lifted slightly. "I should have told you, but. . ."

"We are just getting to know each other, Bishop Graber." Oh, how she was falling for this man. It was a terrible mistake, yet her heart and her head were not going to agree on the matter. "Let me know when the water starts to boil," she said and rushed into the next room before she made a bigger fool of herself.

CHAPTER TWENTY-ONE

The shared bedroom was shaped like a rectangle with pale blue walls, and a hot summer breeze pushing through two open windows. In the corner sat a cradle, made of wood and smoothed by time. Rachel had draped a quilt over the side along with a small white onesie. Stella prayed the cradle would soon be filled with a healthy child.

Only once in all her time with Martha had there been a need to call for outside help. The twins were far too early, the labor too long, and the mother too weary. Like Martha, Stella had no qualms about reaching out, calling the emergency number, if the need came.

Rachel lay limp as yesterday's lettuce in the oak bed, under too many layers of sheets and quilts, grimacing. At her right stood Joel, consoling with kind whispers and holding Rachel's hand. How endearing when husbands stood by experiencing the miraculous gift of Gott with their wives. Rachel's mamm stood at her left, lighting another lamp.

"Are you ready to meet your sohn or dochter today?" Stella asked, smiling. Martha always insisted a smile was required to be a good midwife, helping the mother along. Not all mothers smiled in return, and Stella had already suspected Rachel to be one who would hold on to hers until well after all the work was done.

Stella fetched her spare headlamp from her leather bag. The small blue band was less bulky than the lamp she used to walk over rocky ground at home. She worked the band over her kerchief, allowing her hands to be free for efficiency. Once the headlamp was in place, she clicked the battery-operated light on and gave Rachel a quick inspection progress. Then she straightened, clicking the light off again. It was going to be a long night. First-time mothers either rushed into motherhood or didn't. Only Gott knew the length; a dok simply had to use intuition, acquired wisdom, and a guess.

"Joel, can you help Rachel up and let her walk about for a while?"

Rachel gave her a narrowed look.

"It will help you and the boppli get things moving," Stella assured her. Most couples wanted this time alone. Stella excused herself from the room and slipped back into the kitchen.

Verna and Laura stood at the stove making fresh kaffi as Simon stood nearby, arms crossed talking horseflesh with Willis. They were family. If one had a need, they saw it tended to. Simon was blessed, and for one weak moment, she let her heart drift into that uncharted sea of wishes and wants. She too wished to be part of them, of Simon's lot.

"Kumm along," Lydianne instructed her three young kinner. She poured them each a glass of milk and helped them to sit at the table, their bare feet dangling. Elizabeth set a cookie in front of each child.

"How is she?" Verna asked as Stella moved to pour her a cup of kaffi. Verna's dull brown chore dress accentuated a few freckles Stella hadn't noticed before.

"She is strong and well, jah. It could be a long night," Stella whispered, adding milk to her cup. "Joel is verra calm, though I am certain sure that he cannot wait to meet his sohn or dochter soon." She grinned before taking a tentative sip.

"We will pray for a safe *nacht* for all of them," Verna said.

Verna was a measure of support. Stella admired her dedication to her kinner, even after they grew to become parents of their own. *As it should be,* she reminded herself once more. Perhaps that was why Gott had never seen fit to bestow the same gifts on her. If one wasn't raised to know how to be a godly parent, then how could they teach their kinner to be?

"We will sing songs. When Lydianne was having Sarah Rose, she said it brought her comfort and strength," Laura said. Nearly a teenager, Laura would most likely spend a week helping out the new parents while Rachel recovered. *Because that is what family does.*

"Dok Stella," Joel called, peeking his head out. Stella grabbed a glass of water and returned to the bedroom.

She handed Rachel's mamm the glass. "You may give her a sip." Her helper had now put on a long apron and headlamp, and looked just like Martha, ready for the duration.

Joel began to read from Psalms. "Behold, children are a heritage from the Lord, the fruit of the womb is a reward."

Stella said her own silent prayer, for both mother and child. Nerves, pain, and excitement etched over Rachel's features.

"It is all expected, but soon you will forget the cost paid for a blessing from Gott," Stella encouraged as Rachel's mamm soothed her daughter's forehead.

"When you feel the urge to push, breathe long and slow. We are not ready yet. That's it, breathe like this," Stella coaxed, demonstrating the technique. The longer the mother could breathe through the pains, chances were the hard work of pushing would take thirty minutes or less.

In the dim lighting between soft mumblings of prayers and Joel's consoling, Rachel breathed through the pains. Her eyes remained locked onto Stella for guidance. Outside, voices rose up but did not overwhelm, a harmonious sound of support and love.

As another song sprang up, unable to stop herself, Rachel took a deep breath, bore down, and held her breath.

"Rachel, I need you to stop pushing. Can you do this for me?" Stella urged as she noted the cause for what was keeping progress from moving along.

"Is something wrong?" Joel asked with a worried tone.

"All is well. I only need to help your boppli along some." Rachel's mamm moved to assist. Quietly the two women slipped the cord over the baby's head. Thankfully it was a swift motion, and Stella instructed

Rachel to hold her breath and bear down once more.

It was not uncommon for a cord to put a hold on a speedy delivery or cause Stella's worried brow to twitch, but God was with them as a thatch of dark hair emerged, and in two hard breaths, Joel and Rachel's son was born.

Not all babies entered the world with a joyful cry, which Stella preferred and Martha always insisted was a sure sign of health. In the absence of sound, Stella worked to stimulate the slippery bundle. A finger down the right side of the vertebrae, a tickle to the feet, and then the room filled with cries. Happy tears and praise to God rose and spilled out into the quiet room.

"You both have a healthy sohn. Would you like to cut the cord, Daed?"

Joel's face lit up with the well-earned title while his eyes glistened. His steady hand followed instruction, and the connection between mother and child was quickly severed. Stella suddenly wondered if her own birthday had been celebrated in joy.

Rachel's mamm quickly wrapped the boppli in a thick blanket, then another, and placed him in Rachel's arms. Stella let the little family drink in the first precious moments as she saw over the final chore. Once Rachel gave one last push, all was done.

Stella busied herself to tidy up and then gave the wee one a full scrutiny, checking all the mental boxes Martha insisted needed to be checked. He was healthy, strong, and more comfortable in his mamm's arms than being handled by a dok.

In the absence of her bag, there would be no knowing for certain if Rachel had delivered a nine-pound beautiful child, but Stella was learning to judge that more closely and felt confident to assure the parents that their healthy boy exceeded nine pounds.

Ignoring her own ache for children, Stella was happy for the new parents. Verna was probably pacing just outside, considering all singing had hushed. There would be a few more hours yet of observation, but she'd allot them a few moments alone as a family.

"I will ready Rachel something to eat and a fresh cup of tea," Stella said, carrying a bundle of linens as she aimed for the door.

"Please add honey. You know I don't stomach tea without it." Already as bossy as she was before the first pains.

Stella laughed. "I will, and you both be sure to see the doctor kumm morning. He will need his K1 injection too. I shall never leave home again without my birthing bag," Stella said and suddenly wondered if her birthing bag lay hidden under the debris of wood and metal and one weak oak.

"I'm glad you were here," Rachel said, locking gazes with her. "I wanted you to be here, and here you were. I didn't even have time to worry how long it would take you to bike all the way here."

"Gott has seen Dok Stella where she was needed," Joel said, and Stella swallowed hard. She was here because others were sick. It was a matter of simply being in the right place at the right time. Was it not? Suddenly Stella wasn't sure.

———————— ⚜ ————————

Before the sun dared waking, Simon stepped from the stove, a fresh cup of kaffi in his hand, and slipped back into the sitting room. A lonely lamp sat in the far corner, its flickering flame dancing over the walls.

The household now slept, so he quietly leaned back into the chair and sipped at the hot brew. Across from him, Stella and baby William slept. The tender scene touched him. Had not his own William once slept peacefully in his arms in that same way? Visions of long nights and short days filled his mind. Claire had come so quickly and fussed for months before her cheeks filled out into soft plumpness. William was born with a full head of hair and eyes as dark as a midnight sky. Simon let out a slow breath. He should have told the dok, but he never liked opening old wounds.

The dok looked uncomfortable. Sleeping in a chair was not ideal, but he suspected she'd sleep standing up if that was what was asked of her. She stirred up something heavy inside him. A longing he forgot existed. He didn't like how swift it had come over him, for things that came quickly usually left the same way. But Simon wouldn't ignore what the Lord was telling him. Nee, it was not good for man to be alone, and Simon no longer wanted to be.

A rooster crowed somewhere nearby, and his thoughts drifted to Lizzy. She changed when he became a minister, and more yet when he became bishop. A life serving others was no easy task. But Stella's words had stilled him. He *was* merely a man, with emotions and yearnings. Stella saw him, beyond the duty and grief.

Could the pretty dok be happy with a bishop? Could she be happy with never having children of her own? He was nearing fifty. Did he want more children when they could so easily be taken from him? All good questions.

At a second crow of the rooster, the dok stirred. "They are so fragile." She leaned over and placed a tender kiss on the baby's downy hair, and a lump formed in his throat.

"I made fresh kaffi if you want some."

She looked across the room and met his gaze. "That was verra kind of you." She smiled, and they simply sat in the quiet, eyes locked on each other. A depth of understanding wafted between them. She wanted kinner, he could see that, holding the child possessively as she was. But could she be happy with a life with only him and Michael in it if Gott had no more to give? He had much to offer yet, he liked to think, but was it enough for one as young as the dok? The questions collected in his chest, but hope still filled his heart. He did miss being a husband and missed the sounds of a full house, and he suspected he'd miss it more if the dok returned to Walnut Ridge.

Simon knew better than to mock God as Abraham had. Silas was having his sixth child, was he not? Filling all the gaps and holes in his life, with Stella, was possible. Now if only she'd stay so they could explore the feelings running between them. So he could convince the woman he was courting that she was worthy of love. It tore at him how little she knew on the subject. He felt a grin tug at the corner of his mouth.

He'd be happy to show her.

Stella slowly rose to her feet, careful not to disturb the sleeping bundle in her arms. "I need to ready breakfast. Rachel will need her nourishment when she wakes." Baby William yawned, a small sound escaping that made them both smile. "You should hold your nephew for a spell. He won't be quiet long." She chuckled softly.

"Great-nephew," Simon corrected and shifted nervously in his chair. "I'm a bit out of practice," he admitted. *Not since Claire,* he thought. Stella remained fastened to a spot, waiting. Clearly she was not accepting his excuses. Setting his kaffi on the floor beside him, Simon accepted the baby into his arms.

An unexpected rush of warmth flowed over him.

"You're not the only one, but you must be useful, Bishop, and you never know what Gott has planned for you." She quietly slipped into the kitchen, but his chest swelled in fresh hope. Simon couldn't remember the last time he looked forward to the future, and as he looked down at the child tucked between chest and elbow, he smiled.

A clutch of family and friends arrived at daybreak. It was time to get Stella back to the farm. She needed more rest, and he needed to see over morning chores. "Are you ready, Dok?"

Stella placed her empty cup in the sink and turned to him. She looked tired but happy. They made their way back home as the sun rose over the hilly landscape and the quiet of morning.

"You did well, Dok, and Joel and Rachel were blessed to have you there." He knew the feeling when a new colt was born, especially after a hard birth.

"I'm happy for them. Rachel did well, and Joel is certainly happy to have a sohn."

"But. . ." He shot her an encouraging brow. "I can see how you long for kinner, Stella." It was a bold comment. One she might take offense to.

She let out a heavy sigh. "I just don't understand why Gott gives some a regular life and some not, but I am content in what I have." She need not try to convince him.

"He gave us all life, but what comes of it is often up to us. We don't have to understand, but we must trust. Have faith in His plan."

"Maybe so, but one can reach a time when such hopes are impossible," she said, and Simon couldn't disagree.

"With Gott nothing is impossible, and Gott may see you yet to be a mudder."

"Not all are worthy of such."

Simon brought the buggy to a halt in front of the barn. Morning rays spilled over the farm like a rushing wind. He climbed out of the buggy and made his way to her side. Looking up, he couldn't help but see the hurt etched on her face.

"None of us are worthy, but He gives blessings nonetheless. You are a kind woman, and you keep surprising me." It wasn't proper, pouring on such praise, but Stella clearly had no idea how much Gott had in store for her yet. "You help bring life into the world, restore the sick, and awaken those around you who have been slumbering too long." He offered her a hand.

"Danke, Simon. That was verra kind of you to say." She ducked her head in a quiet blush.

"Don't give up on our community yet," he added with a wink and watched the effects shiver over her. If she only knew how much he admired her ability to help others so freely, her strong will to follow the path she felt God had put before her.

Lizzy insisted they had to be a gut example when he became bishop. That the Lord was watching them at all times. But the Lord always watched, even now as he looked upon a woman tired from a long night with want and hope in his heart. He was flesh and bone first. Just a man, a man whom Gott had put to task and who was coming to enjoy the taste for wilder flavors.

"There are many who need you here, Stella Schmucker." He reached out and let his finger twist around her kapp string. She blinked, and he wished to say more but couldn't find the words.

"I should go see if Lena needs me. Danke, Bishop." She turned and hurried into the house. He rather liked when she called him Simon, but he couldn't help but smile knowing the effect he had on her.

CHAPTER TWENTY-TWO

Rain drizzled over the landscape as Simon pounded metal against iron. They had only been gone a few hours, but knowing how much Stella disliked rain, Simon couldn't help but worry. He loaned her the buggy—it wasn't like the dok would stay put—but why did Mamm insist on shopping in this weather? That's what he wanted to know as a fat drop of perspiration slid from his hairline and aimed for the corner of his eye.

He swiped the dampness away and continued to beat the hot metal until it reached a flattened state then turned it on its side and began creating the shape. His blacksmithing apron felt too heavy, his protective leather gloves too tight. Beside him, the mutt slept, oblivious to what was eating at Simon most.

Bishop Mast was clear—the house was too lost for a simple repair, and it was time to rein in his wandering sheep. Simon knew what that meant, and he didn't like it one bit.

He flipped the piece, now taking shape, and beat the edge with fresh frustration. They hadn't even tried repairing the roof, just covered it with tarps and left it to the elements.

He looked to the hund again. She raised her head and peered his way. "You'll be pestering a new bishop soon," he said, part sarcastically and part regretfully.

This news would devastate her, he knew. Stella loved her home, dangerous or not, and it was clear she held a strong attachment to it.

How long would Bishop Mast put her up before he had her married off? Simon ground his molars until they ached.

At least she wasn't inside when the storm came; for that Simon was grateful. "She'll have a roof over her head," he said. Her bishop would see to that. Simon had to trust that the bishop would have her best interest at heart, and that was why he was struggling.

It was hard being a man of faith but also one of flesh and feelings, and soon Stella would return, and it was his duty to tell her the news. If there was one thing Simon knew, Stella wouldn't like being backed into a corner.

When he heard the buggy outside, Simon went to the opening of his blacksmith shop. The rain had stopped, but *when* it stopped he hadn't a clue as muddled as his thoughts were today. He watched her climb down and help Mamm from the buggy. The sight warmed him as both seemed to be laughing at something.

The hund bolted, just as happy for their return. Stella looked his way and waved. She floated him a smile. Simon waved back and tried to capture that smile to memory. It might be the last she would consider giving him once he told her about her home. It wasn't the first time he had been the bearer of bad news, but this one stung. The last thing Simon wanted to do was cause Stella heartache.

Unless.

As the women slipped into the dawdi haus, Simon crossed the yard to see to the buggy. He didn't have to tell her. . .today.

She cares for me, he silently schooled his anxious heart, and the idea bloomed more profoundly. If he kept the bishop's message under his hat for a few more days, he would know if she felt something more for him. He cared for her. Cared for her well-being, her safety, and what interested her. Jah, courting was a start, but if he wanted her to stay, Simon would need to get busy courting.

They could take a ride. *Rides are romantic,* he thought, and began to unharness David. He'd pack a blanket and a nice lunch. A picnic. Lizzy hadn't favored them, but Simon had many fond memories of such gatherings growing up.

Before Simon could see David out to pasture, his hope for a picnic with the pretty doctor fell to the wayside. A bishop always had to be on hand when needed, but today it was the dok who was being summoned.

Simon stood at the foot of the bed and watched Stella placed a hand on Carlee's forehead and then take up her wrist. The young maedel was a frail shadow of herself.

A rare sense of worry filled him as Stella placed an ear to Carlee's chest. Even he could see that breathing was hard work for her. From the other side of the bed, Susie cried, her hand holding her daughter's as fear etched her features, but Carl stood in the doorway, arms folded and frowning.

Does the man have any emotions at all?

Simon understood heartache. When his family was taken from him, there were moments, small ones, when he wanted to place blame. If only they had all been wearing their seat belts. If only the driver hadn't fallen into a fit of coughs, losing control of the van. But death came to all, in a hundred different ways, and at the Lord's timing.

But Carl couldn't blame the sun for growing tired, letting night come early. This was not their way. The father would have to let go of the son just as Simon had to let go of the past, before it cost them both.

"She needs to go to the hospital," Stella pleaded. Her worried tone filled his heart with dread. If the dok felt Carlee needed to be taken to the hospital, then so be it.

"You are a doktor! Make your tea or something," Carl said angrily. "The Englisch have taken plenty from us. I will not allow them to take more."

"Carl, our dochter," Susie said pleadingly and burst into another heart-wrenching turn of sobs.

Simon trusted God in all things, placed his flock in the Maker's hands, but even as folks grew healthier, this one was hanging on by a thread. All could see it. Gabe gave him a teary look. On bended knees he'd been praying in earnest but now seemed ready to go against the father of the house. Simon sensed the uprising coming and knew he needed to convince Carl to set aside his hardened heart toward outsiders for Carlee's sake.

"Carl, you must listen to reason," Simon said gently.

"I'll take her if you won't." Gabe Schwartz stood determined. Simon's young nephew and Carlee had been courting for some time now, and Simon was aware of their intent to marry come spring.

"You need not decide for what is not yours," Carl threatened.

"Her lungs are struggling. She certainly has pneumonia. Simon. . .I mean, Bishop, please talk sense into him."

"I have authority over my own haus," Carl warned in a booming voice for all to hear.

"A man must take responsibility for his fraa and kinner," Simon said. "He must be selfless in love and deed, just as the Lord has been toward him."

"What can you know of such?" Carl lashed out. Simon felt the stab.

"Let us call an ambulance." Stella tried once more. "Herbs and teas and vinegar baths won't help now."

"We shall pray." Carl's head bowed, but none followed.

"I haven't stopped praying for her since I walked in here! I prayed Gott would tell me how to help her, and that's what I feel He is telling me."

"You know nothing of what she needs. I should have known. A foolish one, you are." Stella flinched, her shoulders dropping as Carl lashed out toward her.

"Not even married with kinner of your own to understand how hard it is to put them in Gott's hand." Carl raised a finger, shook it. "You have been shunned by your own *blut*, pushed out of your community for all your worldly ways. I welcomed you into our home, and yet Gott will see me punished for it."

Simon lifted a brow. *Pushed out of her family? Her community?* When Stella's teary gaze locked onto Simon's, he could see the hurt and some truth within the angry father's words, but before he could put an end to the rising tempers, as quick as the dok came into his life, she bolted and was gone.

"This is not how we speak to others. Dok Stella has done nothing against you, nothing but care for your child. Your dochter needs help," Simon said angrily.

"You think we don't know you have been keeping her. Mary Alice said she sleeps under your roof, sees over your needs. I shall speak to the men of this. You are living in sin. You have led our kinner astray, accepted their abandonment, and now this." Carl flung an angry hand in the air. "You are not fit to be a bishop."

"What kind of man do you think I am?" Carl's words that broke Simon's heart. "I thought you better than one who listened to gossip." Simon couldn't believe Carl's accusations, yet he knew his anger had been holding steam for years, waiting to be let loose. "And Gott decides what is to be done, not one man."

"Jah, then we finally agree," Carl returned. "Gott will heal her and speak to your heart. You should step aside before you lead more astray."

———————— ⚘ ————————

Stella ran away from the words that cut deep. They were the words of her father when nothing went as he planned. He too had a fierce temper when none could reason with his ideas.

Well, she might have been a foolish child but not a foolish woman. Her faith and obedience were sound, yet she knew there were times one had to go against a father's wants.

It wasn't the first time Stella was faced with opposition. Some folks didn't like her teas but had no qualms in buying her remedies and vitamins. Some parents didn't adhere to accepting help beyond childbirth, but they had no qualms waking her in the late of the night when a child was ready to be born. God had set her to task, to care for everyone, no matter how it looked.

"You planted me here to be useful," she spat to the wind as she reached the long white fencing separating one parcel from another. They thought they sent her running, that she was fragile. But they were wrong. She was necessary, and she needed to trust her intuition now. Carlee would die if she didn't do what needed to be done. That's why she ran blindly to the end of the lane, to the corner of the Hooleys' drive.

"Trust," Simon's voice called behind her, but Stella had no time to turn around. She needed to trust her feet to carry her to the phone shanty swiftly. God provided food, sunshine, and the very blossoms and roots and berries that healed a great number of maladies. They helped a body thrive against the elements. God also provided ministers of faith, and healers, but right now Carlee Hooley needed much more.

Stella pushed through the grown weeds and yanked open the phone shanty door, locking it quickly behind her. Chastisement would come soon enough.

Stella quickly told the emergency operator what Carlee needed. She glanced at the mailbox through the tiny door window and recited the numbers. "In Cherry Grove, jah," she repeated. "Please hurry, her breathing is verra weak and she is not waking." The emergency responder promised help was on its way.

Stella hung up the phone, placed a hand on her heart, and felt the wild pounding within. Help was coming.

"Gott be with Carlee and see they get to her swiftly, and forgive me for going against her daed. Be with Susie and bring her comfort. In Jesus' name, amen." *No woman blessed by the labor of bringing forth life should have to watch it be taken away.*

Stella wiped the tears from her face and stepped out of the phone shanty. To her surprise, Simon was not there. Was it not his voice that had called after her?

It took less than five minutes before the sound of sirens echoed between rolling hills and winding dips. Stella stood at the drive, ready to wave them her way, when Carl and Simon both emerged from the house. Looking to the west, they too could hear help coming.

Stella stood steadfast, swallowed hard, and lifted her chin when their heads swiveled her way. This was disobedience, plain and simple. Carl would insist it be dealt with and Simon would be expected to reach out to Bishop Mast, but if it saved a life, Stella would accept any punishment given.

Simon stared at her blankly. In one small act, Stella had severed any chance of courting him. Another tear leaked down the same trail as the previous one. It was a sacrifice, and the right thing to do.

When the paramedics arrived, Stella gave all the details she could as Carlee was placed on a board and carried out of the house. Carl had tried denying any help, but once the paramedic explained how sick Carlee was, Susie stepped up and granted them permission to help her.

"Thank you for being so informative. I'll let the doctor know about what medicines you have used." The young woman slipped a notepad in her back pocket, climbed inside next to Carlee and Susie, and closed the door.

Stella let out a breath, hopeful. Then she closed her eyes and inhaled a deep breath before turning to face the men.

"I will see that Bishop Mast hears of this. You have no right to come into my haus and challenge our faith." Carl took a step forward, panic and fear propelling him.

"Carl," Simon said in a threatening tone, stepping ahead of him. "We are all of the same faith."

"Let us go and be with them at the hospital," Gabe said, gripping Carl's forearm. "Danke, Dok Stella. I'll send word on how Carlee is doing." Gabe urged Carl away.

"They will kill her!" Carl continued to declare as Gabe managed to persuade him into a buggy and both men hurried to the hospital.

"Are you all right?" Simon searched her eyes for the effects of Carl's anger, but it was Carl who needed comfort, not her.

"He finds me no better than the world he fears and hates. His heart is torn."

"But no one should be so quick to anger."

"We all have our weaknesses. I fear mine is an independent mind."

Stella lowered her head shamefully.

"Thankfully so," Simon said, placing a hand on her shoulders.

"Not everyone agrees." His gaze and protectiveness were making her weak-kneed.

"You did what had to be done. God has carried you a long way to be here right now. For that, I'm thankful."

Has He? Stella considered her plight. God had led her home, and He put people in her path to feed her desire to learn, her grandparents and Martha. She had studied hard, read every book she could, and followed the path He had set out for her.

Tears swelled in her eyes as Simon looked down on her, thankful for her. She was more than Samuel's dochter. She was Dok Stella, and she suddenly wasn't alone.

It was always at times like these that life pivoted on one foot and lost its balance. Oftentimes knocking her into a direction that she was a stranger to. For all her knowledge, there were simple matters she had yet to understand fully. She could help a person with sore fingers, cure belly aches with one cup of hot water and a few chamomile flowers, a few leaves of lemon balm, and a sliver of ginger, but she had no remedy for protecting her own heart so far from home.

Stella turned her face into the shelter of his arms, and for the first time in all her life, she cried into another's shoulder.

CHAPTER TWENTY-THREE

Friday had bloomed under a gloomy sky, but the threat passed by quickly, giving in to an overly warm late summer day. Out of the large kitchen windows, Stella watched as Simon and Michael pitched hay bales from the wagon. She should be helping with supper, not fastening an eye on Simon and the way his wide shoulders and strong arms tossed bales effortlessly. He twisted, turned, and latched onto another. Strong arms that knew how to be tender and comforting. Stella let out a sigh.

A fly swarmed her face, and she swatted at it.

"Be sure those carrots don't get too done," Lena said, giving them a jab with her fork. "No one likes soggy carrots." Stella quickly removed them from the back burner. She should have been paying closer attention. The kitchen was filled with the warm aroma of baking bread, the sound of silverware clatter, and minty wafts of tea passing under her nose.

"My sohn might eat like he has a hollow leg these days, but he doesn't like soggy carrots." Lena nudged her shoulder, playfully causing Stella's face to warm. Did Simon like her cooking? He always thanked her, and despite his fearful expressions, he always took a second helping. *And he likes tea.* She smiled at the thought.

He also doesn't think courting you is completely foolish. She sighed again.

Stella went to set the table as the side kitchen door opened. Simon and Michael removed their hats, hanging them on the wooden pegs by the door before stepping farther into the room.

"You two have been working up an appetite today, jah?" Lena greeted while Stella gave her chicken dish careful scrutiny.

"A man must earn his meals," he said, making his way over to the sink to wash up. He smelled of hay, sawdust, and man. Stella tried not to let his nearness affect her.

Stella lifted the lid to the hot dish. She stared at the chicken and frowned. Dipping the tip of her finger into the juices, Stella brought it to her mouth. Without the thyme and rosemary, Stella feared the dish would be bland and tasteless.

"You're studying that hard. Should I be concerned with what's in it?" Simon muttered beside her, a wry grin on his face.

"I need thyme," she replied, breathing in the chicken dish.

"Time?" Simon whispered as he watched her. "Have a change of heart courting me?"

Suddenly Stella jerked to attention. "Thyme, not time. The chicken is bland." His smirk grew into a full-on smile. If there were a rock big enough to hide under, Stella would have done so just then. Clearly flirting was where she lacked most.

Simon dried his hands. "That is good, for me, not for the chicken I reckon." He cleared his throat and moved to sit at the head of the table. He poured himself a glass of her meadow tea. She couldn't help but smile as he gulped down a full glass and aimed for a second.

"I don't care what you put in this. I could drink the whole thing," Michael added, filling his own glass. "They say it was eighty-eight today, but surely it was a hundred." The dog days of August were bearing down hard. Hay sprinkled Michael's shoulder, and his neck looked reddened by too much sun.

Nothing a cool vinegar rag couldn't soothe.

A good meal, bland or not, had the power to induce pleasant exchange. As Lena talked of her time in Ohio with Elsie, Stella wondered what her life would have been like if God had given her sisters and not three bruders with mischief in their hearts.

"Elsie should not touch a cabbage. Her sauerkraut was the worst, and filled the whole house with a mighty stench," Lena continued.

Laughter turned to more serious subjects. Stella had no idea recent break-ins were putting folks on edge. Perhaps if everyone owned a dog, thieves would be more reluctant to make mischief. Remembering herself, Stella stood and began clearing the table. "I can see to these and then tend to the garden for a spell if that is all right."

"Danke," Lena said and stood. "I think you have a green thumb. Everything already looks better under your hand than my crooked ones."

"I don't mind. It is important to be useful."

"You do plenty," Simon said next. It was sweet that he noticed all she did. "If you were home, you would be tending your own garden like as not."

"I would be gathering elderberries down by the creek before the birds have at them." Stella shrugged and filled the sink with water and soap. "It's that time, and I usually spend a full week collecting them."

"There are plenty here, and you can have them all," Lena declared as she sipped on her tea.

"If you make pie, I'll even help you," Michael seconded before reaching for the last roll and making it disappear. His appetite was truly inspiring. "Daed likes elderberry pie."

"You do?"

Without commenting, Simon stood, collected his hat, and headed out the door. Perhaps collecting elderberries here wasn't such a good idea.

"Perhaps it's best I just focus on the weeding."

"Mamm used to make elderberry pie." Michael's head lowered as he laid his fork down. "I've missed it too." Clearing his throat, Michael stood from the table. "Danke, Dok. We appreciate all you're doing, and I do hope you make the pie." Ellie sprang to her feet, her tail swishing in anticipation. Michael laughed, though Stella could see he'd grown uncomfortable talking about the mother he lost. She wouldn't pry but could see the child who missed so many things in the absence of his mother, unlike the man who had collected a thousand memories.

"Can Ellie follow me to finish my chores before I head over to Aenti

Verna's?" Michael asked.

"Ach," Lena said. "You shoot baskets with Alan every night."

"He needs lots of practice." Michael grinned. "Am I supposed to just let him be poor at it?"

"Of course Ellie can go with you," Stella replied. "Danke for including her."

"Always wanted a dog, but. . .we never could have one." With that, the young man strolled out the door, Ellie on his heels. It was a shame, for Michael would have enjoyed a dog indeed.

Once the kitchen was tidy and Lena retired to her knitting, Stella tackled the weeds trying to crowd out tall stalks of sweet corn. Soon it would be time to harvest. It was the right thing to do, canning corn before she left, saving Lena the chore.

Moving to the next row, Stella settled in the fine turned dirt. The beans had long been pulled up, but the tomatoes seemed to have gained a second life. *A second life.* The thought filled her head with a fresh meaning as she continued to pull weeds from the hardened earth.

Summer's humidity was leaving a line of perspiration between her shoulder blades. Michael rushed through his evening chores and hurried along. Stella giggled. She had a feeling he was shooting fewer baskets than he was sneaking looks with Mary Elizabeth Glick. It had not escaped Stella that the maedel lived just next door, and Michael was far too eager to spend time with his younger cousin. The thought made her smile.

Ellie lay nearby, but when her ears lifted and she sprang to her feet in eagerness, Stella knew without looking up Simon was there. A sudden chill ran over her. She hadn't remembered such feelings when she was younger and Burl asked her to take that first buggy ride. In fact, Stella didn't think she had ever been reduced to shivers by a man before.

"An evening as fine as this one is perfect for a walk, don't ya think?"

Inside her stomach, sparrows took flight. "Jah, a walk would be nice." She stood slowly and gave her dress a dusting off.

"Let's go fetch a bucket for those berries, and I can introduce you to Paul and Peter."

So he was going to let her harvest the elderberries and bake a pie. Giddiness bloomed inside her, and she was happy to meet Paul and Peter, whoever they were.

The barn was not overly large as one expected for someone who bred horses, but it was tidy and perfectly laid out to house pregnant mares and newborn colts. Stella approached the first stall, a beautiful chestnut neighing for attention. She ran a hand down the colt's nose and knew his gangly frame would morph into a fine steed in the next six months or so.

"That Peter, he's a difficult one. Doesn't like being separate from his mamm any more than the rest of them, but he'll learn." Simon moved next to her, offering the colt a gentle word.

"He might find himself better off, once he gets used to it," she said, expressionless, her thoughts drifting back to her own mother. Depending on others only led to disappointment. The young colt would soon learn as much.

Simon cast her a worried look.

She reminded herself that she should be mindful of speaking her thoughts out loud and peered up at a spiderweb in the far corner. It was artistic how the lines formed a rare snowflake in the heat of summer. She could always find beauty to rein in her focus when her thoughts bested her.

"Not all mares are good at their duty, but Gott finds each one essential to His purpose." *Perhaps that is true,* Stella thought. If not for her childhood, the many paths she'd traveled, she wouldn't be here right now.

Simon fetched a bucket nearby, a small one used most likely for packing grain. A shower of enthusiasm tickled her that they would be spending time together.

"Don't eat grain. It will make you sick," Simon ordered over his shoulder as Ellie licked from the grain scoop lying nearby. Stella watched her dog narrow her gaze and knew what was coming, but before she could act, Ellie latched her teeth onto the grain scoop and took off in a flash. And here she had been so well behaved, trying to earn the respect of the bishop.

Ellie loved playing fetch and making new friends, but Simon had made it clear he had no interest in either. Not wanting to see Simon have another cause to dislike her, Stella took off after her. When was her stubborn hund gonna learn that tempting a bishop was not the right thing to do?

CHAPTER TWENTY-FOUR

She was light of foot and faster than a four-week-old colt. Simon laughed, helpless against it. She might think herself older, but she was young yet, at a full run as she was. He scratched his beard. *Young enough there is still time for her to marry and have a family. You could be taking that from her.*

He stood at the barn opening, watching, waiting. *Silas was right,* he thought, and his chest fell into a rhythm he faintly knew. It took gumption to do what she had for Carlee, and gumption wasn't always a bad thing. In fact, it would take a special woman to accept a life saddled to a bishop. God had brought her into his life, and Simon had to trust it was for more than just helping others. For as much as he needed her, Simon sensed, the dok needed him too.

Stella wrangled the scoop and scolded the hund, and Simon couldn't help but wonder if she could ever love a man such as him.

"Sorry, she thought it was her stick. She likes to play and is still young yet." She offered him the scoop.

"Jah, she is." But his eyes never left hers, wild and twinkling full of life. She was out of breath, but for a long, drawn-out minute, staring at her, his breath became unregulated as well. The urge to lean over and kiss her snapped Simon back to the present.

"Lena mentioned a creek," she said in a hurried breath.

Simon pointed over the hill and began walking around the house before he did something completely foolish. It was hard to convince others to keep a safe distance from such thinking when it was all he was currently thinking about.

"Lena says you have a forge. Can I see what you make?" She fell in line with his pace, the hund instinctually leading even if the critter hadn't a clue of the destination.

"I make knives, during the winter months mostly." Stella drew to a stop. Simon turned to find her with both hands over her mouth, clearly finding amusement in something.

"I'm so sorry." A chuckle bubbled out of her. "I just had a sudden vision of a bishop wielding knives." She laughed again. He imagined that was quite the picture, and the longer Simon thought on it, the picture now formed in his head too. The laugh came without the ability to retain it.

"Not a common trade." He shrugged as they strolled toward his shop. It was a sight to consider, ironically, and Michael would most certainly agree. He loved that she never treated him any differently than she did anyone else. Far too often folks walked cautiously about him, yet he was just a man, capable of mistakes. Stella was herself at all times. He imagined Gott smiled on such souls as hers.

"Like a doktor, I reckon, but there are a few of us scattered about here and there." He opened the door and let her slip inside. He quickly closed it before Ellie entered. Just because the animal was growing on him didn't mean he wanted her swiping something of importance in here.

Inside, Stella perused the knives, some finished and polished to a sharp shine, others mere scraps of metal he collected when opportunity allowed it. The small forge and anvil sat in the center of the room, his latest piece waiting to be buffed and stamped. He loved the work, the pounding use of muscles he still possessed. The time to focus on creation, not solving a dispute between friends or talking to young men crossing lines their faith frowned upon.

Simon couldn't help but wonder what else was being forged right now and decided to find out. "Why lemon sponge cake?"

"Lena asked if I could bake one," she replied honestly.

Just as he suspected, Mamm was taking advice from Mary Alice about meddling. For that, Simon was grateful, yet he was certain he would have come to the same feelings if she had made. . .meatloaf. Well, maybe not meatloaf. He winced.

"You know, my haus is much bigger." He cleared his throat. "More room to bake in and cooler too. You could dry out a few things if you needed to."

"Oh." She paused at the abrupt invitation and stared over at him.

"I have tried to get Mamm to move in. It's too big for one man alone." He was making a fool of himself. "All I'm saying is it has more room, and I saw those rose petals drying all over Mamm's counter." He shot her a wry grin.

"Perhaps she hopes you will marry yet."

"Perhaps she does." He held her gaze. She was more beautiful now than the day he first spotted her standing over a pot of boiling water.

"Why does Carl Hooley have a bee in his bonnet with you?" Simon's brows lifted as he watched her move about his things. She too was all about getting to the kernel of truth, and he hoped this time together served them both well. "Why does he have such a burr against Englisch as well?"

"We are to be separate," he said. "And it's not proper to tempt a bishop into gossiping." He winked. She wrangled her lip and held her tongue. He liked when she did that, a childish tick that revealed her vulnerabilities.

"His sohn, Jake, and two others left the year I became bishop." He hated to admit it, knowing he could have done more, but honesty was important to him. If Stella was going to open up to him, he might as well lead.

"Free will says we get to choose."

"Jah, we do, once we are of age." She moved to the tools on the wall, inspecting them like a new fantastic language.

"Then Carl is pointing fingers and handing out blame. Not very Christian," she muttered.

"He's hurting, as I would be if it were Michael. I also helped my family build the new apartments in town."

Her eyes widened at the fact. Everyone knew the apartments in town were owned by a former Mennonite who felt it was his sole duty to rescue Plain kids from a life under rules.

"Carl feels I encouraged them," Simon admitted. How many visits Simon had made to help combat Carl's fears, he couldn't count, and how many times had he reached out to each young man, hoping to sway his decision?

"What if his sohn is living a good life outside his home? It is possible to leave and find joy elsewhere." Unlike Jake, Stella had stayed within the community and helped others. Had she wished for a different life?

"I do believe some are called for something else, but to abandon faith is to leave the soul to die. I can respect one who understands a verse differently, but our faith must be sound. Maybe you understand the youngies more than I," he dared to say. "How old were you when you thought of leaving?"

Stella flinched, but she didn't run. No, she didn't run. "I tried when I was thirteen the first time. I begged a neighbor to drive me to Kentucky."

"I take it that didn't happen."

"Nee, he drove me home, but when I started my first job, I learned that as long as I earned a wage, I earned more freedom. When I was twenty-four, I met someone who I thought would give me a reason to want to stay. He didn't," she said bluntly. "I never abandoned my faith, despite how many times I wanted to. Sometimes the rules don't help, but none of that matters now."

"It all matters. I'm sorry," he offered, understanding more how hard that must have been for her. "No child should ever need to leave to survive. We are not a perfect people, but some things should never be ignored."

She stared at him long and hard. "You are a wise bishop and have a care, I see."

"Comes with age," he said as he watched her run her fingers along iron and metal. Fingers that held fragile flowers and newborn bopplin but also had the calluses of one who labored.

"You're not as old as. . ." A blush creeped up her face. Simon could sense the privacy of their talk becoming intimate and felt the first pangs of love burrow within him.

"Most bishops." He chuckled. "You're not so old. . .for a doktor." He lowered his gaze.

"I'm thirty-eight, not so young at all."

"I'm forty-nine," he said matter-of-factly and waited for her reaction. He didn't feel the distance of eleven years between them, only sparks and lightning. Yes, he was a bishop and was thinking about kissing a woman in his shop.

"We are youngies yet!" She laughed and strolled out the door, his heart galloping after her.

Grasshoppers scattered before them as they moved over pasture and aimed for the tree line. In the absence of rain, he hoped snakes wouldn't be too thick, scaring her. This time of year was not the best for hiking to the creek.

"You have so many plants here worth plucking." She waved over the area. "Plantain, nettle, thistle, and mullein, though it is drying out, sure enough." She turned about, searching the landscape. "Queen Anne's lace, poke, and sassafras are turning right now. The pawpaws should be ready," she mumbled. "Look, that's chickweed. You know, I could make you the best mushroom stew if I find any good ones by the creek," she rambled on in one breath. "This late in the year, they face north." She glanced up, taking note of the sun's position in the sky.

"You really do love nature." It wasn't his first observation, and he had to admit he was growing rather fond of her concoctions. The flavors were richer and the dishes more colorful. Perhaps that was what had been missing in his life. Flavor. A Plain man shouldn't care about such, but Simon was beginning to realize he cared a lot.

"I try to be a good steward of the land," Stella replied. "It gives us so much in return."

"So I am learning." Simon offered her a hand to help her over the large dip in the earth, noting how perfectly her hand fit into his.

She talked about milkweed, plucked wild lettuce and nettles like they were treasures and not weeds needing to be eradicated, and shared a sprinkling of her vast knowledge with him. Simon had always been a good scholar and loved learning.

"I am boring you with talk of herbs." She blushed.

"Nee, I find it fascinating and admit I knew nothing of such before you came. Gott created so many useful and wonderful things, I feel dumb for not knowing even a part of it." Simon did still yearn for fun, for love, and for hope. To walk through the rest of his days with someone who shared her view of life with him.

"Oh my, that's a lot of elderberries!" Stella came to a halt, and all he could do was smile at her wide-eyed expression.

"That's why we brought the bucket," he said, brushing by her.

"You have them everywhere," she continued happily. "They grow so big here. They love being near horses and damper soils," she continued. "It's the nutrient-rich earth and compost."

"Compost?" Simon lifted a boot and saw nothing but a mingle of grass and weeds at his feet.

"Manure from the horses." She laughed. "I transplanted over a hundred but barely a dozen took root. I reckon the birds have cleaned them up in my absence."

Simon pulled out two pocketknives in anticipation, handing Stella a smaller one with a slight curve he found matched the woman. He began to cut the stems just below the five fingers of berries and tried not to think about her home that would no longer be. It was important to know her feelings for him were honest before he took future steps.

"Do you keep the leaves for your teas?" He was curious to know. It had been years since he harvested elderberries. Lizzy always made a pie when the berries ripened. It was a faint memory he could barely draw upon now.

"Nee, but they can help with nosebleeds. I would rather gather the elderflowers or berries. They are one of the oldest medicines, and down south they are growing them for many over-the-counter pills. They make great jelly and can send the flu away in a few cups. It's my first ingredient against the flu."

Simon paused and stared at her. "This is how you have been helping folks? With these little things?"

"Jah, and look how many you have. You have all folks need right here. Michael wants a pie, if that is all right with you." She looked up at him and waited.

"Michael misses many things, I reckon."

"I don't want to cause him to think of her and be sad."

Simon didn't either, but he knew his son, and the few memories he had were cherished ones.

"You won't. If anything, it helps him remember her."

"And you?" She sucked in a breath.

"I reckon I will always remember our life together and be thankful for the time we had."

"You miss them?"

"It has been many years now. The wound no longer bleeds when I think of them. It's more. . .a dull ache. One that only hurts when pressed upon. I miss hearing William's laugh." Simon smiled at the loving memory. "He had a laugh that brought a smile to everyone, and sometimes he would get a case of hiccups from it. He liked grapes and strawberries." He dropped elderberries into the bucket and let the past warm over him. He hadn't spoken of his children with anyone but Verna before, and not without sadness. "Claire was a fussy one at first. Kept us all awake for months." He laughed at the memory.

"I'm sorry," Stella offered.

Simon offered her a half-hearted smile. "She had big blue eyes and soft honey hair." Simon swallowed. "I miss them, but I know they are in a far better place than this one. They will never have the flu or be sad. That comforts me."

"I can't know such loss."

"Loss comes in many ways," he said, wondering if she felt a similar loss from being apart from her own family. Stella stretched for a full cluster, and Simon leaned in to help her retrieve it. "How many of these do you need for a pie?"

"Not that many, but Ellie likes jelly, and I want to make more flu syrup in case."

"Let's get them all," Simon said. Everything he needed for good health grew within arm's reach. The cure to what ailed his community and a man who had spent too long missing what was lost.

With a bucket of plucked berries and tinted fingertips, Simon urged Stella on toward the creek. It had been a while since he ventured this far on his property.

"Tell me more about Cherry Grove," she said, touching a yellow-orange bloom from something she called jewelweed. The bloom burst open and shot out tiny seeds. He wanted to know more, finding her world fascinating, but it was his turn to give her more than a glimpse into his.

"If you really want to know more, then I'd be happy to share that with you."

CHAPTER TWENTY-FIVE

Along the narrow path scratched out by small animals and cooled by a soft damp breeze through the foliage, Stella rambled on about weeds and flowers and sunsets that held colors without names. If he found her odd, it didn't show.

Now it was Simon's turn to oblige her curiosity. *Cherry Grove*. Even its name held a wistful note, despite not having a single cherry growing here.

"Freeman, our deacon, was a good friend to my daed." Simon held back a low limb for her to pass. "He tends to give advice even when you don't ask for it. Ervin is much like that too, but don't be asking him for any," he warned playfully.

"Ervin is a fine bruder. I know what it is like to have bruders who aren't." How different her own life would have been with an Ervin in it. "Your eyes smile when you speak of family," she commented.

"I didn't know eyes could smile. . .until now." He drew in on her, and Stella felt a flutter in her chest. He was so handsome, so at home walking alongside her. His voice sounded different out here. At ease perhaps. It also had a way of inducing calm, like nature; its simple rhythm, its timbered tone, surrounded you in arms of contentment. So much so that Stella feared she might share too much.

"Watch your step," he warned, helping her around an ankle-twisting hole sunken in the earth. "It is not like your hillside, but we have pretty things too."

Maybe so, but her hillside would never break her heart. Ellie took off, and Stella heard the splash before she saw the creek. Stella moved under the fence of wild roses, the hips aching to be harvested.

The vein of water spread only six feet wide in some spots, a little shorter in others, but the scent of cool rocks and damp earth filled her lungs and pleased her heart. Wild hydrangea and cardinal flowers flowed parallel to the stream, and something lifted in her chest at the white and red blessings. It wasn't her hillside stream, but yet Stella found it just as beautiful. Especially since it wasn't deep enough to drown in as far as her gaze could stretch over the winding path it had carved into the earth.

God created, even here, the perfect landscape. Comfort for Stella came clothed in low, widespread limbs of oak and maple, and water rippling over rock. Where the air smelled sweet and the sky overhead was the most glorious shades. But Simon was right, beauty was everywhere. One simply had to look closely to see it.

After gulping down plenty to satisfy her thirst, Ellie darted out of the creek, a sopping pup with eyes wildly filled with joy, and ran straight to Simon. He had made her happy, giving her this little bit of joy, and Stella's heart swelled.

The bucket of berries fell to the ground, thankfully not turning over and spilling out their full harvest. Ellie was a hugger and wanted to thank Simon for bringing her here.

"Ellie, down!" Simon barked too late. Ellie did as she was told and ran back into the creek, but not before leaving two wet paw prints on the center of his shirt.

"I'm sorry," Stella said, attempting to use her apron front to absorb as much of the water as she could and trying not to laugh at his scowling expression. When was he simply gonna learn that dogs were just dogs and couldn't be cats?

"It's just water, and perhaps Ellie's thanking me today with something less messy." He winked, and there went her heart tripping all over again.

Stella backed away quickly and fetched the bucket, scooping up a few scattered berries. "You called her Ellie," she said, suddenly realizing he had.

"That is her name, is it not?" Simon grinned sheepishly.

"I knew you'd soon come to like her." *It was only a matter of time,* Stella mused. Lena was right, it was time to let love in, and Ellie obviously approved.

"So how did you kumm to breeding horses and not doing carpentry like Ervin?" Stella liked learning more about him.

"Horses were my onkel's trade. He even taught me blacksmithing. He was a few years older than Mudder, and we boys came late in his life." Simon took a few steps and added, "He had a boisterous voice, and I enjoyed watching the way he could heat and bend iron like a green stick under his boot. We boys used to go over to his house. Ervin liked to challenge him and wrestle, but our onkel didn't give us any slack. He also taught us how to get out of eating pickled beets." Simon made a face.

"Beets are good for you." She wagged a finger his way playfully.

"I didn't say he taught us well. I've eaten my share of them." He laughed. "Mudder always said she was glad she was older when we came along. Wise enough to know our tricks." He winked.

"My parents were verra young." Stella didn't see anything wrong with sharing a little more, as long as she was careful on the how much. She wanted to let the day linger further, drink in the hope filling her heart, but she couldn't share too much of her poor upbringing. How her family truly was. Her embarrassment. A confession might cost her this day. The way Simon was looking at her made her feel love was possible. *This must be what love truly feels like.*

Her folks were just kinner when they wed. Over the years Stella made excuses that they had never known how to be better parents because of it, but even the young grow up and take on the task before them. That had not been the way of it in Stella's family.

"The young know not how to raise kinner when they are just kinner themselves."

Stella stared at him blankly. Was he reading her thoughts?

"Stella, one bad apple cannot speak for the whole tree, just as one good one cannot grow healthy on weak branches."

His gaze drilled through her, and Stella stopped, clamping hold of a willow branch for support. He thought he knew her, but he couldn't know her, the real her.

"You have met most of my family. Tell me of yours. You have bruders too, if I *meinda*."

Panic filled her, making it harder to breathe. "Not all families are like yours. Lena and Michael love you. Verna and Ervin have your best interest at heart. All your family, freinden, think well of you. Some don't love the same way." In his position, Simon probably heard of a great many hardships. Still, Stella was certain he had never encountered a family that didn't have love anywhere within its branches.

"They all think well of you too, Stella. I understand family can be a yoke, as I am reminded of Joseph, and yet he found that through faith and trust, he could restore what had been missing."

"Joseph's bruders sold him," she interjected. "Mine would have if they thought anyone would buy me."

His frown pronounced itself. "You're missing the point of the message." He lifted a crooked brow.

"You are missing that there are some things you can't know." Stella began walking again. A perfectly good evening, ruined. Why had she shared so much?

Nature had balance. There were good fruits and bad ones, but harmony was found. Unlike her family, in which peace was a foreign concept. Stella had often felt like the odd one, forgotten. Until Burl. He had shown her that all families weren't the same. She had learned so much in those three years they courted that her head was filled with hopes that she could sever any wrongs her heart had been raised to believe. Then he pushed her aside for another. A woman born of a solid foundation, not the shifting sand Stella stood on. Simon would soon realize the same. He deserved better.

"You could tell me."

"You cannot understand such things." *Courting is a very bad idea,* she told herself. Her place was high on the hillside where birds nested and water didn't rise. His was tucked between valleys and pastoral fields and fresh, flowing creeks.

"I don't know the full of it, but I know you have been hurt."

"Hurt?" That was worth a laugh.

"I may surprise you yet with what I understand. I have heard a good many hardships from others, and I want to help you. You didn't jump, and I don't believe you fell in that water," he said bluntly. Stella's steps faltered as her heart sped up at the terrible memory.

"Why do I see fear in you? Like an orphaned colt ready to run." His voice was calm, his hold on her steady, but Stella couldn't muster up a word to respond. He placed a hand on her arm to steady her, and she hated knowing he could feel the trembling she had no control of.

"That's why you have bad dreams and were afraid when we drove through the water to Ervin's. You have endured much, but you don't have to do it alone anymore."

She swallowed hard and closed her eyes. The sound of roaring water filled her ears; the scent filled her nostrils. Simon deserved to know everything. That was what courting was, getting to know each other, but talking about her past always lowered her confidence and brought about a sense of dread.

"You are shaking, and I don't like that. Why is a schee woman with so much knowledge and strength afraid to speak of her family when she can speak so freely with me about other things?"

"I. . .I. . ." She couldn't.

He brushed a kapp string from her face, waiting.

"You want things that I cannot give you, Simon," she finally said.

"I want nothing more than what you are willing to give." He kicked at a dirt clod.

"I have nothing to offer you, Simon," she admitted. Years of herbal remedies hadn't smoothed out her fears or calmed her breaths. Panic and terror still came unbidden, and despite believing Simon truly cared and wanted to help her, Stella knew he could not change the past.

"You have already given me so much. I will never ask for more than that." He cunningly slipped her hand into his. There it was again, sparks and heat and. . .hope.

"I think you and I have both forgotten what is important, that alone little is done, but together much is accomplished. Danke, Stella Schmucker, for reminding me that no burden is too heavy when shared."

"I did nothing but be plainspoken. . . to a bishop and refused to answer his questions." Her shoulders sank.

"I appreciate that more than you know. Folks tend to be closed off, fearing what I have to say. It's nice to speak without that between us. Courting is best done with honesty." He held her hand as they walked, and Stella had to admit, honesty did feel rather pleasing.

"Then you should honestly know there are better choices out there than me." She felt the warning was needed to give Simon a chance to come to his senses.

"I reckon that works both ways." He winked. So were they courting?

"How did that man ever let you go?" he said, shaking his head. Dumbfounded.

"He thought boiling water was a little strange." She tried to smile, but thoughts of her past always made the simple act harder to conquer.

"Well, I like clean water, and I like green nettles in my supper." He winked again. "You make courting wonderfully hard work, Stella Schmucker."

"I don't know how to do this, Simon," she admitted shamefully. "I may be a terrible girlfriend. Surely Gott has a better plan for you." Though deep inside, Stella hoped not. Courting Simon would be such a pleasure. Her heart was already being lost to him, his family. It was a scary feeling, a vulnerable risk.

"I think you an interesting girlfriend." Again, a wink.

Simon was nothing like anyone she had ever known before. Her own family had a million reasons why she wasn't worthy of love, and here he was, fighting for a chance to love her. No matter how she tried to sway him, he was clinging tighter than Ellie to a stick of jerky.

"I thought bishops were to be steadfast and solid and not such risk takers." She tried removing the seriousness, a habit when vulnerability wormed its way over her.

"Like someone who would live in a house dangling off a cliff." He leaned closer. Close enough that Stella felt the warmth of his breath crowd her.

"I trust Him in all matters. I am trusting Him now and only ask that you do the same."

"Not so easy sometimes," she whispered, feeling her body gravitate closer. She was about to be kissed.

"Nee, but that is what faith is. That is what love is. Trust. Trusting in something you cannot see."

Her breath quickened.

"Trust me with your heart. I know you feel what I feel."

In her fear-driven hesitation, Simon let go of her hand. "I guess there are worse things than courting a bishop." He began to walk away, taking her heart with her. Simon was opening her up, offering her something she had ached for all her life, yet she was doing nothing to accept it. What was she so afraid of?

Summoning a bit of courage and recklessness, Stella called after him. "I do," she called out after him. "I do care for you, and I think you're a fine bishop, and even a better man, but—"

Simon marched up to her so quickly, Stella had no time to react. His lips crashed into hers before she could change his mind. The kiss deepened, and every doubt disappeared under the incredible sensations and overwhelming love she had so quickly been wrapped in.

"Stella," Simon whispered in a shaky breath. "I should have asked, but—"

Stella placed a finger to his lips. How could she have been so wrong? He was a man worthy of knowing her yesterdays and being the center of all her tomorrows.

"I trust you." The words came out slowly, floating in a quiet breath, but what they said suddenly changed everything.

CHAPTER TWENTY-SIX

Heavy winds were making a chore out of doing even the simplest task. Stella wrangled the last of the laundry into a basket and quickly went to help carry some of the buckets Michael had filled to feed the thirsty pumpkins and remaining garden. There were only a few root crops left to harvest, and peppers that could carry well into colder weather.

Looking out toward a looming sunset, she wondered if Simon would be much longer. Since that kiss, he'd been gone more than not. No sooner had he finished her chicken and rice casserole this evening had he left to meet with elders. He hadn't even tasted her hot apple cobbler. Now it was cold, which wasn't the same at all.

"Daed says if you want rain, just water the garden," Michael jested as he poured the last bucket over a row of thick sunflower stalks. The birds had nearly emptied the bloom heads, but the bright yellow gave the space a sunshiny appearance.

"But one who waits for rain clouds may never see the first drop," Stella replied.

"No wonder," Michael said, staring at her with the same deep blue eyes as his father's. He had the same sideways grin as Simon too.

"No wonder what?" Before Michael could reveal the rest of that thought, Ellie barked three times ahead of a buggy as it worked into the drive.

"That's Rob Glick's rig," Michael said, sounding alarmed. He set down his bucket, and Stella did the same, and they went to the drive. Stella quickly recognized Betty Glick, who was very much in the family way and loved lemons without sugar. Michael immediately offered Betty a hand out of the buggy. Her rounded belly made a chore out of the simple task. Seven-year-old Stephen and five-year-old Levi sat curled in a blanket. Betty hadn't come in search of a midwife but a doctor.

"*Was iss letz?*" Michael asked in a worried tone. Yep, just as she suspected, Michael was sweet on Betty's daughter.

"I'm glad you're here." Betty reached in and pulled Levi into her arms. "Levi hasn't felt well, but it is Stephen who concerns me most. This weather has his asthma kicking up. I don't like the sounds of his chest."

"Ach, I am sorry to hear that, Stephen." Stella offered the young boy a sympathetic smile. "Kumm down and let me help you get breathing better."

"I got him." Michael fetched him out of the buggy and sat him down. "Levi can help me see to the buggy while Dok Stella starts boiling water." Stella shot him a narrowed look. Like father, like son.

Stella led the way into the house. Inside Betty urged Stephen into a chair at the table while Stella put water on to boil. "How long has he had asthma?"

"Since he was but a wee little one. It's verra expensive to go to the doctor so often. If you feel it's best, we will, but I was hoping you could help him."

"I'll do what I can. I have just enough elderberry and mullein leaf left for a few cups." Stella didn't make promises, even if she knew her remedies would work.

"I often mix mentholated ointment and plantain leaf. Rob's mamm claims it's a fine cure."

"The eucalyptus in mentholated ointment is a good choice, but mullein is good for clearing the lungs, and peppermint and lavender can help with an episode." As Stephen sipped on warm tea, Stella massaged his back with a mixture of eucalyptus and lavender oil. Betty had relaxed in a nearby chair. Stephen's coloring improved in just a few short minutes.

"I'll send you home the rest of the oils I'm using now, but if he gets worse, don't hesitate to see the doctor."

"Can I go help Levi and Michael?" Stephen asked. Betty looked to Stella.

"I'm sure if you promise not to run or do any chores, you can watch." As Stephen headed for the barn, Stella couldn't help but laugh. "Boys don't like missing out, but it is *dochtern* that give us the most fits."

Betty rubbed her middle. "It's a wonder Mary Elizabeth doesn't give me indigestion yet. She comes home from a *singeon* in one buggy and a gathering in another." Betty blew out a long breath. Stella tried not to let the comment stir her, but she felt partial to Michael and didn't like knowing the girl he might be courting was courting another. The same deception had once changed her whole life.

"Michael is gut with the kinner." Stella had noticed that too, and a sudden sadness crept into her heart as she began cleaning up everything. It was best to scrub everything extra, to prevent the spread of germs, just in case more than the weather played a part in the young boy's poor health.

"The bishop might have more kinner yet." Betty leaned forward and added quickly, "Once he marries again."

"Ach," Stella stammered out. Stella remembered the look on Simon's face when the new colt was born two days ago. New life sprang forth fresh hopes, and it showed he agreed with the old adage.

Betty had lifted a hope Stella had long put under her pillow. Betty was but six years younger, and Stella had helped women even older than her. Fresh warmth sprang over her. Perhaps it was not too late for a dream to come true, but just because the bishop wanted to get to know her didn't mean he'd. . .marry her. Burl Hilty sure had a change of heart. Simon might soon find her unconventional ways too much to overlook. Nee, she was better saddled with Leon Strolfus.

"Everyone is talking about it and how you helped Carlee Hooley. The Keim sisters have a contest going on if you will marry at Christmas or in spring. I think a Christmas wedding sounds wonderful."

"Betty, he and I are freinden. We're just getting to know each other.

You should remind those Keim schwestern that gambling is a sin," Stella finally replied, but she couldn't hide her own grin. Marrying a bishop suddenly didn't seem so far-fetched.

CHAPTER TWENTY-SEVEN

While Deb and her new foal lumbered outside their stall, Simon shoveled and scraped the concrete with fresh angst. Stella had named the new filly Ruthie. She sported one large white spot and three smaller ones. A mirror of her mamm.

He had been looking forward to talking with Stella after supper. He had made leaps in unraveling the woman within and admired her more and more as each layer revealed a life hard lived.

Unfortunately, Simon was neck deep in horse sales with Silas, forging knives for the shop in town, or working alongside the elders to decide on a dividing point for a new community. Stella was constantly being summoned to see over everything from insect bites and rashes to being called upon by anxious mamms thankful to have a dok near so they didn't have to travel all the way to the clinic in the next town over.

Hopefully this evening no one would have need of either of them long enough for Simon to take her on a ride. Perhaps they would go get ice cream. He knew she liked strawberry since that night at Verna's.

These last couple of weeks, Simon's world had gone from existing to living again. He looked forward to each new day. Simon felt younger, capable. Not nearly a man of forty-nine at all. And, he was courting.

"Courting," Simon said with a half laugh and moved to set both animals out to roam the front pasture alone. "Kumm," he instructed the dam and her shadow. He needed to put down fresh bedding. Perhaps he and Stella could stop by Bulk Foods. Simon wanted to see if anything brought out an extra sparkle in her brown eyes. Those teacups had been on his mind a lot of late, and if he was going to take a step forward and let love into his heart again, then he had to have the perfect gift to encourage Stella to do the same.

Deb was usually one to easily follow orders. She had been born to him more than twelve years ago, so it came as a surprise when she stomped a foot defensively and then two more in warning. Her years had been catching up to her, but Simon knew she was only being protective. She would never hurt him.

He stepped forward, slowly lifting a hand to her, but instead of welcoming his touch, the horse reared. "Whoa, whoa, whoa," Simon called out, but she reared again, this time too close. Simon stumbled back, his straw hat falling behind him.

As Simon reined for balance, the silver blur raced by him. He had little time to react. How could he forget his welcomed guest had an unwelcome companion? The last thing Simon needed was the hund making an unsettling situation dangerous.

"Get back!" Instead of listening, the hund started with a percussion of high, yipping barks at both horses. She bounced on her front paws and advanced forward. Deb seemed unconcerned and stomped again, and Ellie backed away, placing herself between Simon and the unsettled dam. The horse snorted and stomped, growing more agitated with the smaller species.

Simon reached out for Ellie's powdery blue collar, but she only barked again and began driving Deb backward in a series of determined threats and growls. Stella's beloved pet was no match for a horse weighing roughly twelve hundred pounds.

Deb threatened to advance a second time, and Ellie backed away, touching Simon's leg. She trembled, but only briefly, and to Simon's utter amazement, the mutt found her courage.

For as scared as she was, Ellie lunged forward again, holding steadfast to the few short feet between him and his unhinged horse. It soon became clear that she was risking her own life. . .for his. Between bouncing and driving and snapping and barking, Deb continued moving farther away, and before he knew it, both the dam and her colt were out of the gate.

Simon moved quickly to secure the latch and let her settle. Breathless, he turned to face his unexpected help. It had all started and ended in a matter of a few short minutes, but it had left Simon just as rattled as the trembling mutt. They stared wide-eyed at each other for a few measured heartbeats. The foolish mutt nearly got herself killed, and no way would Stella appreciate losing her pet under the hooves of one of his horses.

Accidents happened in the blink of an eye, he well knew. He could have been seriously injured or worse, leaving Stella alone. That sent a fresh appreciation deep in his chest. . . for the mutt.

Ellie sat on her hind legs and stared up at him with an odd, lifted brow. Her long pink tongue hung out of one corner of her mouth as she panted. She looked a bit goofy, a whole lot dumb, and he couldn't help but shake his head. Simon had clearly misjudged this rodent-wrangling critter.

She was seeing over his groundhog problem, keeping Michael company during chore time, and offering companionship to his mother. The silvery, slippery, stinky mutt provided friendship and safety to the woman he cared for. And she very well might have saved his life.

As teal eyes continued to stare up at him, Simon realized the dog, like the woman, sought approval and love. Both of them gifted love in act and in deed.

"Danke, Ellie," Simon finally offered. Ellie's tail immediately went wagging in fierce excitement as she wiggled and walked to him in a sideways dance. She was kind of cute, a whole lot smelly, but Simon surrendered, reaching down and offering her a hand. When her paw landed in his palm, an instant friendship was made.

"I guess that makes us freinden," Simon said. "Might as well stay in here where it's cool while I finish up," Simon told her and burst out in laughter when she began inspecting every corner for pests.

Whistling, Simon began the chore of putting down fresh bedding when a car pulled up his drive. Between the logo on the side and lights situated on top, Simon knew his plan for teacups and ice cream would have to wait yet again.

It wasn't every day a man was paid a visit by the local sheriff.

Sheriff Mitchell was a mountain of a man who held the respect of nearly every resident in Pleasants County. Simon thought him a fine fellow, serving both the Amish and Englisch with equal respect. But the last time the sheriff had paid Simon a visit, a car was stolen, a barn set on fire, and Alan Beechy learned a hard lesson about sowing wild oats.

Ellie wasn't sure whether their newest visitor was friend or foe, and she gave a low-throated growl as the sheriff stepped from his car. Simon flattened his palm toward her as he'd seen Stella do on occasion. It worked, sort of.

"Sheriff," Simon greeted and offered his hand. Like the man, the shake was firm but friendly. As expected, Ellie marched between them, sat, and narrowed her eyes at the sheriff. It was that same untrusting glare Simon had once received too.

"Bishop Graber. Nice animal you got there." The sheriff bent and gave Ellie's head a friendly pat. She didn't even attempt to take his hand off.

"She's better at pest control than visitors," Simon replied and darted her a disapproving brow.

"I hear you're the man to see today," the sheriff began as his eyes roamed their surroundings. A pumpkin patch ready to harvest and haul over to Verna to be sold at the bulk store, a cluster of daisies and cornflowers lining the fence. A young colt finding his legs as he raced circles around mares and dams munching lazily on pasture. Between the house and barn, laundry flapped into the warm autumn breeze. Braided rugs of deep blues and grays hung over the porch railing. *I'm not the only one feeling more ambitious today,* Simon thought with a smile, knowing Stella was feeling more at ease here, and the thought warmed his heart considerably. Thoughts of sharing a home with her made his ears warm.

"What seems to be the trouble?" Because only trouble brought the sheriff. *Which youngie was going to be the cause for indigestion today?*

Simon mentally grumbled. Since Nelson Beechy's son jumped the fence three years ago, all had been relatively quiet.

"Got a call about a young couple stranded in a cornfield." The sheriff gave Ellie another pat, as if knowing she deserved a little extra affection today. "I called the tow truck, but they insist I come to deal with the perpetrators."

Simon lifted a perplexed brow. A tow truck meant a vehicle was involved. Simon tried not to let his disappointment show, but he wasn't sure he could deal with another Alan Beechy right now.

"Our folks don't drive. . .cars," Simon reminded him. Now he was more confused. Being Amish didn't always come with welcomed interest. Some complained about manure on the roadways or how many felt the Amish had been given more jobs than Englisch locally.

"Seems someone disabled their car." The sheriff cut a wry grin. "It's just over where your folks are putting a new place. Next to the fish farmer." The sheriff's face pinched. He obviously held Simon's position on such a livelihood.

"That would be Joe Shetler's place." The young man had lost his ability to walk when he was barely a teen. Jumping into the murky waters of a nearby swimming hole, Joe hit the rocks underneath, leaving him crippled. It had taken John and Linda a long while to help the young man accept life as it was, but now the twenty-five-year-old was ready for his own home and to start making his own income. An archery shop made about as much sense to Simon as a fish farmer, but he had been proud of the young man's will to not let his disability be his lot in life.

"In such matters I know how you folks like to tend to your own, so I thought it best you come along."

Simon appreciated his understanding of how separate they were, but if a serious law was broken. . .a swirl in his gut was already forming. "Let me get cleaned up, and I'll be right along." It was time to put on his other hat, as the Englisch would say. No sense in facing a problem smelling like a barn.

Complaints came and Simon always tried to address them accordingly, but as he stood next to a worn-down silver car in the newly made drive leading to the construction site, he wanted to chuckle. He wasn't alone in that thought. While the young man angrily explained how he and his female friend had only stopped to take a brisk walk after driving all day, only to return to find their car incapable of driving, the sheriff too was straining to remain composed. It was no secret that many young folks found themselves at this end of the community, sneaking private moments together in the cloak of tall corn and unknowing eyes.

"And you decided to stop in the middle of nowhere and take a walk on someone's property?" the sheriff questioned as he looked over the young man's identification. "You're from Pleasants County, young man, and trespassing is illegal."

Simon stood quietly by, letting the sheriff do his job. He looked to the car again. Both back tires had been removed and placed flat on the ground. The car now rested on both tires. A prank as sure as he was standing here.

"It's a free country, and walking isn't illegal. Someone sabotaged our car. I think you should be arresting them and not trying to make us feel bad for enjoying the fresh air," the young woman disputed, and Simon could see the sheriff was hiding a grin under his newly grown beard.

"You want me to dust the tires for fingerprints?" Neither of the pair appreciated the sheriff's humor, but Simon respected him all the more for it. Tense situations could easily be avoided if one restrained the urge to feed it.

But his being here was still questionable. Aside from the car being disabled on Amish land, there were no. . .perpetrators in sight. That's when he looked up the long drive where the skeleton of a home was being erected.

There were only a few souls in sight that could have been responsible for this. Perhaps the sheriff did have cause after all. Simon shook his head as his gaze locked onto Joe's bruder Levi, Mark and Ethan Schwartz, and his own brother, Ervin. All four were currently sitting on the back of a wagon, munching on sandwiches, grinning with the cunning of guilty men. Simon frowned deeper when he spotted a fifth culprit. Sitting high on a fence board eating a sandwich, with a grin as wide as the horizon. . .Michael.

"Well, I'm not arresting anyone, unless you want me to take you in for trespassing." Neither of them responded.

"We will at least help you get these tires back on"—Simon began rolling up his sleeves—"and get you back on the road." He would not be buying teacups today, that much he knew. A bishop had to set an example, but Simon had a feeling those watching weren't learning a single thing.

CHAPTER TWENTY- EIGHT

She was courting the Amish bishop, making new friends, and finding new footing on centuries-old earth. Each new day was a surprising gift waiting to be discovered. The Keim sisters had recently gifted her one of their braided rugs with rusted colors of brown and red. Carlee was gaining strength every day according to Sadie, and Stephen's breathing had not been worrying sweet Betty Glick into an early labor. The sun was shining and birds were singing. That's why Stella found herself humming old songs in new surroundings as she finished pinning the last sheet on the line.

When the sound of buggy wheels and the familiar cadence of hooves approached, Stella squinted against the sun to make out who was pulling up the drive. It was early yet for Michael to be home, not with the new haus barely under roof. Simon had left shortly ago with the sheriff. Hopefully it was nothing too serious. It seemed that doctors weren't the only ones who made house calls at all hours, but Stella warmed knowing Simon always put his duty to others before himself.

As it should be.

It was ridiculously wonderful, but love had bloomed right under her nose without her knowing its seeds had even been sown. She wasn't sure if she had Pricilla to thank, or Mary Alice Yoder, but Simon had opened his heart and awakened hers to new possibilities and a second chance.

Lifting the empty basket from the ground, Stella made her way to the house to keep anyone from waking Lena. Her elder was resting at this hour, or knitting as she called it, but her steps came to an abrupt stop when she recognized the older woman stepping out of the buggy.

"Hello," Stella greeted. "Lena is resting, and Simon was called away to deal with a matter, if you need the bishop." Something told Stella that Mary Alice would not admit to needing anything despite everyone needing something. Yet, from the foiled package in her hands, it seemed she had come to see the bishop nonetheless.

"You're still here." Her hello lacked gratitude. "It wonders me how long it takes for a roof to be mended. When Harvey and I married, he built a whole house in less than a month." As Stella approached, she realized she hadn't even thought about her home once in the passing days. A fact that both surprised her and suddenly made her feel homesick.

"I see you have brought something for Lena. How kind of you." It was always best to show kindness even if your stomach knotted with some more than others.

"Pricilla asked that I drop this off. . .for Bishop Graber."

Stella opened the door and let the woman go ahead of her despite knowing Mary Alice came under false pretenses. As hard as it was to have a mamm without a care, Pricilla was born with a mamm who had too many. She respected the older woman even if her methods needed to be corralled and sorted.

"I can see to this. I know my way about the bishop's. I see no one has been tending to his needs." Mary Alice frowned as she looked about at the drying herbs. Her nose crinkled at the fresh scents of lemon and thieves oil that still penetrated the air.

Stella once read about the benefits of dandelion, but she didn't like dandelion leaves. They left a bitter taste in her mouth. However, she always tossed in a few young leaves in her salads to help her cleanse her liver, gallbladder, and kidneys. Sometimes it was best to take the bitter quietly if one wanted to be healthier overall.

"I wish Pricilla had come too. I was glad to meet her. I hope she and the kinner are well."

"Jah, they never get ill," Mary Alice said defensively. "But I know for certain she was out late last night. . .courting. It does this old heart gut to know she and the bishop act young yet."

Stella took a deep breath. Was this just another one of Mary Alice's attempts to see her daughter happily wed? Stella didn't know, but it wouldn't be the first time she was looked over for a better maed. If Simon was courting her and another, Stella knew one thing for certain sure. She would be the one to sit aside. In fact, Simon had been coming and going at all hours recently. She inhaled a deep breath. Mary Alice knew if Pricilla was courting a bishop or a pig farmer. The sudden jolt to her gut brought about a string of nausea.

"It wonders me why you ain't married. I hear you have many vying for you. . .in Walnut Ridge." Mary Alice nailed her to a spot with a look of disapproval. "I remember when you jumped into that flood. It was a terrible thing you put folks through. All those menner out searching for you. My own mann as well. Where are Samuel and Bertha living now?"

"Baltic, Ohio." Stella barely got her reply out when Mary Alice continued on.

"Ach, I do recall someone saying as much. And those bruders of yours—they were fine kinner, if I meinda." The air was thickening, and Stella felt her insides tremble. "I reckon your folks miss ya. Living alone here makes little sense when you have family of your own. One should always be with family."

Stella twisted the side of her dress into her fist as Mary Alice continued.

"I hear you stirred up a bees' nest with Carl and Susie too. I have never known those two ever to not look at one another with affection, especially with Carlee on the mend." It was a left-handed compliment if ever there was one. Stella might have helped Carlee, but had she also stirred up division within the Hooley household? Mamm always said she was terrible at stirring strife. She felt the tears of her sinful forwardness sting her eyes.

"I never meant to. . ."

"Mary Alice, how nice of you to visit." Lena appeared in the doorway, Ellie at her side.

"Jah, Pricilla wanted to see I dropped this off on my way to Verna's for sewing needles today. She has a mind to start quilting on a new marriage quilt. I'm hopeful, for certain sure."

"Jah, as you should be. There is nothing better than seeing our kinner happy."

"Ach vell, I best be going. Pricilla isn't one for being idle and will want to get busy today." She looked at Stella and added, "We best not be growing roots in another's orchard."

Stella couldn't help but nod. Jah, it was best she see about returning home even if the roof wasn't finished. The last thing Stella wanted was to come between Simon and his own happiness, and Michael would benefit greatly from siblings. Stella had no more to offer either of them but a cup of tea on a rainy day.

"We will enjoy the meatloaf. You can thank Pricilla for me." Lena urged Mary Alice to the door, but Stella's feet were stuck to the spot. When Lena limped back into the kitchen, she immediately went to inspect Pricilla's gift to Simon.

"Hamburger casserole. Simon will be pleased, I reckon."

"I think I will go see the Shetlers and Grabers, and perhaps call Bishop Mast to hear word about my roof."

"Simon will be returning soon and would be glad to take you."

"I have been seeing to others without help for a while. It's best I do what I came to do and return. . . ." Emotions had a habit of being stronger than a person at times, and Stella couldn't hold hers back. As tears presented themselves, she hid her face in her hands.

"Stella." Lena moved to her, placing a hand on Stella's forearm. "Do not let her words trouble you. She only wants what all mothers do."

"Pricilla can give him—"

"Many things, I reckon, but you give him what he needs," Lena quickly put in. "You must open your heart and trust Gott has you right where He wants you. You cannot ignore the Lord."

"The sick brought me here, and they are getting better."

"Your home was destroyed."

"A tree fell on it in a storm," she said a little too harshly. Gott would never destroy the only place in the world meant for her.

"He controls the seas, the wind, and even you. You and Simon are only getting to know each other. I am old, not blind. I see the sparks of love move between you. I see how he worries over your past hurts and how you worry over his. He has had time to heal but has yet to open his heart to another—until now." Lena grinned.

Stella sucked in a shaky breath at Lena's words.

"Mary Alice speaks her thoughts more than one should, and the Hooleys have been at odds since their sohn jumped the fence. You did the right thing. All think it's so. You are a blessing, for certain sure, and leaving helps no one. Especially you."

"My mamm would disagree with you."

"Then I would sure like a word with her, for she raised a fine dochter," Lena said pointedly.

"My family did little to raise me, but danke for the compliment, Lena. It means more than you know."

"Your family doesn't see all the good you have brought to us. I feel sorry for them. But *they* are not here, Stella. You are."

Stella inhaled a deep breath and lifted her chin. She was here, right here.

"You have a duty, as does he, but I know the two of you will bring great support and comfort to each other as you follow the Lord's will for you. He cares for you, and you can write that behind your eyes. Just be open to love."

"What if I don't know how to do that? I know so little about love, really." It was a terrible thing to admit to another.

"Ach, my child. Love is everywhere, even in a cup of tea made to help another. Especially when a man who dislikes tea drinks three cups." Lena winked. Lena had such a way with words, it all seemed possible. It was time to set her insecurities aside. Simon deserved a second chance, and so did she. It was time to forget the past and fight for her future. Her family had no hold on her, and Mary Alice was slowly becoming more inspiration to Stella than nuisance. A mother who loved that deeply was worthy of respect.

Stella lifted her chin. "He does like my tea, but I'm still working on him liking my chicory kaffi." They both chuckled at that knowing, for Simon wasn't truly convinced.

She was Dok Stella, not a woman unworthy of love.

CHAPTER TWENTY-NINE

"Never been on a picnic." Simon stuffed Stella's comment deep into his pocket as he helped her down from the buggy. "We're about to remedy that," he said, removing his Sunday coat. He had prayed for good weather, and the Lord delivered graciously as September arrived much cooler than the previous weeks of miserable heat and humidity. He retrieved the heavy basket Mamm had packed so discreetly.

"It was kind of the deacon to visit folks today," Stella said, walking alongside him. Freeman and Judy were happy to pay visits to those not present this Sunday. Judy had insisted it was the least they could do for love. A comment that had sent a hot streak straight to his ears. Simon barely sat still through the three-hour service and refused to do more than nibble at his plate during the fellowship meal. The moment a quiet escape presented itself, he had Stella in his buggy and halfway to Twin Fork Lake before anyone could bat an eyelash.

"We often take turns," Simon replied. Twin Fork Lake centered the county of Pleasants and bordered the town. The drive was long but well worth it to see Stella view the way the wind blew over the water while sitting under one of the shady maples nearby.

It wasn't crowded, as he predicted. A couple of johnboats on the water, a few walking the pavement-to-dirt trail surrounding the lake.

A faint scent of pine mingled with the warm water and earth. Stella strolled to the water's edge as he spread out a blanket. He should tell her about her haus. It was wrong keeping it from her so long for selfish reasons. He simply couldn't accept being an option when she had so few left. For as much as Stella needed the love he had to give, Simon too wanted to be loved without conditions.

Stella turned and looked down at the blanket on the ground with a smile that had the vein in his wrist pulsating. He asked, "Are you just gonna look at it or open it?"

"You bought me a present?" Her voice hitched, and her features bloomed into a pleasant smile.

"I did." Simon had considered it long and hard, but in the end it was Driver Dan, not Verna who helped with the purchase. *The man has a serious romantic side for a retired Englisch professor,* Simon mused.

"It's not my birthday or anything."

Simon laughed as she lowered to the blanket and took up the pretty purple package. She pressed her lips together thankfully as she peered up at him with pure appreciation. Simon agreed with Verna, the purple suited her.

"Don't shake it." He knelt beside her. While she worked the ribbon loose and tape free from the paper, Simon set out the ham sandwiches, chips, and Mamm's blackberry cobbler. Mamm had no trouble spilling Stella's secret obsession with potato chips.

"Let me set everything out." Stella reached for the basket, but Simon stopped her and chuckled.

"I'm afraid nothing in here will do us any good until you open your gift."

Giddiness radiated off her. Jah, he wasn't so old he'd forgotten how courting went. Simon pulled a knife from his pocket and cut through the tape he had placed around the box.

"I can't believe I'm nervous," she said in a half laugh as she lifted the flaps and peered inside.

"Simon." His name came off her breath in utter surprise.

"You bought me. . .a tea set!" It went against the Ordnung, an unwed woman touching an unwed man, yet her arms encircled him in a hug so fast, Simon blamed slow reaction for not moving away sooner.

Then again, he had been the one to break the rules first. The memory of that kiss now came with a fresh yearning for another. They were tempting places best saved for forever commitments, but in his heart, Simon would declare her his fraa tomorrow, if he could.

"This is the first present anyone has ever given me," Stella blurted out and let go. Simon was certain she hadn't meant to share that, caught up in the moment as she was, but as he watched her slowly handle each dish, he couldn't help but frown.

———————— ⚜ ————————

They were the color of blackberry syrup. Inside each cup, a different design. Chicory, ginseng, and yarrow. Stella ran a tender finger down a fiddlehead drawing before reaching in and discovering a fresh new herb, this one a flowering dandelion. They were all the herbs she knew that healed, and they were hers. Not one was chipped or cracked, and at the bottom of the box were a mortar and pestle for grinding herbs.

"I figured a dok might need tools of the trade," Simon winked.

"You made these," she said, noting the handmade pieces. No one had ever given her such a precious and thoughtful gift.

"My young niece Mandy likes to play with dirt and clay." He shrugged. "I just told her what I needed, and it gave her an excuse to spend three days doing something other than canning beets, but I don't think Ruthanne minded. Mandy is terrible in a kitchen unless one has a hankering for noodles."

"I think I'm glad I agreed to court you, Bishop Graber." Stella grinned playfully. Lena had been right. All she had to do was let love in and trust all would be right.

"I'm glad you did too, Dok Stella."

Under a cloudless blue sky, they ate sandwiches and cobbler, and Stella munched on potato chips. "I hear you both about got that Shetler haus finished," Stella said.

"Jah, it would have been done if my bruder acted his age. One must keep a close eye on his flock, closer on his kinner." Simon grinned as he leaned on an elbow and studied her.

"Michael was awful flustered when you got home." Stella chuckled.

"Someone has to see that his time is well spent, and having me as his shadow did get his dander up."

Of course, no young man wanted to be chaperoned by the bishop, but it was sweet that Simon set aside the time for his son. If only her daed had spent more time with her bruders, perhaps they would have been as wonderful as young Michael.

"So you help stranded motorists, can frame a house in three days, minister to a whole community, and sell horses."

His deep chuckle made her smile.

"I help stranded motorists because mei bruder forgets he's no longer a youngie." Simon had shared the details of the recent prank. Stella blushed, knowing full well two single people weren't taking a walk in cornstalks for the fresh air. Her experience with such was limited, but as the sun moved toward the west a little farther, she was anticipating what tomorrow might deliver.

"I can swing a hammer, and Michael is less likely to participate in mischief with me glued to his side." Stella had to admit, it was good parenting advice. As far as she could see, Michael was a well-behaved young man, albeit one with an endless appetite. The thought of pizza came to mind. Surely he would enjoy a wild mushroom pizza. It was the one thing her family argued over that she welcomed gladly.

"What are you thinking about?" Simon asked, pulling Stella back to the present.

"Pizza," she replied and popped another chip into her mouth. Something happy flickered in his eyes.

After spending a full afternoon watching fish jump, listening to Simon tell stories of his boyhood, and eating potato chips, the rest of the week fell into nothing short of bliss. Each evening after supper, Simon took her and Ellie for walks down by the creek. The water had dried to barely a trickle, nothing at all dangerous about that. Stella found that Simon enjoyed learning about herbs and truly wanted to know her thoughts on how to help Carl with his stagnant personality. He wanted to help Carl heal and wanted a healer's thoughts on the matter. It meant more than Simon could ever know that her thoughts were heard.

Stella had a perfect remedy for helping one stop smoking. Ginseng had been proven very effective according to her lost remedies book, and there were a great many herbs one could take to heal the anxiety and stress that often followed on the heels of surrendering to a habit. And there was prayer. Stella and Simon both prayed Mahone Miller would no longer lean on tobacco for support when he was blessed with everything he needed already.

On Wednesday, Lena had arranged a tea with Sadie and Verna, and Stella enjoyed a full afternoon of foraging rose hips, picking more elderberries, and fellowship. Business had also grown. Stella had set up to make elderberry syrup in Simon's kitchen during the day for the many who stopped by hoping for a remedy to ward off any flu or cold symptoms in the future. And she welcomed new faces, like Driver Dan. His wife Greta was becoming Stella's best customer. Her bouts with gout had driven her to new levels of insanity, she claimed. Stella found her as normal as a bee on a thistle bloom and focused on her gout and not her mental state.

Simon spent more time in his knife shop, but with the birth of his last foal, she assumed that was his regular routine. There were so many things she had yet to know, but Stella, for the first time in her life, was eager to learn everything she could about another.

On Thursday she helped Michael deliver pumpkins to Verna's. Stella said nothing but knew the money would go straight to Carl Hooley to help his family with medical expenses incurred during Carlee's illness. And soon Stella would be present to see the young woman marry Gabe. Once Carlee was of full health, Simon was eager to announce them.

Life had pivoted again, but this time Stella was too happily consumed to notice how swift one day ran into the next. Outside, crickets chirped the first sounds of the season, and as she lay in the quiet, Stella couldn't help but think of her home and what her grandparents had given her. They would be disappointed if she didn't return, would they not?

The best course of action would have been to never fall for the bishop at all, but now that she had, Stella felt pulled in two directions. Soon she would need to return home. Only now, the one place that made her feel most loved wasn't the four walls of her grandparents' home but at the right hand of a man who valued her.

Prayer was the best way to relieve one of a heavy burden. Isn't that what Mammi used to say? *"Take it to the Lord in prayer, Stella. He knows what is best for us even when we haven't a clue."*

Lord, I never imagined a life more full, but how can I abandon my home and grandparents' place? Do I truly belong here? I trust You have all the answers and will reveal them in Your time. I've been here awhile now, living among them, falling in love with them. Please show me which path to follow and quick, before more hearts are broken besides mine. Amen.

Stella slipped under a thin quilt and found her spot on the couch where she slept best. Trust, that's what Simon asked of her, and that's what she would do. Surely the Lord would reveal His plan for her soon. He knew her, and that brought a weak smile to her face as she stared into the moonlit room.

He'd taken her on a picnic, given her teacups, and with that thought, sleep came swiftly.

CHAPTER THIRTY

"I'm heading to bed," Michael said. Simon remembered the long hours spent working alongside his bruder. He also knew what it felt like to get a Friday wage for his labor. Ervin had nothing but praise for Michael and his work. Time went by so fast, his son would soon be making a life and family of his own. The thought once scared him, but right now Simon was happy to see he had done well being both the daed and the mamm.

Michael opened the refrigerator and gave the inside a thorough scrutiny.

"Thought you were going to bed," Simon teased.

"Just seeing if there was some pizza left. I reckon it would hold me over until morning."

Growing men had endless appetites, but so did courting ones. Simon smirked. "I finished off the last piece."

Michael closed the door and gave Simon a disappointed look. "Just as well. Onkel Ervin said someone broke into the Glicks' and stole his tools."

"They stole more than tools. They took a money safe, Rob's two shotguns, and a few dishes Betty was partial to," Simon shared. Thankfully the family had been gone to a wedding in Missouri and weren't there.

"It's crazy what folks will do for some fast money. I hope Mammi and Stella ain't worried." He glanced out the window, inspecting the shadows.

"Ellie won't let anything within three feet of that door if she thinks it's a threat, but it is important we pay attention and lock up at night."

Simon had called a meeting of the elders for Saturday. With the thieves getting braver, stealing in pure daylight, it troubled him to think how far they would go.

"Not everyone has an Ellie, that's for certain," Michael said with a grin. Simon hoped his son did too, but how did a man go about having such a conversation with his son? "Onkel Ervin said they took Rob's planer? That thing had to weigh a ton. Not so easy for just one man alone."

"Jah. They left little behind. They even took Betty Marie's lemonade pitcher." *Of all the stuff.*

"It was a riddle for sure and certain. Who would want a sour lemonade pitcher?" Michael made a face. "What if they knew Betty Marie made sour lemonade?" Michael added. "If it's one of our own, I hope you hand them a stiff punishment, but don't give them up to the sheriff. They are doing many a kindness by taking that pitcher."

Simon ignored his son's remark. "I'm certain it's not one of our own."

Michael lifted a lid and noted one piece of pie sitting under it and smiled. "Well, it's not pizza." He lifted the wedge and took a healthy bite. "You know, if you married her, we could have pizza every night and pie every day."

Simon lowered his teacup and stared at his son, speechless. Of course he knew Michael was aware of how much time he and Stella were spending together, but they hadn't really talked about it.

"Don't look so shocked. I'm sixteen, not six. It isn't like you're very good at keeping courting private anyhow. Joe Hostetler has been telling everyone about your picnic last week." Michael rolled his eyes.

Joe Hostetler needed to mind his own. "Guess I just wasn't sure how to bring it up with you." Simon saw how the Miller boys treated Ida when their daed remarried. Of course they were all under ten, raised with no firm hand to guide them. Not all children were happy to have a stepmom when they would rather have the mamm lost to them.

"You never asked." Michael stopped chewing. "It's too quiet around here, and if you married her, we'd eat plenty good, I reckon." He resumed chewing and grinned. "And if you get hurt, it's nice to have a dok handy, like as not. You are getting. . .older." Michael chewed again, grinning.

"Don't talk with your mouth full," Simon said. "I ain't marrying her just so you can stuff your stomach."

"Then do it because she makes you go on picnics." Michael chuckled. Ervin was not a good example to be around, as the two had much of the same humor. "You really bought her teacups?"

Simon nodded. "So you wouldn't mind?" He didn't need Michael's permission, but if they were going to be a family, Simon wanted his blessing. Michael took another bite and chewed slower this time. He was thinking. Was he thinking of Lizzy?

"I miss them too, but at least I was young enough not to remember every little thing like you do." So Michael had fewer memories than Simon thought he did.

"If there is anything you want to know. . .about them, I'd be happy to talk about it anytime you want."

"That would be nice," Michael replied with the same sorrowful expression he bestowed on an empty plate. "No one expects you to be alone forever. I ain't no youngie and might want a place of my own one day."

"I reckon you will." His son had grown into a man in a blink, and Simon wasn't sure he was ready for that.

"I don't like seeing you alone either. If you have feelings for her, if she makes you happy, that's good enough for me, Daed. Mamm would want you happy, in case you didn't know that."

"Danke, Michael."

"Oh well, don't thank me." Michael strolled to his room. "I'm in it for the pizza until I find a woman who can make it with sausage and peppers." The door shut, and Simon couldn't help but chuckle. Michael was a smart fella, thankfully, and he approved.

Simon knew his heart was ready, and he couldn't imagine a life without Stella in it, but he needed sleep, too many long days running into a blur with the next one. He fetched the jar marked SLEEPY TEA and grinned. Stella had lined his counters with all her dried concoctions. He should build her a shop, a place of her own for all her things. *It would be much nicer than a laundry room full of drying nettles and fuzzy mullien leaves,* he scoffed.

He spooned out what portion he felt equaled Stella's, glad he paid attention to details, and let the leaves fall into the nearest mug. Once the water heated plenty, he flipped off the burner and poured hot water on the dried leaves.

I'll let that steep, he thought with a smile. Two months ago he hadn't a clue what steeping was, or that one could eat flowers and weeds.

Once he drained his cup, Simon checked the locks and turned off the propane kitchen light, and then he aimed for his bed. In the distance, the sky rumbled. Stella hated storms, and he hoped this one moved over swiftly.

CHAPTER THIRTY-ONE

Simon cleared his plate, loaded his newest knives into his buggy, and hurried off for another meeting with the elders. Stella had hoped to spend some time learning to knit today, as Lena had been ever so eager to teach, but she'd barely had time to clean each dish before it was her being summoned next.

Young Elaine Shetler had been cleaning the schoolhouse and found herself with a three-inch splinter embedded in her palm. Her younger bruder had made it sound as if it were life and death, which is why Stella harnessed Michael's horse and rushed the two miles to get there. A dab of ointment and a bandage later, Stella was entertained by hearing how much Elaine dreaded the new school year and how the large upper room needed a fresh coat of paint. Painting wasn't Stella's favorite chore, but Elaine was injured and terribly flustered to be a teacher, and the first day of school was in a few days.

Since she already had the buggy, Stella next visited the Millers'. Simon would be gone most of the day, meeting elders and selling knives in town. Mahone Miller didn't think her remedies were helping with his not-so-secret tobacco habit, but Stella was glad she stopped by for Ida's sake.

Ida Miller seemed to have a new energy since her last visit. Her color was looking better after Stella talked to her about adding more iron to her diet, and though Ida didn't seemed rattled one bit by the boys since she was now a mamm too, Stella was.

It's a wonder how either parent wasn't two toes into the grave keeping up with those four kinner. Between Josh and Martin chasing cattle out of the fencing and seven-year-old Willy getting stuck in that tree, no wonder it took more than thirty minutes to find four-year-old John in the attic shredding old copies of the *Budget*.

Stella paid a visit to two more homes before returning to the farm. She hadn't even bent Gott's ear one bit when she had to rub camphor and eucalyptus oils on Gemma Shetler's toenails all morning. Helping others filled an empty place in her chest. Even the smallest kindness had a way of making one feel good inside.

However, Stella couldn't help but wonder why after so many good deeds God had still seen fit to send Mary Alice Yoder to pay an unexpected visit. . .on a Saturday.

Fungus was much easier to stomach than an unexpected visit from Mary Alice Yoder. But, with exasperated annoyance, Stella served Mary Alice sunshine tea and biscuits with fresh apple butter and listened for a full hour to how Mary Alice was convinced her Englisch neighbors were the culprits of the recent break-ins all because they were gone well into the night and never returned until morning. Explaining that some worked nightly shifts didn't faze her theory one bit.

"Well, I should be off. Danke, Lena, for biscuits. I fear you may have added too much cinnamon, but they were good," Mary Alice said as she worked her way to the front door. Stella was glad Lena didn't tell Mary Alice it was Stella's recipe, but the tea had seemed to do the job, as Mary Alice left with a smile on her face, and not once had she broken out into a mournful tune or inserted a single word about Pricilla and the bishop in her windy conversation.

Perhaps the day was going to turn sunshiny yet.

"It wonders me if that woman should focus on finding a mann yet to fret over." Lena chuckled as she began cleaning up the table. "She should be happy Pricilla is getting married. It's what she wanted, rightly so."

Stella smiled as she began filling the sink, adding a healthy pump of homemade dish soap she'd recently made after Lena shared her love for fresh scents. The lemony-scented bubbles multiplied, and Stella dunked her hands in and began scrubbing.

"Simon's a good catch. I can see her stubbornness in it."

"But he is already taken," Lena said flatly. "And Pricilla is marrying Shep Ebersole. All know it, and you do too." Stella hoped that was true. Her heart was Simon's, but just like that tingling in the back of the throat during hay season, she felt a prick of uncertainty. Simon and Michael could always do better with another. She hated her doubtful thoughts. If only Gott would simply tell her how the story would end, she'd be more open to enjoying all the chapters.

There was something to be said about asking the Lord for answers. For as soon as the thought came to her, Bishop Mast was standing in Lena's tiny kitchen. From the moment Mary Alice appeared out of the blue on a Saturday, it was as if all the air and sky and earth were telling Stella that something was afoot.

"Let me make us some kaffi," Lena said and offered him a seat at her table.

"Just a half cup. It doesn't agree with me well." Bishop Mast motioned for Stella to sit. She dried her hands and lowered cautiously into the furthest away chair. As small as he was, bent by years of hard work and worry, he still was much taller than her and as intimidating as Stella had always found him to be. His being here meant her home was ready and her time in Cherry Grove was over. She didn't expect to feel downtrodden but rather happy to return home. *But it doesn't feel like home anymore.*

"I'm assuming my haus is ready to return to now. You should know that I have been saving. I hope it is enough to repay you for all you've done."

The bishop lifted two bushy, perplexed brows. "Your home is better kindling than home. Cullen and the menfolk have seen to packing what few things were salvageable, but living there is not best any longer. I already told Bishop Graber such weeks ago. He agreed to give you shelter in return for you seeing over folks here." Bishop Mast looked to Lena, who suddenly appeared blank.

Stella was certain her ears must have gotten clogged up from all of Mary Alice's ramblings this morning, or maybe it had been the camphor and eucalyptus she inhaled from working on Gemma Shetler's toenails. She wasn't certain. Either way, Stella believed her bishop just said Simon knew her home was beyond repair. Had the men struck a deal without even discussing it with her?

"You have not been to church, and many have concerns."

"Stella hasn't missed a service yet," Lena put in. "She's even helped ready things here for Sunday as well as helped ready the schoolhouse rooms when Elaine got a splinter." The bishop ignored Lena's praise.

"I am told there is little need left for you here."

"There is always a need, Bishop," Lena reminded him, and the bishop nodded, though he never appreciated being reminded. "It wonders me who has been telling you such."

Stella clenched her teeth as both elders continued chatting. Simon knew she didn't have a home to return to and yet hadn't told her. Lowering her head, she clasped a hand over her fist and squeezed. It was the best way to harness her sudden heartbreak.

Had he lied to her, or was Simon offering charity to an unwed woman with no home? Simon liked helping others. It was one of the things she loved most about him. But the truth was a hard punch to the heart. He wasn't courting her out of love but out of pity. Burl Hilty all over again.

Stella felt her skin turn hot before a chill ran over her. Simon knew she had no home to return to, no family to depend on. And what of Michael? Was he keeping this from her in exchange for better meals and his shirts mended? Stella had cooked him pizza and packed his lunches and baked his favorite elderberry pie and chocolate cake.

The bishop needed to remarry, but for companionship and wants. All those long talks, asking Stella's opinion, suddenly felt like she was being interviewed for a job at the local market. It was as clear as Lena's freshly washed windows that she was being lured into a marriage of convenience and not one of love.

"Stella has been a great help, and I would be happy to let her stay here as long as she likes. In my old age, it's been a mighty blessing to have her help reading everything for Sunday service, and as you know, Bishop, we have no dok here. Folks already think of her as one of our own." Stella warmed at the offer, but staying with Lena, as badly as she wished she could since coming to love her as she did, was not right.

"There are proper ways of going about it, as you know, and you have kinner yet, do you not? Dok Stella will continue to see over those in need." The bishop turned to Stella. "I've kumm to share that your family has written."

If the bishop thought to make a terrible day even harder, he had just succeeded. "I no longer speak with my family, Bishop Mast. It is of no concern to me what they have to say to you." Bishop Mast deepened his scowl, but he did not drift from the reason for seeking her out. Stella lifted her chin and braced her heart for what came next.

"Your father is ill."

Stella inhaled a long breath and held it. Regardless of her lack of love for her family, she hated to hear of her father's illness. He would be sixty-three next month, barely an old man, but his lack of physical labor and poor eating habits had always told her his health would decline terribly early on. Perhaps that was why she insisted on eating so healthy herself.

"He has been for some time, according to the letter they have written to me. Your brothers can no longer see over them. Your mamm struggles helping him about alone. I do recall her being rather small and your daed a man of. . .a certain girth." The bishop cleared his throat. "They have reached out to me with this concern and feel it is best you return to Ohio and care for the both of them."

"My bruders thought it best." Of course they did. Since she was old enough to wash a dish without breaking it, she had always been the one to finish what they started.

"They have families to provide for, and you do not. You have declined offers of marriage within our community." Stella winced. She knew what the bishop was about to say. "I feel it is best you do as expected." She clamped her lips tight. Did the bishop know what he was asking of her? When she asked God to direct her path, Stella had no idea He was leading her back to one she had long left.

"Cannot her parents kumm to Cherry Grove to be cared for?" Lena asked in a desperate voice. "Perhaps Bishop Graber would like to know of this." Poor Lena, trying to find a way all could be happy when happy wasn't even possible right now. Her bishop wanted her to return, back to a life she had worked so hard to forget. Her childhood was stained with sorrow and washed in muddy water, and she didn't see it changing even after all these years.

"This is of no concern to your bishop, but a matter between Stella and her family. Stella has no home to offer them. It is our way, Lena, you know this."

He was a bishop, deserving of her respect. It was a good enough reason to school her tongue. She had long felt that family who didn't feed and love their kinner didn't deserve her love. Simon had shown her differently. In her time among his family, Stella had learned a great deal. Family came second next to Gott. It was her duty to see to her blut. And what choices did she have? Stay and love a man who deceived and pitied her? God had a plan, and though she didn't like it one bit, Stella had to follow. Oh, how life changed and ebbed. Her life was like standing in the wind and thinking to change its course.

Outside, Ellie begged to come in, but Stella knew the moment the bishop pulled up, it was best to keep her outside. "Nee, it is my duty. I must go."

"You have been a great help to many, and now you can see over your own." He stood, his firm expression not leaning one way or another, always steady. "I will give you a minute to pack your things. You will stay with me until they fetch you," Bishop Mast said before stepping outside.

Stella struggled to her feet and fumbled shakily to gather her things. It was all for the best. She didn't belong in Cherry Grove. Simon deserved real love. Even if he had asked to marry her, which he hadn't, she reminded herself, what did she know about family, about being a wife and mother to Michael?

A tear sprang forth. The thought of returning home and living out her days with her parents rebirthed a fear she had spent weeks apart from. "The Lord decides our path," she muttered, shoving a fresh pair of socks into her bag. Staring down at her feet, Stella noted the shoes. They weren't hers. Nothing here was. She was a woman without a home, and heartbroken.

"I don't want to see you go. Simon will want to know of this. He will speak to your bishop and your family and. . . ," Lena hurried to say.

"Nee, I must go," Stella insisted, thankful he was gone today to sell his knives to the Englisch dealer in town.

"He cares for you. You cannot be asked to marry if you leave. You have Simon and Michael to consider now."

"He never asked," Stella said flatly. "He's lonely and was only offering kindness to another," she spat as she fought the zipper on her bag. "Simon was doing his duty, helping another, and now I must do mine." But would he be lonely when she left? She couldn't think of that now. Not with Bishop Mast, one not known for patience, waiting outside.

"Stella?" Lena pulled her into a hug. Tears soaked into her shoulder. "I will pray for your quick return. This is your home. I hope you know that." Hope was important, despite how many times hers had been yanked away.

"Hope will see me returned, perhaps, but Gott is the only one who can decide that." Without hope, she would have never worked so hard to learn all the things she did. Hope was what brought her back to Walnut Ridge, where no one thought her a failure. But now as she was coming to know Verna and Sadie and Lena, Stella was discovering freindschaft could be found in other places too. Maybe Gott would lead her back here someday. Or maybe her future was meant to be like her past.

"Danke, Lena, for being a good friend," she replied and took in one last look of the small house. Stella closed the door, but she'd never forget the people she had come to love like family.

Life was filled with many chapters. Stella feared hers would fade into a tangle of skipped-over pages no one cared to read.

———————— ⚓ ————————

With a cool wind in his face and a pocket full of money, Simon aimed for home. David was feeling the change in the season, as he trotted along more briskly. *What a glorious day the Lord has made,* Simon thought as he worked out a few scenarios in his head. He would add on to his knife shop. The little shop in town was happy to expand their collection, even opening a virtual store, which meant Simon would be spending more time forging out knives than mucking horse stalls. Reason enough for a man to whistle.

He couldn't wait to tell Stella. He couldn't wait to plan out their life together. If she would agree to be his wife, they could start right away on her own shop. She would need ample space of her own for drying all those herbs.

God had taken Simon's loss, his grief, and extended him the grace of a second chance. A man didn't waste second chances, and a future alongside the pretty dok was one he couldn't wait to start living. He loved her so much that Simon was tempted to thank Mary Alice Yoder.

He probably should have told her about her home, but since their kiss, Stella seemed no quicker to leave than Simon was to see her go. He had to know her heart was his, and now Simon did.

As Simon pulled into his drive, pondering the best way to go about asking the dok to be his fraa, the hairs on his arms shot up. Something was wrong. For one, Ellie hadn't run up to greet him.

Second, Mamm was waiting on the porch for him with that same worried look she had the day Lizzy and the kinner passed away.

Simon quickly secured his rig. "Was iss letz?"

"She's gone. Her bishop took her back to Walnut Ridge. Her family reached out to him." Mamm began to cry. "Ach, Simon, her *fatter* is in poor health and has called her to return to Ohio."

Simon listened to the details with a mix of despair and astonishment. Of course Stella agreed to leave. She could never decline caring for others, but the very thought of her returning to a family who tried ravishing her heart and put self-doubt in her head didn't sit well with him.

"Sometimes His answer is no. I shall pray for her safe travels," Simon said before turning, and then he went to unhitch the buggy. What more could he do? Stella was a woman old enough to make her own choices. And she had made her choice.

That evening Simon couldn't eat. Sinking down in his chair at his lonely table, he dropped his forehead on the table. For as much of a reprieve from his loneliness spending time with Stella had been, Simon should have known Stella could not be swayed.

"I don't see why you don't go over there and speak to her bishop," Michael insisted as he pushed his warmed-over chicken casserole aside.

"She has the right to choose," Simon reminded him. "You best eat that. It's the last of the leftovers." Michael's face crinkled at the fore-warning. It was oatmeal and egg sandwiches now.

"She was gonna make roast with gravy," Michael continued.

"At least finish the salad." Simon did at least put that together, though it was lacking the flavors and color of Stella's.

"Better a meal of herbs and wilted lettuce than a fatted calf." Michael lifted his fork and inspected the torn lettuce with a scrupulous expression.

"Not sure that's how the proverb goes."

"How about. . .whatsoever you desire, pray and believe you will receive it, and it shall be yours."

"That's not right either. Perhaps you should help me tidy up, and while I ready for Sunday's sermon, you can learn a scripture that doesn't involve your stomach."

Life would go on, Simon knew, but like his sohn, he did wish it went on with the healer among them.

CHAPTER THIRTY-TWO

The Amish had many traditions. Sundays were for gathering and worshipping. Mondays were set aside for washing, and Tuesday was a day for ironing. Wednesdays were shopping days. Fridays were commonly reserved for baking, while Saturdays were set aside for cleaning a house from the ceiling to the basement floors.

Stella didn't have a calendar, but she knew good and well Cora Mast needed one, and if she was here come Saturday shopping, she was buying her a calendar with big bold lettering.

Here it was a Monday, and Stella had already scrubbed all four bedrooms on the top floor.

"My husband asked me to tell you that your bruder, Matthew, will be here by the noon hour. Best start gathering your things," Cora said, leaning the broom in one corner to give the couch cushions a few hard slaps. They were fat with knitted flowery fronts and as orange as a firelit sky.

Bishop Mast conducted his home as he did his work, with a firm purpose. His fraa certainly had no quarrel with that. Stella was not one to complain, but living with Bishop Mast was far from sleeping on a couch. As she finished up the last windows in the *schtupp*, making sure she left behind no streaks, she thought of Simon.

He asked so little of others and appreciated even the smallest kindness. Joshua Mast didn't even thank her for washing the insides of muck boots. For sure and certain the sense of smell must diminish with age.

It might have taken Simon a couple of weeks to warm up to Ellie, but he had come to appreciate all her fine qualities as Stella did. The Mast household had fifty rules, and Stella hadn't memorized them all yet, but no dogs inside or free to jump on visitors was one the bishop planted firmly from the start.

Outside, Sugar Mountain rose up at the back of a far field. The narrow valley had her feeling off balance. Perhaps it was the fact that a heavy rain would swell the creeks surrounding them, or a fire could leave them no way of escape. Jah, she had never been particularly content sleeping this low on the map.

She looked out searching, for what she didn't know, and cringed at the dark clouds clinging to the uppermost heights. *He never came,* she mentally grieved. *He's a verra busy man,* she concluded. *But it's been two days.* If he was coming, he would have been here by now.

Stella scrubbed a little harder. Happy endings didn't exist for everyone.

"Don't scrub so hard. You'll leave streaks," Cora fussed.

Well, if being married to a bishop made one work harder than needed, Stella should be glad Simon hadn't come. She only glanced out the window because the bishop had a likable view. That was all.

Stella had a box full of herbs and a leather bag. Neither constituted as time consuming. "I'll see to cleaning the rags and feeding Ellie first," Stella said, ignoring the *harrumph* as she slipped into the kitchen. Any mention of Ellie was met with such displeasing sounds. The Masts had no care for dogs, but they did have three cats that at any minute Stella feared she might step on, as needy as they were.

She quickly scrubbed and rinsed all three rags and hung them to dry on the back porch line. Then Stella immediately shot to the barn, where Ellie was contained in a stall. For as much misery as Stella had being here, Ellie had to be in total agony being confined as she was.

"Oh my sweet Ellie." Stella opened the pen only to be met with two happy paws and a few dozen slobbery kisses. "I know it's hard to stay out here, but you have all the horses and calves to keep you company."

Ellie cocked her head disapprovingly. "I know. I know." Stella bent and wrapped her in a hug. "I miss you too. I don't know if Matt will even welcome you. I'm so sorry. This is not how I wanted things for you and me." Stella cried on Ellie's shoulder, her only friend in the world. A friend she might have to part with for Ellie's own good. Her tears multiplied at the thought.

Stella recalled the day the local game warden showed up and threatened to charge her father for animal cruelty if they didn't surrender her brothers' dogs. Stella would have helped take better care of them herself if not for the fear of losing a finger. Just like the brothers, each one could never be trusted.

Ellie deserved better than living in Ohio. She couldn't bear parting with her constant companion, but when you loved something this much, it was right to do what was best for them.

Wiping the dampness from her eyes, Stella urged Ellie out of the back of the barn. She needed all the freedom she could get until Matt arrived. As they stepped out onto a gravel drive looping around the barn, Stella gave the gravel a kick. Ellie needed a proper home.

There was Grace, but Stella wasn't sure her husband Cullen would approve. Her stomach twisted. In the end, Stella knew what was best for Ellie, and for Lena. . . . Michael adored Ellie, and Ellie did bring an extra sparkle to Lena. "Would you like that, Ellie?" Stella asked as Ellie ran up and down ahead of her. "You could live the life I wish I could," Stella said. She shouldn't be feeling sorry for herself.

He didn't love her. A fresh tear came every time she thought about the man with a wry grin and storm-blue eyes. Her life was like riding in that fast-moving buggy away from her dreams. Ellie would no longer be at her side. While folks worked their fields, continued on as if she was but a blur in a short moment, she would be in Ohio. Mary Alice's woeful song filled her head, and the tears came harder yet. She was afraid, admittedly so. Her future would be one flood after another, raging waters, and Simon would not be there to carry her out of the storm.

"Don't leave me, Lord. I'm afraid."

———————— ⚜ ————————

In the glow of firelight from the block and firestone forge, Simon set aside the small hammer and replaced it with the heavier one. He began pounding the red and yellow blistering metal down to a flattened state. He'd awakened before dawn, a night short on sleep but long on thinking. How long he had been out here, he wasn't sure. He just didn't want to think about the woman or that she'd be leaving soon.

It would be easier not to think about it if Mamm and Michael had something else to talk about these days, he scoffed. Perhaps he'd been wrong and her past made it far too difficult for her to accept love when it came without conditions.

The sun too had refused to wake, hiding away as it was. Even it felt a tinge of despair, he reckoned, as shadows danced along the three walls of his shop. He looked to the far corner, the only empty spot in his cluttered shop. He even missed the cantankerous mutt.

Turning the metal, Simon proceeded pounding, anger and irritation driving him forward. That's why he didn't hear the buggy approach. He'd already forged out more knives this morning than he had in the last two weeks. God may have not seen fit to give him what he wanted most, but he did give Simon good health and the ability to continue work he enjoyed. So why wasn't he enjoying it?

"A man in hiding usually isn't heard from three miles away."

Simon lifted the heavy hammer and jerked his head to the open shop doors. Carl Hooley was the last person he wanted to see today.

"A man who wants to eat must work," Simon said bluntly, dunking the flattened metal into the quench.

"Jah," Carl replied, removing his hat and stepping inside. At his height, he ducked his head a few inches. "A man with troubled thoughts does too." His judgmental gaze moved slowly over the cluttered shop where knives were in various stages of being made. Simon was in no mood for ridicule, but when he followed Carl's gaze, taking in the room, he too frowned. He hadn't looked up much in the last couple of days. Didn't have much to look up for, heart aching as it was, but now Simon could plainly see what continuous clutter surrounded him. His shop was in utter disarray. If a head could open up and spill out, this was probably how his would look. Nothing was where it should be. Simon closed his eyes, dropped his shoulders, and let out a heavy sigh.

"I can see you have been at it. . .hard," Carl kindly added.

"I hear Carlee made a full recovery," Simon said, removing his heavy elbow-length gloves. He wasn't going to start another project until this mess was sorted. A bishop was to set a good example, and suddenly, with Carl Hooley blocking what little light seeped in on this cloudy day, Simon felt ashamed.

He began with the table to his left, a scatter of scrap metal, bone handles, and drawings he had put together late into the night that looked nothing like he wanted at all. Jah, his head was as cluttered as an auction house.

"She is strong, like Susie." Carl kicked at the dusty earth floor. "And as forgiving of her father for taking so long to accept help when it is given." Simon paused and stared at his old friend. Carl was beginning to accept his shortcomings, and for that, Simon was thankful. It had been long overdue.

"I reckon my dochter seems ready to marry. *Eager* is the better word." Carl chuckled. "Already got her mamm sewing up dresses, and that gaggle of freinden of hers has been over every day since she got home."

"A full house of gaggling maeds should make any man happy."

"Or ready to pull his hair out," Carl jested. "But all that baking is worth having them about," he added, running his thumbs through his suspenders.

"Gabe will make her a fine husband, and the Lord will bless you with many grosskinner soon enough." That earned Simon a wide smile. It almost looked unnatural on Carl's face, for as long as it had been since Simon saw the man smile. The thought of grosskinner had powerful effects.

"Your nephew is a fine man indeed. He sat on the porch with me, asking and all." Carl shrugged. "He also reminded me we all have a choice in life." *Blessed Gabe,* Simon thought, knowing he most likely made a difference in Carl's life.

"I reckon you've kumm to ask me to announce them next service." A little good news would do well within his community, but Simon couldn't help but think of Stella and how much the dok would have enjoyed being there when he shared it.

"I've come to ask for forgiveness," Carl said flatly. "I have been lost and angry and have not been such a good friend to you"—Carl glanced about—"when you clearly needed one more than I do, by the looks of things."

"It's yours, then. You and your family have been through much," Simon replied, ignoring the latter comment.

"We both know I can't get off that easy," Carl said with a smirk and began setting anything that looked to be done on the polishing table to the left of the shop opening. That was the Carl he once knew. A man who didn't shrug at helping others.

"Verna gave Susie a check when she stopped by the bulk store last week. Did you really grow pumpkins for her to sell?" A dusted-over brushy brow lifted cockily.

"We are all family. Carlee was verra ill, and I know how much hospitals cost these days."

"Jah, you do," Carl said sorrowfully. "Danke for it. I cannot stand being a burden to others, but I was. My heart has been lost since. . ."

"Having a son leave would leave any father aching."

"Yet, you too have lost a sohn and did not let it harden your heart." The men simply stared at each other.

"You have lost much more than I have. I still have Susie and Carlee, and I have not treated them as I should have. I have been selfish, wanting my only son back, but Jake had a choice. I have blamed you for what is mine to have. I always knew he would seek life out there." He waved a hand to a rising sun. "He always had big ideas. Scared me to death every time he shared them with me. I held on too tight, pushed him to love what I did, until he hated all of it. He wanted to see things, and with that mouth he could have taken a job as auctioneer over in Miller's Creek, but I was against it. Wanted him to help with the farm, not follow what Gott called him to do."

Simon nodded. He remembered the young man who could ramble a thousand words a minute and wondered if he should share that Zach had found his place in the world, going from community to community as an auctioneer.

"But I wouldn't allow it. I couldn't see past my own farm to even notice he was aching." Carl sniffed back his guilty emotions, but Simon knew he wouldn't drop a tear.

"He loves you still, Carl. I should tell you that I get a letter every few months or so. He asks how you are, his family."

"He writes you but not his mamm?" Carl stiffened.

"He would love to write to all of you if he felt the letters would be received gladly." A range of emotions flitted over Carl's face, from shock to anger and then finally acceptance. That's when the strong man crumpled and burst into tears. Simon went immediately to him, placing a strong and supportive hand on Carl's shoulders.

"I would gladly accept word from him. Just to know he is fine, that he is alive!"

Simon couldn't help but feel his own heart tug for the father. "Then I will arrange it. Perhaps he might even return for a visit. He seems to miss his family and friends."

"He would be ashamed of me and how the farm looks since he left. How unhappy his mamm is, not knowing if he is alive or safe or even happy."

"It is not my place to say, but you should know this much. Zach never left his Amish faith." Such news sent the man into a harder fit of tears. It was a blessing, for sure and certain, to know your child had never swayed from his faith.

"He is still the upright young man you raised. As far as your farm, I have a thought about that." Simon offered Carl a seat, and for the next few minutes he shared with Carl Stella's idea of a cherry orchard.

"That ground is good for it, I reckon, and Susie does make a fine cherry pie." Carl looked over at Simon. "That dok is smarter than both of us. I should have never spoken to you or her like I did." Carl shook his head sorrowfully and looked to Simon. "I knew the morning Mary Alice came calling she was spreading gossip. Everyone knows she hoped you'd have eyes for Pricilla when here the woman and Shep have been courting for months."

Simon smiled.

"We all want our kinner happy, and some of us go about it the wrong way."

"True. You and that dok make a fine match. Folks sure seem to like her and, better yet, seeing you courting again. Did you really take her on a picnic?"

"She has a kind heart for others," was all Simon said. He didn't want to talk about picnics or rose petals or lemonade or that kiss. He just wanted to put it behind him.

"Jah, but it seems you made an impression. I was certain sure Nelson would try snagging her up if you didn't. You know, Bishop, you've been alone too long, so I hope you are not as foolish as me. Don't let her get away before telling her how you feel."

"She's already gone." Simon stood and resumed organizing. He had done his duty, helped a grieving father find his footing, but talk of Stella he could no longer listen to. Mamm had been doing plenty of that.

"Where to?"

"Her bishop came to fetch her. Her bruder will fetch her back to Ohio to live with her folks. Though I cannot pretend I'm happy about it." No, he couldn't even pretend that. "From all I know of her folks, they haven't been the kindest to her." Just the thought of her choosing to return to the very folks who put such hurt inside her made him want to start pounding metal again.

"You're just letting her leave." It wasn't a question, but Simon answered it anyway.

"Her folks are getting older. Her kin all have families, so she's expected to tend to them."

"Getting married and raising a family is expected too. There is still time for that, you know." Carl lifted a brow. "Wasn't like you two have been quiet about your feelings for each other. I figured you'd be hitched by spring anyhow."

"If she stayed, I would have," Simon admitted. *But she didn't stay. She didn't even say goodbye.*

"So you asked her to marry ya, and she left anyhow?" Carl's head moved from side to side sympathetically.

"She left before I got around to it. No matter, it was Gott's will."

"Gott's will?" Carl harrumphed. "His will would have been for you to not drag your feet," Carl said bluntly. "I reckon if He put her at your doorstep, and you both have a mind for it, then you'd wed. Never thought you to be slow as I was. How do you know what she wants if you don't ask, brother?"

Simon didn't need another lecture on romance.

"Stella has a mind of her own." Carl didn't know Stella as well as he did.

Then again.

Stella was obedient, desperate to please, with the exception of life-or-death situations. She'd also never had a present before. She was afraid of rainstorms. She said she loved being alone, but she had Ellie, so she was never alone. Most of all, Simon knew without a shadow of a doubt she loved him, and he hadn't asked. Carl was right. Stella hadn't been given a choice, and he was an idiot. He hadn't even gone after her.

"I'm not a smart bishop," Simon blurted out.

"Nee, you are a good bishop but a terrible boyfriend. Maybe you still have time to correct your ways and sweeten the offer." Carl grinned. "Go after her, or you will be sitting in regrets just as I have for the rest of your days."

Simon quickly began untying his heavy apron. His friend was right. He hadn't given Stella a reason to stay. Loving her wasn't enough.

Telling her, choosing her, was the only way. No one had ever chosen her. . .until now.

"Excuse me Carl, but. . ."

"I'll hitch your buggy. You best go fetch an umbrella and put on a clean shirt." Carl chuckled and headed for the barn.

CHAPTER THIRTY-THREE

On the other side of Sugar Mountain was the low valley filled with rich emerald fields and swollen summer creeks. Simon veered his horse up the long and winding gravel drive. Bishop Mast owned a vast amount of land and yet had no sohn to help maintain it.

Cattle roamed lazily along one side of long white fencing while horses ran playfully on the left. A slow rain misted softly, but a sound of distant thunder told of heavier rains heading their way. *Stella is afraid of storms,* Simon thought as he secured his rig and marched up the bishop's steps.

"Wasn't expecting to see you today," the bishop welcomed, surprised from the far end of the wraparound porch.

"Good to see ya again, Joshua," Simon greeted, turning his way.

"Kumm sit. It's the best view for a man seeking a change in weather." Simon found a seat, though he was seeking for something, or rather someone. A quick glance about showed no signs of the dok or Ellie.

"What brings a man out before a storm?"

"I have come to speak to the dok." Simon didn't hesitate to answer. Joshua Mast was small in stature, but his gaze held strength few could muster.

"She is inside, helping with the canning and readying lunch." He leaned forward. "At least until that bruder of hers arrives to fetch her, but you can stick around and share the meal with us."

Simon looked to the front door then set his eyes back on the landscape. He wasn't hungry but suddenly felt like a youngie asking a father's permission. Perhaps it was his respect for the man who had cared over so many for more than forty years. Perhaps it was because he wasn't sure what to say next.

"What time is he comin'?"

"He's late already, so that I cannot say. I feel you have come not to seek my wisdom but a woman before she leaves." His perceptions were keen.

"I am." Simon lifted his chin to his elder. "Or I hope to."

"Hmm. You know her family is in need of her now. Gott directs us in our duties, does He not?"

"Jah," Simon agreed. "But she has a choice, and a good friend just reminded me that I failed to give that to her."

The bishop turned slowly, angling his body toward Simon. A twinkle of amusement glinted in his pale gray eyes. "And what would that be?"

"She can go see over her father or let her bruders care for him as they live next door. She can stay and. . .marry." Simon didn't like the laugh that followed. He need not prove his worthiness to Joshua Mast.

"If she wanted to marry, she would have done so by now. Many have tried to turn her head. Stella is more concerned with flowers and foolish thoughts than caring for a family of her own."

"I disagree."

"You know her place is with her family. It is the way of it." The bishop waved him off as if the matter had been settled. It hadn't.

"Gott's timing is not ours to decide, Bishop Mast. Perhaps she didn't care for them or didn't think herself deserving of such. I've learned in our time together that there is much about her that isn't as it should be. I don't want to see her return to a family who wasn't kind to her."

"Ach, the flood." He shook his head. "I knew that day her brother pushed her in. Paul, I suspected." He stroked his beard. "That one had a meanness in him I saw nowhere else. Samuel ran off to Ohio and plucked up a fraa before returning home. Bertha was barely a teen. Youngies have no thought of what marriage means." He shook his head. "I asked Stella what happened, but she refused to say. I admit I hated to tell her the news of her fatter and how they had need of her. Her bunch was odd, and Samuel never lifted much of a hand for another, but he sure held one out plenty so. When they left, I dusted off my feet with it."

"Well, I don't feel that is what I can do." Simon stood. He had dusted his feet off plenty, but it didn't wipe away what had been ingrained in his heart. Stella deserved a life better than the one being forged out or her.

After a long minute, the elder finally spoke. "So be it, but you will find she isn't interested in any men here."

"I had no plans of talking any of them up."

"She's inside, but in case you fail, don't forget the hund on your way out. She's of a mind to leave her with Lena instead of taking her along." The bishop motioned a thumb to the door and went back to his view.

If Stella was leaving Ellie behind, then she was saving her from what awaited her in Ohio. She would never part with Ellie aside from that. Simon didn't hesitate stepping inside the house. He had someone to save too.

———————— ⚓ ————————

Stella wiped her damp forehead with her apron front. Steam from the canner on the stove mingled with the thick air in the room, adding more discomfort to her day. With the windows all open, she could hear Ellie barking from the barn. The urge to rescue her was growing by the minute.

"That hund of yours is making such a fuss," Cora complained.

"I need to walk her. She has never been penned up before," Stella replied. She turned off the burner. It would take a good half hour before it cooled enough to remove the jars inside.

"Best go to it, then, before you leave. Though I do hope Joshua sees her on over to the Grabers' soon yet." Stella nodded. When discouragement found its way past her defenses, there was only one thing to do. Stella drank tea. Tea was always gut, unless one only had water to make it, and Cora insisted the scents from Stella's leather bag induced plenty of headaches.

Stella needed a few lasting minutes with Ellie. Matt wasn't to arrive until just right before noon. That gave her a couple hours to say her so-longs to her best friend in the world. Bishop Mast thought her fickle and complicated, but he had promised to see Ellie delivered safely to Lena.

Slipping out the back door, Stella ignored the rumble in the sky as she made her way to the barn. The moment she opened Ellie's kennel door, she sprang out and aimed for the woods near the road. Poor thing, she had to be frightened to death with all the changes in her life.

"Ellie!" Stella shouted after her, but her dog simply wouldn't comply. Stella had no choice but to run after her. A caged animal certainly refused to give up its freedoms. Stella wished she could run too.

When she reached the first set of trees marking the woods that ran thick into the next county, Stella stopped to listen for which way Ellie had veered. Two barks instantly alerted her left beyond a thick patch of dried brambles. The road wasn't too far, and Stella quickened her pace. Ellie had to be so scared she wasn't aware of the dangers lurking just around the corner. The very thought that a car might hit her suddenly twisted in Stella's gut.

Stella followed the barks until she found herself at the edge of the road. Narrow asphalt split right down the middle of woodland, and on the opposite side of the road sat Ellie.

"Ellie," Stella called out breathlessly and bent to urge her back. She was always obedient, never unfaithful, but in that moment her best friend in the world remained stone still. Ellie cocked her head and looked west before fixing her teal gaze on Stella once more.

"I know you don't like the barn, but I promise Lena will never put you in one." Ellie didn't like being caged any more than Stella liked having her life chosen for her.

"What do you want me to do? It isn't like either of us has a choice." Stella patted her leg and yet Ellie remained still.

"He doesn't want us," Stella said. Thankfully no one but the squirrels could hear her talking to her dog as if she understood. Ellie barked, bounced as she was prone to do when eager for an adventure.

"He didn't even come to see us," Stella reminded her and grew more tense at the darkening skies overhead. This time Ellie stared blankly at her. "Get over here, and let's go home." Ellie's ears perked at the mention of home, but her feet stayed roughly planted in the pebbly roadside.

Home, Stella's heart whispered. She hadn't felt very much at home anywhere in a long time. The little wooden house that was no longer had only been a reminder of what family was. Well, that was until she met Lena and Michael and Simon. Something else Stella had discovered suddenly—in all her anger at Simon's deceit, her heartbreak at his absence, she too had done nothing to change her course.

"I never told him, did I?" Ellie's jaw opened wide in a yawn-like fashion, expelling a sound Stella could only describe as mockery.

"I never told him I loved him. What if he didn't pity us? What if he too was. . .scared?" What if she was completely wrong? Was it so hard to imagine a grown man scared. . .of love?

"We should tell him, jah?" She was talking over major life decisions with a dog. Fine, she had reached a new level of ridiculous, but she trusted Ellie more than she did most folks. When Ellie barked three times, Stella knew.

Stella glanced down the road. "It's a good seven miles," she mentioned. Ellie looked too, returning her gaze to Stella as if saying seven miles was no hardship at all for four legs.

"Bishop Mast might have you whipped yet for such crazy thinking," Stella offered as the foolish idea continued to fester. When her friend showed no lack of fear at such a threat, Stella couldn't help but laugh.

"You reckon for us to go back and tell him we have sparks for him?" Ellie barked and ran to her, her wet noise nudging Stella to get going.

"He will laugh at us." Stella placed her hands on the sides of Ellie's head. "You know this, jah?"

Ellie began panting and drooling like she did when Lena filled her plate at the supper table. It was anticipation, and Stella was feeling it too.

"It's not going to be easy, and do you see that cloud there?" Stella pointed. "It looks like rain. Do you really want to get caught in the rain, leave without telling anyone where we are going, and get rejected all over again too?" Stella had been accused of worse, and taking risks was not new to her, but she would never know if Simon truly cared for her if she didn't at least try. Ellie was right about that.

A half hour later, goose bumps rose on both of Stella's arms. The strange silence, the absence of wind and birdsong, sent an internal warning that this was a very bad idea. She was a fool for trusting Ellie with matters of the heart.

They took the old road over the mountain to cut the miles shorter, but a sudden crack of thunder reminded her she was very far from Bishop Mast's farmstead. If she had only stayed on the main road, where buggies were more common, her heart wouldn't be beating so hard right now.

There were no barns or houses nearby, and a sense of urgency came over her. It was best to turn around. It couldn't be more than three miles back, and she might make it before the storm arrived if she hurried. But just a few more miles ahead was Simon. How did one choose between common sense and yearning?

"Nee." She stomped a foot. "It's rain. It feeds the earth and flowers, and I won't melt. We can't turn back," she told Ellie with fresh determination. "We have to try."

She loved him. There was no denying it, and he might be waiting. Waiting for her to decide an answer to the question he had never asked. In her heart she knew he loved her too. "He bought me teacups!" With that, Ellie took off, leading the way.

Back was not forward, and rain or not, Stella wanted forward. She picked up her pace but had only gotten a few hundred yards before the heavens emptied. Thunder crashed, lightning striking earth in fast streaks. Her kapp grew heavy, soaking up the rain, and the puddles formed in swiftness.

Showers of an old memory, the one where Daed insisted she get over her fear of storms, reemerged. All those hours she had to spend sitting on a lopsided porch, eyes closed while rain beat overhead in a deafening sound.

She spotted a phone shanty up ahead. The Zooks had left the shed unattended, but surely the roof held up. Stella picked up her pace and aimed for shelter. She was soaked to the bone and shivering like a wet cat in winter when she heard her name howl through the trees. Ellie stopped, not minding the rain at all, but cautious as to the approaching buggy.

Stella wiped her face for a better visual and felt her chest explode with relief when Ellie took off. Simon had barely stepped out of the buggy when she climbed up him like a coon climbed a tree and delivered a hundred slippery kisses. He was soaked and now muddy, but he didn't look one bit angry.

Simon had come.

"What are you doing here?" she called out. When he reached her, Simon pulled her into his arms.

"Hoping I wasn't too late. I came to tell you. . ." Thunder roared, drowning out his next words.

"Tell me what?"

"Don't go. Stay. . .with me." A single plea, but what was he truly asking?

"I don't want to go!" Stella admitted in a tearful confession. "I never did. I don't want to watch storms or give away Ellie. I don't want to go back."

"I know," Simon said, removing his black hat and setting it on her head. She had no recollection of where her kapp had gone.

"I want to stay, and I love you, and I should have told you, but I was afraid, and Mary Alice said—"

Simon placed a finger to her lips, shushing her. "I'm a bishop, remember? It's best I don't know what Mary Alice said to you, and I love you too."

"Really?"

"Of course I do. But I must know one thing."

"What?"

"Stella Schmucker, will you court me?"

"But we are already courting, Bishop Graber," she said with a laugh. *This man.* Life would never be the same. Thankfully so.

"Then I guess it's time we move on to the next step. . . ." His lips found hers in the pouring-down rain, but Stella Schmucker didn't feel a drop.

Dok Stella's Sunshine Tea

INGREDIENTS:
2 parts chamomile
1 part lemon balm
1 palm each lavender flowers and rose petals

Combine dried herbs and store in a jar. For tea: Boil one quart water and spoon in 1 ounce dried ingredients. Steep 30 minutes. Strain and drink.

Stella's Wild-Crafted Breakfast Omelet

INGREDIENTS:
2 to 3 eggs
1 cup trimmed and washed nettle leaves*
1 wild garlic, washed, trimmed, and chopped
Salt and pepper to taste
1 tablespoon olive oil
Shredded cheese

*Please research proper handling and identification of nettles before collecting.

Beat eggs fully; then add nettles, garlic, and seasoning. In a warm frying pan, add olive oil. Fry egg mixture and turn when you can easily flip it. Sprinkle with shredded cheese and let cook a couple of minutes before folding it in half and removing from pan.

Violet Shortbread Cookies

INGREDIENTS:
1 cup (2 sticks) unsalted butter, room temperature
½ cup sugar
1 teaspoon vanilla, or lemon zest
2 cups flour
Violets (about 25), stems removed

Mix butter with sugar until well combined. Add vanilla or lemon zest and flour. Knead until well-blended dough takes form. Cover bowl and refrigerate for 30 to 60 minutes. On floured surface, roll dough to ¼-inch thickness. Cut out your desired shape and size. Decorate each cookie with a violet. Bake at 325 degrees for 7 to 8 minutes.

Bestselling and award-winning author Mindy Steele is a welcome addition to the Amish genre. Not only are her novels uplifting and her characters relatable, but they touch all the senses. Her storyteller heart shines within her pages. Research for her is just a fence jump away, and she aims to accurately portray the Amish way of life. Her relationship with the Amish enables her to understand boundaries and customs, giving her readers an inside view of the Plain life. Mindy and her husband, Mike, have been blessed with five grown children, ten wonderful grandchildren, and many great neighbors.